THE TRUTH ABOUT FIRE

Also by Elizabeth Hartmann

A Quiet Violence: View from a Bangladesh Village
(co-authored with James K. Boyce)

Reproductive Rights and Wrongs:
The Global Politics of Population Control

THE TRUTH ABOUT FIRE

ELIZABETH HARTMANN

CARROLL & GRAF PUBLISHERS
NEW YORK

The passage from *The Jewish Wife* by Bertolt Brecht is from the translation by Eric Bentley in *The Jewish Wife and Other Short Plays* by Bertolt Brecht (New York: Grove Press, 1983).

THE TRUTH ABOUT FIRE

Carroll & Graf Publishers
An Imprint of Avalon Publishing Group Inc.
161 William St., 16th Floor
New York, NY 10038

Copyright © 2002 by Elizabeth Hartmann

First Carroll & Graf edition 2002

Book design Michael Walters

Library of Congress Cataloging-in-Publication Data is available.

ISBN: 0-7867-1021-7

Printed in the United States of America
Distributed by Publishers Group West

To Jim

Acknowledgments

I am deeply grateful to all my friends, colleagues, and members of my immediate and extended family who offered valuable support and suggestions on the manuscript. I would particularly like to thank Yvonne Dubbers-Albrecht for taking me to eastern Germany and helping me on the sections of the novel set there; Rajani Bhatia for her assistance on the German sections; my past and present colleagues at the Civil Liberties and Public Policy Program at Hampshire College for teaching me about the Far Right through their courageous research and activism on reproductive rights, especially M. J. Maccardini and Marlene Fried; and the members of my writing group, Mordecai Gerstein, Roger King, Joann Kobin, the late Norman Kotker, Marissa Labozzetta, and John Stifler, for their excellent comments and support throughout the writing process.

Finally, I would like to thank my agent, Linda Roghaar, for all her help and calm persistence, and my editor at Carroll & Graf, Philip Turner, who with great efficiency and keen editorial insight has seen the book into print.

Contents

The Truth About Fire

FIRE WATCH

By the time Johnny reached the fire tower, the Forest Service jeep was coated with a layer of dust so deep he could write his name in it. It was the hottest and driest August he could remember. Even Lake Superior was swimmable, and tourists swarmed as heavily as the mosquitoes. The campgrounds were fully booked and fire risks were high.

Global warming, maybe. Or El Niño. Or just another fluke of nature. Whatever the cause, the drought made him feel more useful. His capacity for watching and waiting took on more heroic proportions. He'd already nipped several brush fires in the bud and doused a few illegal campfires. Drunk kids and fishermen. Dumb.

He climbed the ladder to the top of the tower and hung his backpack on the railing. From the front pocket he took a joint and a lighter—he never used matches. Getting stoned aided his vision;

it was a secret of the trade. Later, when he was assured the woods were safe, he would take out his sketch pad. Yesterday he drew a hawk; he was still waiting for an eagle.

The forest took a different form every day. Sometimes in heat like this the treetops melted together in a green haze like fog on the sea. Other times the trunks stood out, separate, stark, like poles in an unfinished fence. Or he hardly saw the trees at all because he was following the migratory pattern of geese or watching a deer drink from a stream. He had learned to become so still that nothing feared him.

He smoked the joint down to the very end, crushing the roach carefully between wet fingertips. He took a swig of water, then started looking with his binoculars, trying to distinguish smoke from haze. His eyes watered from the effort, and he was suddenly conscious of how hot he was. He unbuttoned his uniform shirt, letting the breeze tickle his chest. North was clear, east and south were too, but over in the direction of Ironwood he thought he saw a thin trail of smoke. He got out his compass and marked the location roughly on the map. It was in the National Forest, but there was no campground over there. Shit. He wasn't ready to leave just yet. No time to even start a drawing.

Back in the jeep, he radioed headquarters to tell them he was going to check out the smoke. Lonna took the message, but she sounded as if she couldn't be bothered. He didn't trust her. She came on to him, then yanked away, played him like a yo-yo. Maybe she looked down on him because he was Ojibwa, or maybe she was just plain weird. He could never tell which it was with white women.

He had never been too stoned to drive before, but this afternoon might be the exception. The ruts he hadn't noticed on the way in threatened to wrench the steering wheel from his sweaty palms, and he hung on as if he were driving a wild bumper car in an amusement park. His concentration seemed to jump from one side of his brain to the other. He caught himself looking too long at a fly on the dashboard. A second more and he would have been off the road heading for a tree.

It was those kinds of seconds that determined your fate, his friend Michael claimed. Sudden flashes of chance, he called them. Michael had gone all philosophical after the buck totaled his car on New Year's Eve and almost took him with it into the next world. Was there chance there too, or did it die along with you? He wished he'd asked his mother that before she lost her memory to Alzheimer's. She'd known everything there was to know about such things. Although she went to church every Sunday, she never believed in the white man's heaven or hell. "Even if only a tiny fraction of your blood is Ojibwa," she told him, "you're going to the camping ground of eternal bliss, where you can hunt and fish wherever you want. No one can stop you." But here in this life it was his job to stop people, so he'd better keep his eyes on the damn road.

The intersection with Forest Road Number 17 reached him before he reached it, and he had to slam on the brakes to make the turn. A couple of miles down he turned left on an unmarked logging road that cut off to the west. He noticed fresh tire tracks in the dirt and felt confident he was on the right trail, heading toward the source of the smoke. Of course the fire might be out by now and the culprits long gone. That would be fine by him; he got no thrills from busting people.

He crossed a dry streambed, after which mixed deciduous forest gave way to pine plantations, some already logged, leaving behind ugly stump land. In another year or two the brush would take over and the wildlife would return. Despite the hard winters, or maybe because of them, nature was resilient here. You only had to look at the hardiness of the mosquitoes and blackflies, their eggs surviving months under ice.

Less than a mile down the road he spotted a blue pickup pulled over on the side. He parked behind it, noticing it had Illinois license plates. Poor out-of-staters probably, hunting deer off season, "government beef" they called it around here. It was the only way some families could afford to put meat on the table. He considered radioing Lonna his position, but he didn't want to hear her voice again and be reminded of the way she bent over sometimes so he could see clear up her legs. He stuck the radio in his pocket and set off into the woods.

He had a knack for trailing people just like he had a knack for spotting smoke, knowing how to let his senses take the lead. Even when he was five and trapped in a sudden blizzard in the woods, he found his way back home before his mother had time to worry. Now she was so lost even he couldn't find her. He brought her gifts from the forest, pine cones she turned in her hands or seed pods she shook like a rattle.

There was no path this time and no footprints really, except for a few indentations in the pine needles. He swatted at a mosquito on his chest and rebuttoned his shirt. On the way home he would reward himself with a swim in the lake and pick up a pasty and some cold beer for dinner. He needed to call Michael back. Maybe Sunday he'd drive up to the Keweenaw to try out the new kayak.

Michael was always trying new things, sailing last summer, fly-fishing the summer before that.

He smelled smoke, but it wasn't wood smoke, too metallic for that. Could be illegal dumpers—it happened sometimes—although usually they just dumped whatever it was without bothering to burn it. A surge of adrenaline cut through his stoned stupor, and he patted the radio in his pocket.

He heard a small explosion and then the sound of laughter. Must be kids with fireworks. He had done the same once and was busted by a cop who turned out to be a poker mate of his uncle's. Nothing on his record, just a slap on the wrist and ten hours of community service.

He approached quietly and, when he saw them, hung back behind a tree. They weren't kids but two grown men, and whatever they'd set off looked bigger than a firecracker. Scraps of metal were scattered on the ground, and the acrid smoke burned his nostrils. He turned on his radio and spoke softly, but there was too much static. When Lonna shouted for him to speak louder, the radio screeched.

The men looked around. The one with the ponytail and the scraggly beard saw him first, locking his eyes on Johnny's face. "What the fuck you doing here?" he shouted. He was wearing a denim shirt with the sleeves cut off, and there were tattoos all up and down his arms.

Johnny stepped forward. "Shouldn't I be asking you that?"

"You some fucking Forest Service goon?"

"Fire warden. Are you aware that there's a high risk of forest fire today?"

"Guy thinks he's Smokey the Bear." The other man laughed. He was more clean-cut and wearing camouflage pants. Ex-army, Johnny thought, easier to deal with. He heard Lonna shouting at him and shouted back his position.

"Turn that fucking radio off," the man with the ponytail warned.

"So what you guys up to?" Johnny asked calmly, hoping the ex-army man might answer.

"I said, turn that fucking radio off," the guy with the ponytail repeated, moving toward him.

Johnny obliged. "You're on government property, you know."

"Ain't my government, asshole. Ain't yours either by the looks of you. At least you got a reservation to go back to. I'd head back fast if I was you."

"No more fires," Johnny said, feigning a smile.

"Yeah, yeah, Smokey," the ex-army man said. "We get the idea."

"OK, I'll let you off this time."

"Gee, that's awful nice of you. The Reverend will be real pleased, won't he, Al?"

As Johnny turned to walk away, he saw his own death before it happened—the man with the ponytail reaching into his pocket for the gun, then lifting his arm and taking careful aim. He felt grateful that it would be fast, one of Michael's sudden flashes of chance.

But he was wrong. It was the other man who shot him, and his death had nothing at all to do with chance.

CHAPTER I

THE JEWISH WIFE

It used to be you had to take a ferry between the lower and upper peninsulas of Michigan, but progress came by way of the Mackinac Bridge in the late 1950s. It's a stunning bridge, the seeming connecting line between Lake Huron and Lake Michigan, whose waters meet under its steel girders. Huron's waters are a deep emerald and Michigan's a purer blue, and that first time I crossed I looked up to see if the sky was divided too.

I tried to point out the view to Marcy, but she was busy switching radio stations. We had spent the night in Detroit en route from Boston, and Marcy had uttered maybe five words over dinner. Now her silence, combined with the inanity of late-nineties teen radio, was getting on my nerves. I wished I had a ferry ride to recover, though standing alone with my face in the wind would have probably only deepened my sense of foreboding.

It didn't help that everyone I knew had told me it was a mistake to accept the job at Keweenaw University in Houghton, Michigan. "It's the North Pole up there, geographically and intellectually," a colleague advised me. "You're going to go nuts." But sometimes the only choice you have is to make mistakes. I'd been denied tenure at Boston University because of a conservative dean who didn't think my work was academic enough, and Keweenaw had the only opening in German history in the country. I couldn't go back to Sajit. Only by living in different places could we sustain the illusion of marriage for Marcy's sake.

How much longer I could sustain that illusion I didn't know. All during the drive from Boston, Sajit had been on my mind. It was as if the more physical distance I put between us, the closer he became, and I replayed my past while Marcy played her music.

I was back at the very beginning now, watching myself climb the steep stone staircase to Sajit's office in a crumbling annex of the Oxford college where I was spending my junior year abroad. I was in two kinds of shock, I guess—sad and exhausted from the shock of my father's death only a month before and in culture shock too, allergic to the damp air, the greasy food, and the curiosity of the English students, who found me an amusing ingenue, a New World mascot for their Old World debauchery. I knocked on Sajit's door and he told me to come in. Then, glancing up briefly from a book, he gestured for me to take a chair.

I sat there for five minutes while he continued to read. Finally, he closed the book, placed it on top of a pile of papers, and stared at me. "They added you late to my list," he remarked, "and I already have too many students." He paused, and if he smiled, it was not kindly. "I hope you're good."

I must have blushed. I had heard he was a cruel tutor and would literally tear essays into shreds and throw them at you like perverse confetti. "I'm American," I said. "I'm on the Wellesley Junior Year Abroad Program."

"Does that make you good?" he asked, taking a pen from his pocket.

"No, but it doesn't make me bad either."

He twirled the pen between his fingers. "What's your field?"

"German and history."

"Does that mean German history?"

"Maybe."

"What do you mean by maybe?"

"I haven't decided just how I want to put them together."

He shook his head in disbelief. "It always astonishes me how long American students have to make up their minds. Very different from this system, you know. Unfortunately, my field is twentieth-century Indian history. I know very little about Germany. I'm surprised they assigned me as your tutor."

"You're the only modern historian in the college," I replied. "Professor Humphrey studies medieval German manuscripts."

"So why did they assign you to this college in the first place?"

I shrugged.

"You really don't know?"

"No."

"Because the master of this college is very clever and knows how to make money off rich Americans. Although I daresay he chooses to invest most of it in the wine cellar and not in fixing up the buildings. If you look behind me, you can see the damp spreading down the wall. My books mildew just as badly here as they did in Calcutta."

I looked at the patch of damp but felt no pity. "I'm not rich," I stated.

"Perhaps not, but Wellesley is. Do you know how many

mediocre American students I have had sitting before me in that same chair?"

"Any more than mediocre British students?" I quipped, surprised at my nerve.

"On a percentage basis, yes."

"Professor Mukherjee—" I began.

"I'm not a professor yet, I'm a mere lecturer."

"Dr. Mukherjee"—I began again—"if you really don't want to be my tutor, I can try to find someone else."

He leaned forward, pushing away an empty teacup. I couldn't tell his age. He had no wrinkles or gray hair, but there was something about the skin around his eyes, tight and a bit sallow, that suggested he was beyond his twenties. "That's not the point, Miss Grace," he said. "I'm only hoping you'll prove me wrong and modify my estimation of your compatriots." He started twirling the pen again, though this time it slipped and fell on his desk. He picked it up and put it back in his pocket, careful to secure the clip. "Next week I want you to write an essay on why you've chosen history as a field when the job prospects are dismal and politics or literary criticism is far more fashionable. As many words as you like. Let's see how you write."

I noticed we were the same height when he stood up to let me out the door. He threw me off guard by shaking my hand. His palm was damp and warm.

The next week I turned in a one-sentence essay. When I went to his office to discuss it, he was reading a play. "Do you like Brecht, Miss Grace?" he asked as I sat down, and I nodded. "Can you read him in German?"

"Yes."

"Ah, I envy you then. I grew up on Brecht in Calcutta, but I always felt something was missing in the translation. I read your essay," he continued, "and I gather you've been forewarned of my reputation. One page makes less confetti than ten, was that your logic?"

"I didn't employ logic."

"What did you employ then?"

"Truth. Historians are supposed to be interested in the truth."

"'I am studying history because I like it.' Is that sentence your idea of the truth, Miss Grace?"

"Yes."

"I suppose it's better than the usual nonsense I receive when I ask that question." I watched as he fastidiously folded my essay into a paper airplane. "Let's see where it lands," he said, as he launched it from his desk over my head. It hit a bookcase and fell on the carpet. "Well." He sighed. "It seems we are off to an auspicious start."

Starting next week, he told me, we would read a collection of short Brecht plays at the beginning of every tutorial. First I would read passages in German, then he would read the same ones in English, and I would comment on the translation. And then we would study German fascism together. One of the leaders of the Indian independence movement, Subash Chandra Bose—or Netaji, as he was popularly called—had sought assistance from the Axis powers in his fight against the British during World War II. Sajit wanted to understand fascism's appeal better. He hoped to understand why an intelligent man like Bose would go down that road.

I didn't read from Brecht. Instead, I substituted long lines of German swears decrying Sajit's arrogance. *Verpiss dich, du arro-*

ganter Arsch. Du hast nichts im Sinn. I told him the English translation certainly lacked the passion of the original. Soon I tired of
swears and began a stream-of-consciousness monologue about my
father's death and how lonely I was.

Then something changed, though I can't put my finger on
exactly what it was. We were reading *The Jewish Wife*, a short play
about a Jewish woman preparing to leave Nazi Germany and the
passive response of her gentile husband, who lets her leave
without him. She's practical; she packs; she understands the rules
of survival. Somehow I got into her character and stopped my
game, reading this passage to him in German:

> I don't want you to tell me not to go. I'm going in a
> hurry because I don't want to have you tell me I *should*
> go. It's a question of time. Character is a question of
> time. It lasts for a certain length of time, just like a
> glove. There are good ones that last a long time. But
> they don't last forever.

I felt his eyes resting curiously on me and wondered if he knew
German and had been aware of my subterfuge all along.

When we finished the play, he got up to put on the electric
kettle. He made us tea but forgot I didn't take milk and sugar.
When he sat down again, it was on the couch, not behind his
desk, and I had to turn my chair to face him. He had on a maroon
sweater, and his thick black hair was slightly disheveled. Through
the leaded window, a dim ray of evening light crossed his shoe,
and I noticed it was badly in need of polishing.

We had our tea. He even offered me a biscuit. And then,

unprompted, he began to tell me about his father, who had died during World War II. As an officer in the British Indian Army, he fought in Burma and was captured by the Japanese. In the prisoner-of-war camp, Bose's followers recruited him to the Indian National Army, and he died fighting on the fascist side. "I'll never know whether he joined Bose because he really believed it was the only way to gain India's independence," he said, setting his empty cup and saucer on the floor, "or because it was the only way to survive. He probably would have starved to death in the camp; maybe he thought he had a better chance in battle, even if it was on the wrong side. You see, I don't know. I always thought my father was a man of character, but character doesn't last forever, as we've just read. Perhaps Bose's men genuinely convinced him right was on their side, but my father was a smart man and a great believer in democracy. He didn't like Hitler."

"His views could have changed under duress."

"Do we all pack up when we're under duress?"

"It's the husband who's guilty in the play, not the wife," I said.

"Aren't they both guilty of a lack of passion? That's what unsettles me most about that play." He looked at me, not as a professor should, but we were both shy so we returned to history.

History became our passion and we didn't need Brecht anymore. Sajit was a good storyteller and transported me to Bengal in the early part of the century. Then we would shift to Germany, and he would make me talk about what I read. I analyzed the rise of the Third Reich from every possible angle, and then he made me compare historians, forcing me to have my own point of view. Soon our stories intertwined, as Bose escaped from India in 1941 and made his way to Berlin, where he set up a Free India government. We searched through his papers and broadcasts, trying to understand how such a fine mind could go so wrong.

As the days grew even darker and damper, I dreaded the end of Michaelmas term and the long Christmas holiday, when my sessions with Sajit would be suspended. I had decided not to go home to Pennsylvania for Christmas—the plane fare was too expensive, and in truth I had little desire to see my mother because she would remind me of the father I no longer had. The college said I could stay in my room, and a nice but boring girl invited me down to her family house in Surrey. Both options seemed dreary.

One unusually warm afternoon I decided to take one of the college boats out on the river. I rowed up the Cherwell into the University Parks, maneuvering under overhanging branches and around the ducks and grebes. The current was stronger than I'd anticipated, and by the time I turned around it was starting to get dark. My arms were tired, and I was hungry and thirsty and lonely and sad.

And so Sajit chose that moment to appear, though of course it had nothing to do with choice, it was just the warm afternoon that drove him outside. He was standing on the high arched bridge that spans the river at one of its widest points, watching something in the water. "Miss Grace," he called, "will you be so kind as to give me a ride back?"

I pulled over to the bank, grabbing hold of a branch to stop the boat. As he put one foot in, the boat edged away and his other foot landed in the water. "*Verpiss dich!*" he swore.

"You never told me you knew German," I said, as I extended a hand to help him.

"Oh, I know a bit, enough to recognize a few swears."

"So you knew."

"Knew what? All I know at present is that my shoe is wet. It's no matter, anyway. I was casting sticks to see if I should go to High Table or not. The first that came out the other side of the bridge would decide it; long was yes, short was no. But they both disappeared. And now my only pair of decent shoes is wet, so *that* decides it. Shall I take you out for an Indian meal?" He paused, then quickly added, "part of the tutorial; you know, local color."

I gave an indeterminate nod and concentrated on the next push of the oars. As I pulled them back, I said that would be nice; I'd never had a proper Indian meal before. Then we both fell into silence, watching the darkness spread on the river like spilled ink.

The rest is history, as they say, but it's not really, because I remember it differently every time and I'm supposed to be a historian, trained to be objective about my own subjectivity. However, it's impossible in this case because the subjectivity itself is constantly shifting, depending on the particular detail I pick or the mood I'm in. Start with the geography. Is it the walk on Cowley Road that softens me up because I am finally in the "rough" neighborhood the privileged students warned me about and I like it? It's England, not Oxford, small storefronts with bright pink nylon saris in one window and plantains in the next.

Or is it the weather—still warm, clear enough to see a smattering of stars? Or my body, weary from the rowing but pumping endorphins and hormones and the still-fast blood of youth? Or the food, the lovely food? Sajit knows the owners personally; they speak rapid-fire Bengali with each other and plan a feast for me of flavors I've never tasted before. There is fresh ground chili in the fish, tamarind in the potatoes, and they pour wine like it was water. I cool my mouth with Chardonnay.

Our knees touch under the table and we both pull away, but not fast enough to prevent the touch traveling up to our eyes.

Is this really the way it was? I don't know. Only the letter that came the next day stands as genuine historical record:

> *Dear Miss Grace (or may I call you Gillian?),*
>
> *I am writing to tell you that I can no longer be your tutor, even though you are one of the best students I have ever had. I should not even see you again. I have done something terribly wrong and I beg your forgiveness. I have fallen in love with you. I do not expect you to reciprocate; in fact, I am trying very hard not to hope for it.*
>
> *Next week I leave for Devon, where I am renting a small cottage by the sea. I will be alone there, working on my book about Netaji. If for some reason—oh, but I should not hope for it—you have similar feelings to mine, I am enclosing directions on how to get there. I always leave the door unlocked. It is up to you; everything is up to you.*
>
> *Please do not feel you have to respond to this letter. I am sorry I cannot help myself from sending it. As Brecht wrote, character is a question of time. Passion has finally got the better of mine.*
>
> *With love, Sajit*

I still look at that letter to remind myself it was I who made the choice. Nowadays I suppose I could plead undue pressure and sexual harassment, but it wasn't the case. I chose, freely and willfully, to go to Devon.

It was so unlike the choice I was making now to go to Houghton, Michigan. No passion in the decision, just cold calculation. A job, a house, a new school where Marcy wouldn't be labeled for at least a few weeks. Epileptic—they knew how to deal with that, but not with the other part: wild, troublemaker, sexually precocious, "at risk." "Your daughter is at risk," the counselors in Boston had kept telling me. *I know, I'm not blind,* I'd wanted to shout at them, *but aren't we all at risk in some way?*

CHAPTER 2

A Christian Wife

The lake is so still, Lucy can see fall coming on it in the reflection of the red maples. The tomatoes are almost finished and the cornstalks are short and tatty, their worm-infested ears like bits of stiff sponge. Nothing grows well here except berries and birches. In the winter, snow piles up so high you can hardly see through your windows.

If she closes her eyes, she can see winter on the lake too, and she knows it's time to pack up the camp and move back to town. Her husband, Hank, still uses the place in the fall for fishing and hunting. He waits for the first really bad snow to nail down the shutters so no snowmobilers can get in and piss beer on the floor. But she likes to get out early, before she feels that sense of everything closing in. It's almost physical. Her lungs get tight and short of breath at the start of fall.

She'll begin packing today because there's nothing else to do. She should be at the store, but Hank won't let her work there anymore. "The Reverend wants Nelson to help out," he told her. "He thinks you should stay at home." But they can't afford to hire

Nelson, and besides, Hank can't run that store without her. He has no head for numbers. All he knows is fish and tackle, and all Nelson knows is guns, polishing them until they shine. But people up here don't care if their guns shine or not, they just want to bag a couple of deer for the freezer. Nelson doesn't understand that. The Reverend says Nelson was sent to them for a reason, but she can't figure out what it is.

There are either too many reasons for things or no reason at all. Maybe it's all God's doing. He likes puzzles, she's sure of that. It's his occupation, like the people who make up crosswords for the newspaper. The Reverend wouldn't like to hear her say that, but never mind, she doesn't always like what he says either.

She pours herself another cup of coffee and sits on the porch in her father's old rocker. The camp belongs to her and could be worth something someday with all those rich people from Chicago and Detroit buying up land for summer places. Pretty soon there won't be any land left on the Lake Superior shore, and they'll start looking out here. A nice little private lake to fish in. But she'll never give it up, because she hates those people; a lot of them are Jews who own the banks they get their mortgages from. Lending themselves money. It isn't fair.

She hears a car on the dirt road, but it's not Hank's pickup; she'd recognize that. Maybe one of his buddies coming to fish, but usually they call first, especially now that everyone in the Sons of the Shepherd has a cell phone. She goes inside so she can look through the window. Never good to advertise you're a woman alone, even though she's never had a problem. A tan Jeep Cherokee comes into view. Looks like the Reverend's, so she tucks in her blouse and straightens her hair. Maybe he's had second thoughts about having Nelson replace her in the store.

He parks next to the shed and gets out, stepping carefully around the puddles left by last night's rain, the first in a month. He's not wearing a suit today, but his white shirt's either pressed or new because the folds are where they ought to be. He's left his dog in the car. She hates that dog, something's wrong with it; it has crazy eyes like her Aunt Betty when she drinks too much.

She feels a little nervous—the Reverend's never come to see her alone before. The Sons of the Shepherd is Hank's thing really; she goes to the Sunday services because he wants her to, but she misses the Lutheran church where her sister belongs. However, Hank's stopped drinking, and she's thankful to the Reverend for that. She waits until he knocks on the door to open it.

"Good morning, Lucy," he says. "May I come in?"

"Of course," she replies. "Want a cup of coffee?"

He shakes his head. "Nothing, please. May I?" He points to a chair.

"Of course," she says again, sitting down opposite him on the couch.

He spreads his hands on his knees. They're fine hands, slender and smooth, more like a woman's than a man's, or at least not like the men she knows who split wood all year long. He fixes his eyes on her, smiling like he does when the children march in to be blessed at the end of service. She smiles back, but it's not natural, and she wishes she were making him coffee so her back would be to him. That tight feeling in her chest comes and she coughs. "I guess I'd better get some water," she says. "Sure you don't want some?"

"All right," he answers.

She turns on the tap so it runs cold and gets two glasses from the cupboard. "Hank has confided in me about your problem," he says, as she hands him the water. "We've prayed together about it and I've prayed alone. There's no greater earthly burden for a woman than to be barren."

Her chest constricts again. "I'm not the barren one, Reverend," she says. "Did he tell you that?"

"He said the tests were inconclusive."

"You should be praying for *him*."

"I'm praying for you both." He takes a sip of water, sets the glass down, and wipes his mouth with his handkerchief. "I came here to pray with you."

She wishes she'd left the door open to let in the breeze. She doesn't want to kneel down beside him. She doesn't pray that way; she prays alone, lying in bed or working in the garden. There's something so strained in the Reverend's face, like his muscles are trying too hard to hold his jaw together. She hears the dog barking in the Cherokee, but he doesn't seem to notice. He gets down on his knees and she joins him, because if she doesn't she'll have to explain something she doesn't know how to explain. She listens as he prays for Hank and her, but she knows, the way a woman knows, that he wants something else.

CHAPTER 3

CANALS

In Oxford, Sajit and I lived in a house bordering the canal that parallels the Thames on the northwestern side of the city. From my study window I observed the itinerants and hippies who made their homes on houseboats there. In warm weather I envied them their rooftop gardens and easy life, but in winter I imagined the damp and cold seeping up through the floorboards and the air stale with coal dust and reeking of kerosene.

In Michigan, my new office in the history department overlooked another canal, the Portage, which bisects the Keweenaw Peninsula as it juts into Lake Superior. On the southern side of the canal is Houghton, home to the university, a town that strives to be cosmopolitan although the most visible worldly signs are a strip of global franchises: Pizza Hut, Blockbuster Video, McDonald's. Along the main street, its historic wood-frame houses—once home to rich copper-mine owners—have been converted into fraternities, and they wear their Greek letters like the mark of a foreign beast. It is Houghton's anomalies that are most charming: the Lebanese deli with vats of homemade hummus and

babaganouche; the 1930s bar that looks like a dive from the outside but inside boasts walls painted with intricate hunting motifs;
the crafts gallery, where, hidden in back of the copper kitsch,
handsome raku pots and wall hangings sell for much less than
they would on the East Coast.

Across the drawbridge lies the twin town of Hancock. Despite
economies of scale, Houghton and Hancock's two school systems
have never joined. Hancock still feels like a Finnish town. It has a
Finnish college, and whether it's illusion or reality, its inhabitants
seem blonder and beefier than the people on the other side. Local
lore has it that north of Hancock there are people who have never
crossed the Portage Canal and are proud of it. They are citizens of
the Keweenaw, not of Michigan's upper peninsula, or UP as it's
called, or the United States. "From sea to shining sea" means from
one shore of Lake Superior to the other.

I was pleased the department had given me an office with a
view—they didn't have to do that. So far my colleagues had been
almost too nice. It was a culture shock after Boston, where people
never had time to linger by the coffee machine or ask you how you
were and wait for an answer longer than "swamped" or "pretty
stressed out." I'd already received four dinner invitations and
many more offers of help.

It was Marcy's first day of school, and I felt a mixture of appre-
hension and relief as I unpacked my papers. I'd already met with
the school nurse, who assured me they knew what to do in the
unlikely event of a seizure. "Marcy hasn't had a seizure for over
three years," I told her, as if it were my own achievement. She
looked at me the way nurses do, with a sympathetic yet conde-
scending smile.

I put my books in the bookcase, attempting some kind of order that I knew would break down as the semester's pressures accelerated. I used all my force to yank the cabinet drawers open. They smelled musty and unused. One by one I inserted my files on the German neo-Nazi movement. The older ones were from my Ph.D. research on groups in western Germany, my current research focused on the fascist resurgence in the eastern part of the country. Not a pleasant topic, but there aren't many when you study modern German history.

Or, as in my case, when you have a Jewish mother who doesn't want to let you forget the Holocaust because she has. My Presbyterian father never forced my mother to assimilate; she did it willingly because she has a chameleon nature. As a child I never knew which color she'd be: blue-blooded WASP, green-thumbed grower of resentments, or red-hot tempered—which I preferred because then she screamed and was done with it. She lives in a retirement community in Arizona now and is the color of tan panty hose.

As I stood up to stretch my back, I heard a knock on the door. I was expecting the department head, Mark Nicholson, but standing in the doorway was a younger man I hadn't met before. "I'm Michael Landis," he announced bluntly.

"Come in," I said. "Want to sit down?"

"I came to make an appointment, unless you have time to talk now."

"I have a few minutes anyway."

I cleared some files off a chair for him and sat myself on the edge of the desk. I was glad I was perched above him. He was physically intimidating, tall, with a back that was almost too straight, and muscular limbs he advertised through a tight black Lycra cycling suit. He was carrying a helmet, which he set on top of a box.

"What can I do for you?" He looked at me as if I had just asked a stupid question. I tried again. "What's your relation to the department?"

"I'm a graduate student," he said, "and I'm looking for a Ph.D. supervisor."

"What's your field?" I noticed his face was red and sweaty from exertion and his eyes hazel like Marcy's.

"American history."

"Mine's modern German history."

"I know. I came to your job seminar."

I didn't remember his being there, but then again I'd been in a fog after the flight up in a twenty-seater plane that landed in blinding snow. "I don't think I'd be very much help."

"No one here is," he said.

"But there are several American historians—"

"Copper mining at the beginning of the century is about as con-temporary as they get. Plus they're afraid."

"Afraid of what?" I could see they might be afraid of him, since I hadn't seen him smile once.

"Afraid to find out what's really going on around here."

"And what's that?"

He leaned back, assessing me, then began. "My best friend was murdered this summer by a couple of guys experimenting with bombs." I knew he wanted me to look shocked, so I didn't. When he paused and looked down for a moment, I thought maybe I'd read him wrong and he was the type who broke down on you after the initial bravado. He looked up and past me to the window and the canal view. The shock registered then: His best friend had been murdered. Like the Turkish man I'd interviewed in Berlin last year, whose best friend had been trapped in a blaze set at a guest workers' hostel.

"He was Native American—Ojibwa," Michael continued. "I met him in grade school. My dad ran a gas station near the reservation in Baraga. We went separate ways in high school, but in college we became friends again. He did a degree in forestry and ended up working for the Forest Service over near the Porcupine Mountains. He was on a fire watch when he spotted smoke and went to check it out. They found his body near the residue from a couple of pipe bombs."

"I'm sorry," I said.

"I'm not sorry. I'm angry, angry as hell."

"Do they know who did it?"

"There were some tire tracks, and the office relayer heard a few male voices on the radio, but she didn't record them. So, no, they don't know who did it. Specifically, that is. And they aren't trying hard enough to find out. But it's no secret that the area over near Ironwood is a militia stronghold. Lots of Forest Service agents have been harassed in the last couple of years, tires punctured, that kind of thing. But no one had been hurt. Johnny's the first."

"I'm sorry," I said again. The clutter in the office suddenly seemed oppressive and I wanted to sweep it all away, start this conversation over again in a tidy room, with me behind the desk, not on top of it. Then it would be easier to say no because I knew what he was going to ask and I was going to have to be the cool voice of reason: Finding your friend's murderers is the subject of a police investigation, not a Ph.D.

But he was clever; he approached it another way. He wanted to study the recent rise of the Far Right in Michigan, looking at parallels with the populist movement at the turn of the century. He turned on the academic language as effortlessly as changing gears on a racing bike, citing all the right authors. He was playing me for a fool, but that's the game after all. The graduate student must impress. The graduate student must flatter. I was the perfect supervisor, of course, since I studied neofascist movements in Germany. "That's a very different context," I insisted.

"I know that, but you can teach me your research techniques."

"I still think you're at risk—"

"At risk of what?"

"Your best friend was just killed."

"So I'll be too personally engaged?"

I was glad he said it and not me. "Yes."

"Hasn't that ever happened to you in your research?"

"A few times, yes."

"And what did you do about it?"

"I pulled back."

"You tell me to pull back and I will."

I didn't believe him, so I left things hanging. I told him I wanted to talk to other people in the department and read some of his previous work before I made any decisions.

"They'll be delighted if you take me off their hands," he said, as he buckled his helmet. "I'll check in with you next week."

Later that morning when Mark Nicholson stopped by, I asked him about Michael. For the first of many times I watched him roll his eyes. I liked Mark; he was appropriately cynical, but not in the sharp East Coast kind of way that cuts too close to the bone. His body was soft too; his stomach looked like a down pillow you could easily rest your head upon.

In so many words he told me Michael was their most difficult graduate student but also the smartest. In college he was All-American in Nordic skiing, then ran a ski shop in Calumet until he got tired of snow and discovered history. "Calumet was the center of the mining industry around here," he explained. "It's even got a beautiful old opera house where Sarah Bernhardt played. Michael helped start the ball rolling to make a national historic park up there. I met him on one of the park committees and was impressed. I encouraged him to come study here."

"Are you still impressed?" I asked.

"Oh, yeah, I'm still impressed, all right—the guy's the most stubborn person I've ever met. We've told him a hundred times he's way too close to his friend's death to do any research on the subject, and he accuses us of being a bunch of cowards. He's still grieving; he's not rational. I leave it up to you. He's been through everyone else in the department. If you last more than a month, I'll buy you a drink. Just don't let him get to you. Don't blame yourself if you can't handle him."

All I needed was someone else I couldn't handle. As if Marcy wasn't enough, or the husband I pretended I had, who pretended he wanted us back because he wanted to believe it. Some men just can't sustain love on a daily basis even if they want to. Somewhere between the breakfast dishes and the first dirty diaper they turn off—and then on again in bed a few times, maybe even a few years, until they flicker and the electricity supply runs out.

Mark took me out to lunch in the faculty dining room, and then I went home so I could be there when Marcy got off the school bus. Just to make sure—of what? That she hadn't collapsed in a seizure or run back to Evan, her punk boyfriend, in Boston? I don't know. Maybe just to watch her step off the bus and walk up the drive swinging her backpack like any normal kid.

I watched her from the kitchen window. I don't think much about my own looks anymore, maybe because I see enough of myself in her. She has my height and broad shoulders, and even my nose, just long enough to be interesting, as my mother used to say. Otherwise she is Sajit's child—she has his almond-shaped eyes and dark hair and skin, and there is a delicacy to her movements that belies her large frame. When she was little, she hated her dark skin because the kids on the school playground in Oxford taunted her. "Paki, Paki, go back home!" they shouted, throwing gravel in her face.

Sajit was outraged they thought she was Pakistani, not Indian, and he transferred her to an elite private girls' school. But the girls there were really no nicer to her, because she wasn't smart enough. "The epilepsy drugs affect her performance," Sajit kept telling the teachers, and he hired private tutors, which meant she never had time to play. I tried to tell him that not all children of scholars are born scholars, whether they have epilepsy or not. He made her feel dumb, and alone in the privacy of my study I screamed silently at him and the school.

That was another reason I moved to Boston. In the Cambridge public schools Marcy finally fit in, and when she reached adolescence she learned to play her difference for all it was worth. Ten holes in each ear and skimpy tie-dye T-shirts that revealed her long, gorgeous dark arms. Marcy the Exotic: the boys followed her like the Pied Piper, but they were still children, half her size. Until Evan, three years her senior, hit on her. Sex, drugs, rock 'n roll, B's to C's, C's to D's.

So I moved to Houghton and found myself standing by the kitchen window, hoping when she opened the door she'd cross the threshold to a Fresh Start. She'd smile at me as I set out juice and crackers and we'd sit at the table, mother and daughter, and be close.

"How was school?" I asked, as she threw her backpack on a chair.

"What I expected."

"Which was?"

"Do you really want to know?" I nodded. She turned her back and grabbed a soda from the refrigerator. "It sucks. The teachers are boring," she said, pulling the tab, "and the kids, they're worse. They're totally superficial. At lunch all the girls talked about was brand-name clothes or they giggled about boys. It was like I was back in seventh grade."

"It's only your first day, Marcy. There must be a lot of different kinds of kids."

"The geeks, you mean? They all hang together in geek classes and look down on the rest of us. It's apartheid, Mom, and I'm stuck in the underclass."

"It'll get better."

"That's what you always say, and it never does."

"That's not true."

"What's not true, that you always say that or that it never gets better?"

"Both."

"Bullshit."

That was usually a signal that we were going to fight in earnest or disengage, and I wasn't sure which I wanted. I reached into the cabinet looking for something to open and seized the first thing there, a bag of pistachios. "Want some?" I asked.

"They ruin my nails."

"But you said you wanted some when we were in the grocery store."

"I forgot about my nails."

"Pistachios are expensive, you know." I wished I could tell her how I hated her long nails, but instead I opened a nut and ate it. It was dried up, bitter. "What do you want for dinner?" I asked, cracking open another.

"Anything."

"Chicken salad?"

"Didn't we just have that?"

"Spaghetti?"

She made a face.

"Well, what then?"

"I'm not hungry."

It was time to become the Invisible Mother, vanish in a poof, and materialize elsewhere: out on the road for a walk, by the computer, in the bath. But I wanted more from her. I wanted her to ask me about my day, but she never would; it was beyond her. "I didn't want to move here either," I remarked, regretting the words as soon as I said them.

"So why didn't we go back to Oxford?"

"I think you know the answer to that question."

"I think I don't."

"Your father and I do better living apart."

"Some people get divorced, you know. It's easier to explain to people that your parents are divorced. When I say you're separated, they ask for how long, and I have to say six years. Evan says it's weird."

"What does Evan know?"

"A lot more than you give him credit for. You moved here to get me away from Evan, didn't you?

"I moved here because I needed a job."

"Thought a little separation would do us good, but I'm not you, you know. I don't like to be alone."

"Marcy." But she was already down the hall, opening the door to her room.

CHAPTER 4

SINS

The Reverend's body feels much heavier than Hank's though it isn't really; he's probably a good twenty pounds lighter, but his arms don't support his weight as he rides her, grabbing her breasts like saddle horns. "The Lord wants this union," he keeps saying. All Lucy wants is his seed. It was faster last time—he came in a few minutes—but now he's sweaty and so damn heavy and he's trying too hard. So she starts to pretend that she likes it, even though she just wants to get up and pee and take a shower and put on something clean, a sundress and a white cardigan sweater. Make dinner. Something light, chicken salad, maybe with a few grapes thrown in, seedless ones.

Finally, it's over and he rolls off, saying again how the Lord wanted this. She hates how he can't keep his mouth shut. You've broken a commandment and committed a sin, she wants to tell him, just to see his face go pale. But she doesn't say anything, because she needs him to keep coming over until there's a baby growing inside. She'll pray tonight that it happens fast so she doesn't have to keep sinning. Lord have mercy, make my sins short, make my sins sweet. There's no sweetness in the Reverend; she can see why he doesn't have a wife.

A fly settles on her arm and she brushes it away. It's on the Reverend's back now, perched on a mole. If it were Hank's back, she would blow it away. There's a little sweetness left in Hank, not much after all the drinking, but enough to spark a memory here and there of when they first got together and he thought she was everything.

The Reverend brushes off the fly and sits up, pulling the sheet over his private parts. "That was nice, Lucy," he says. "I have to go soon—the shepherding circle's getting together at five. Did Hank tell you he'll be gone this weekend?" She shakes her head. "There's a meeting over in Ironwood."

"We were planning on moving back to town this weekend."

"I told Hank I'd come over and help you tomorrow. I'll borrow Nelson's truck and we can do it in one run."

"You sure you have the time?"

"I'll make the time. The Lord wants this, Lucy. Don't worry, He wants me to be with you."

He stands up and, with his back toward her, puts on his boxer shorts. He's built square, with short legs and a rear end that sticks out more than Hank's. He looks better with his clothes on than off, and she's relieved when he's finally zipping up his pants. He doesn't have many muscles on his arms, and she wonders how good he'll be lifting boxes. She's got the sheet pulled up to her neck.

"I'll come at ten tomorrow," he says, turning back toward her. "You'll pray tonight."

"Yes, Reverend."

"What will you pray for?"

"The souls of the unborn, like you told us to do on Sunday."

He nods but moves hesitantly toward the door, as if he's waiting for her to say more. "You don't feel bad about this, Lucy?" he says, as pushes the screen door and holds it open.

"No, Reverend, I know the Lord wants our union."

"You feel it in your heart?"

"Oh, yes," she lies.

"You won't tell Hank."

"Of course not, Reverend."

He calls good-bye to her from the porch, and then she listens to him start up the Cherokee. No barking—he hasn't brought the dog today. When she's sure he's gone, she gets up and takes a shower and even brushes her teeth to rid herself of his smell and his taste. He doesn't make her feel dirty exactly, more like a glass you left water in too long and it started to get a little yellow and slimy and you have to wash it with really hot water to get it clean. She likes things clean, that's why she likes numbers; they're a lot cleaner than words.

Hank told her he'd ask the Reverend if she could still do the store accounts at night. Hank knows he needs her help, but he has to run all decisions by the shepherding circle, and the Reverend has the last say. They have too much power over Hank, but he doesn't drink anymore; she has to keep reminding herself of that. Once, shortly after Hank joined Sons of the Shepherd, he got so drunk he hit her, and the next day the Reverend made him get down on his knees and beg her forgiveness. She still likes to think about it. He got down on his knees and begged and cried, and she didn't cry; she just stood there.

After getting dressed, she puts two chicken breasts in a pot of boiling water and dices up some onions and celery. She washes grapes in an old enamel colander she inherited from her mother. Her mother's dead of lung cancer from smoking too many cigarettes. Sometimes she wonders if that's why she gets that tight feeling in her chest, if she's remembering her mother and the way she coughed near the end.

Just as she's draining the chicken the phone rings. It's Hank, who says he's bringing Nelson home for dinner. She wants to tell him no, she doesn't have enough food, but she knows Hank will insist the Sons of the Shepherd are like family, and it's their duty to share their food with them like the disciples shared the bread and wine. So she boils another piece of chicken and sets three places at the table and then sits down in the rocker on the porch, planning what she'll do when Hank's gone for the weekend. She'll call her sister, Diane, and maybe they can drive to the mall in Marquette. She hasn't seen her in a long time. Diane doesn't like how the Reverend's taken Hank and her away from the Lutheran church.

Diane surely wouldn't like what the Reverend's doing to her now, either. And she wouldn't understand why Lucy's going along with it. Diane's babies came so easy, she just doesn't know what it's like to want one so much and never get one. All she does is complain about her three kids, but that's a privilege, that kind of complaining.

She looks out at the lake, which each day seems to get smaller and smaller as the fallen leaves thicken around its edge. She feels peaceful for a moment until the Voice comes to her. It's a voice she's been hearing for over a year now, and she's scared to tell anyone about it because they'll think she's crazy. But she's not. It's the voice of God or an angel or some spirit up there that watches out for her. The Voice warns her that something's about to go wrong.

That night at dinner Hank announces Nelson is going to move into the cabin next week because he needs somewhere cheap to live. She wants to say no, it's her cabin and she makes the decisions, but how can she in front of Nelson? She serves them both chicken salad, taking only a little for herself. There's a hairline crack on her plate and she follows it with her eyes, like a river on a map.

CHAPTER 5

BLOOD AND SOIL

The next day Michael sent me a collection of his papers, which I read late at night in the bedroom that still didn't feel like mine. Maybe it was the ugly gold color of the carpet or the banality of the light fixtures that made me think I was in a cheap motel, in transit, but to where?

His papers were good, it was true; he possessed the kind of raw intelligence that professors seize on like dogs pouncing on a hunk of meat. His style was rough in the first year, but he had gradually learned to dress his arguments in designer fashions, a little post-modernism here, a little subaltern studies there—at least until his most recent survey of the Radical Right in Michigan. Here he was entering my territory; I had made my name through painstaking documentation, not theoretical flourish. But unlike him, I was much more detached from the subject matter. Yet, even so, I had crossed the line.

It happened on my first trip away from Marcy, who was five at the time. Sajit's mother was visiting and more than happy to take over so I could do my research. In truth I think she wanted to have her son to herself even more than her granddaughter. By reducing him to a spoiled little boy, she would have the pleasure of commanding two children. I was glad to get out.

It was amazing, sitting alone on the bus to Heathrow, then the plane to Munich, and then the train into the city, with only my own demands to meet. And they were few and far between, since I'd learned to compress my own desire until it was like a piece of paper folded into so many tiny squares it would never open again without creases and tears.

I slept the night in Munich, then took a bus up to the ecocommune in the Alps founded by New Age antihero Gustaf Schmidt. I was investigating neofascist influences in the Green movement in Germany, something environmentalists generally don't like to talk about. Nazism has always had a green streak, with roots in the *Völkisch* movement, whose nature mysticism and hostility to urban culture ultimately translated into hatred of the Jews. Some top Nazi officials like Rudolf Hess promoted organic farming and nature protection, but of course the homeland they were protecting was for the purebred alone. Hitler was a vegetarian.

So was Gustaf Schmidt. Word was that in between planting his gardens, shepherding his hippie flock, and writing his philosophical tomes, he was starting to make alliances with certain neofascist groups who shared his passion for ridding Germany of consumerism and foreign influences. He had consented to an interview even though I was from the land of all evil, the United States of McDonald's.

He met me at the bus stop in an old VW van, dressed in jeans and a faded work shirt, with graying hair down to his shoulders. He was tall and thin with a sharp nose, and his face was gaunt yet ruddy. A string of coral beads was wound tightly around his neck. He walked with a slight limp and I noticed the heel of one shoe was higher than the other.

I didn't want to like him, but he was more relaxed than most Germans I'd met, and on the dirt road to the commune he kept stopping to show me a particular species of wildflower or the view down into a forested gorge, where a waterfall glinted in the sunlight. By the time we reached the commune, I didn't mind that he helped me out of the van or carried my bag.

We sat on his cabin porch, drinking Riesling and eating fresh cherries. I convinced myself that the wine would loosen his tongue more than mine, and besides, I had nothing to give away since I was the interrogator. But he kept turning the conversation back to me, inquiring about my family and my work, and I even admitted to being half Jewish. When he asked me my views on the ecological crisis, I refrained from telling him the only crisis that concerned me was domestic, the growing chasm between Sajit and myself. But he figured it out anyway. Maybe he read cherry pits like the I-Ching, because he knew by the end of an hour that I was vulnerable.

"I don't know how anyone could accuse me of being a Nazi," he told me. "I've never been a fascist or an anti-Semite, and I never will be. Yes, I'm a German, and yes, I believe in a German identity, but it can save, it doesn't need to destroy. I believe Germany will be in the vanguard of a new ecological consciousness. We've suffered so much already from the cruel disease of modernity—we know what we need to do. But we need strong leadership with a spiritual vision. Our politicians understand nothing of this."

When I asked him if it was true he was making contact with

neofascist groups, he shook his head vehemently. "They made contact with me, and so I spoke to them. And then it's broadcast all over the country that I'm a fascist, and the Green party throws me out. Many of these groups, they're made up of lost young people, alienated, without jobs. I'd like to show them another way, and so I take the opportunity to speak with them. Is that so wrong? Is it wrong to try to persuade them that they need to find themselves through nature, not through violence? Who will speak to them if I don't?"

After we drank the bottle of wine, he gave me a tour of the commune. I wish now it had been a rainy day with people slogging around in mud boots and the dirt paths rivulets of slime. Instead, the afternoon sun cast everything in a *Sound of Music* glow. The adults put hoes to the soil, children frolicked in the orchards, and everyone—even the goats, it seemed—smiled happily at me. Gustaf kept placing a hand on my shoulder: fatherlike, at first, and then with a touch of something else. I looked at my watch and told him it was time to return to town for the bus. He told me there was a later bus and invited me for dinner. I told myself maybe it was a chance to learn more. After dinner and another bottle of wine, he invited me to sleep with him.

That's when I learned that the danger of folding up your desire is not that it will never open again, or that when it does it will disintegrate and tear, but that it returns with a vengeance so that you lose control and find yourself in bed with a man who some say is a fascist and you don't care, because he's a good lover and your husband isn't. But after you're sated and he falls asleep, you have second thoughts.

So you get up and rifle through the papers on his desk, hoping to find proof of his unsavory affiliations. And perhaps you might have if he hadn't woken; perhaps you would have fulfilled your childhood fantasy of being a spy. Instead, he stands and confronts you, grotesque in his old hippie nakedness, and accuses you of being a paranoid Jew. That's where all the rumors about him come from, he says, paranoid Jews. And you have to spend the rest of the night sleeping in the same bed, where the sheets smell sour from stale sex and the blankets are coarse against your skin, and you become Jewish in that moment, no longer half-blood, no longer Presbyterian, and travel back, back, back, along the long road that led you to commit this act of betrayal.

But that wasn't punishment enough. When I returned home a week later from my research trip, exhausted and hating myself and hoping a hug from my daughter would somehow set things right, the house was empty and there was a note under the door from a neighbor that I should go immediately to the pediatrics ward of the John Radcliffe Hospital. Marcy had experienced her first seizure that morning and was in the hospital for tests.

Now she was down the hall, asleep, I hoped, and safely medicated, all sixteen years of her.

I put Michael's papers on the table and turned off the light. A nod from me would be a nod for him to cross the line, because he would, of course he would, but who was I to stop him? We all have to make our own mistakes, I told myself, knowing it was a lame excuse. I'd crossed the line into a little stupid sex, that's all. He risked more—maybe even physical danger. But I wanted to watch him, to follow him, because I needed a diversion from all the emptiness that filled me in this ugly room, this ugly house.

A few hours later something woke me, and as I came to consciousness, I thought I heard Marcy's voice. I sprang out of bed, frightened that she'd had a seizure. But as I approached her room, I realized she was talking on the phone. "It's past two o'clock," I remarked angrily, as I opened her bedroom door.

"I have to go now, Nicole," she said, putting down the receiver. "Nicole just wanted to know how school was going."

"At two A.M.?"

"She stays up late."

I knew it was Evan who stayed up late, not Nicole, but I was too sleepy for a battle. "Go to bed," I said.

"OK, Mom," she mumbled.

I slept fitfully after that, dipping in and out of dreams that were like fragments of one long unfinished sentence. When I logged on to my e-mail after breakfast, there were two messages: a reminder of the department picnic that evening and a few lines from Sajit, wondering how we were settling in.

"Everything's fine," I wrote back, though I knew he would see through that. I pressed the SEND key, polluting cyberspace with yet another little white lie.

When I arrived at the picnic, the department volleyball game was under way. Michael was serving, and the ball flew over the net with such force that it was impossible for the hapless players on the other team to return it. "Hey, go easy on us, Mike!" Mark Nicholson shouted. "This isn't the Olympics." He spotted me and waved me over. "Dr. Grace has arrived just in time to save us."

"Oh, no, I'm a terrible volleyball player," I said.

"Doesn't matter. We can use all the help we can get against these young upstarts." I noticed then that the teams were firmly divided between faculty and graduate students. "Come on in, you can't be any worse than I am."

Michael's next serve was softer and directed at me. I managed to hit it just high enough so Mark could punch it over the net, and the service returned to us. "See, you did save us, Gillian." Mark gave me a pat on the back.

We managed to lose the service on the first volley because of a spectacular return by a young woman who dove for the ball, setting it up for Michael to slam it. They hugged each other after that success, and as the game proceeded I began to suspect they were more than just fellow team members. They anticipated each other's moves, moving in and out of each other's space as if they'd been there before in more intimate circumstances. She was petite, with a ballet dancer's body and a pretty face, the kind of girl I hated in high school because each one seemed to twirl effortlessly through cruel cliques on the toes of pink satin shoes. I hated her now because she was still young and graceful.

Maybe at her age I would have been graceful too, if Marcy hadn't been conceived in the cottage in Devon. Maybe I would have been able to dive for the ball like her and rise to accolades instead of coos at the baby in the baby carriage. I became invisible in my early twenties and had to fight my way back to recognition.

When I stood behind her in the line for barbecue chicken, I discovered she wasn't so pretty closer up. Her mouth and chin were too small and her voice was shrill, her laugh teetering on the edge of nervous. She kept looking over at Michael, who was in another line, but as far as I could tell, he didn't return her gaze. Nor did he look at me. The wind was picking up, and he'd donned a dark

green fleece after the game. I chided myself for noticing everything about him, down to the color of his socks.

I sat at a picnic table with a group of faculty wives; the only
other female faculty member was on sabbatical this year. The conversation centered on their kids' sports activities, with a few
digressions into music. Did the Suzuki method really work? Well,
it did for Sarah but not for Libby. Libby was a reader; she wanted
to read the music from the very start. Ethan's soccer coach was too
negative; Peter's was nice but without any serious skills. They
asked me if Marcy played sports and I said no. Then they asked
me if she played music. "On the CD player," I replied, and they all
looked embarrassed. I got up, claiming I was going to get another
piece of chicken. The men were all huddled around the ham-
burger grill, drinking beer.

After throwing my plate away, I followed the path to the
lakeshore. It passed through a mature birch grove, where I
stopped to pick up a piece of shredded bark, pulling it taut
between my hands. The underside was a light pink, the same color
as the sky. I felt stupid because I wanted to cry. Maybe my period
was coming on, maybe the barbecue sauce tasted like childhood,
maybe it was just that Marcy didn't play the Suzuki violin like the
little girls squeaking their parents' way into rapture. When I was
pregnant, someone gave me a book about having your baby listen
to classical music in the womb so it would come out a virtuoso.
What did Marcy listen to, our fights or our silences? Or maybe I'm
forgetting that we were still happy back then.

The beach had no sand; it was composed of tiny little rocks,
smaller than pebbles, all a uniform dark brown. Later someone
would explain it was stamp sand, the man-made residue of rocks

processed for copper. Pieces of driftwood lay about like lazy animals, and snared in an old fishing net were a few bottles and cans. In front of me a breakwater stretched about a hundred yards into the lake, and I made that my goal.

I stood at its end, watching the waves crash against the rocks on the side. The sun was going down and the pink was deeper now, cooling into purple like bruised flesh. The spray stung my face and I could almost imagine I was by the sea, tasting salt on my skin. I knew I should go back—they would probably be packing up the picnic soon—but I preferred the lake to human company. Moving water; I'd sought it out ever since I discovered the brook at the bottom of our road and my mother found me there at twilight, sculpting clay from the bank into little animals. She thought I was dead, drowned, abducted, and warned me never to stray again. But stray we must, lovers of moving water.

I heard a voice behind me. "I thought I'd find you here."

Startled, I turned around, then tried to sound casual. "Oh, hi, Michael," I said.

"The party's just getting lively—the kids are roasting marshmallows."

"I don't like marshmallows."

"Neither do I. Nice view of the sunset here." I nodded. "The beaches are better farther down, though—white sand." I nodded again. He paused, putting his hands in his pockets. "Have you read my stuff yet?"

He seemed vulnerable for once. "Yes."

"What did you think?"

"You're a good writer, but you already know that."

"So will you work with me?"

"I think it's going to be hard."

"Of course it's going to be hard. That's why I need your help."
He had become full size again, hands out of pockets, ready to
return the serve. But I just stood there, hanging on to the ball,
because I knew it might be the last time I exercised any real power
over him. If I said yes, I would become his accomplice; if I said no,
he would just turn and go. "I'm going to a big Christian rally in
Ironwood this weekend," he said, breaking the silence.

"What do you think you'll find there?"

"A place to start."

"You'll go as a researcher?"

"I'll go as a God-fearing Christian, just one of the crowd."

"You'll stick out in a crowd."

"There are going to be thousands of men there. Look"—he
came a step closer to me—"I'm going to do this project whether
you help me or not. You don't have to feel responsible either way."

"It's my job to be responsible."

"Then help me."

"All right," I replied, "but on a trial basis."

"Fine. Whatever it takes."

The children were still roasting marshmallows when we got
back, and I stood by the fire to warm my hands. Michael's girlfriend, if she was his girlfriend, approached with two helmets in
her hand. "We should get going now," she scolded him. "You
know I don't like to ride in the dark." He introduced her but
mumbled her name, so I wasn't sure whether it was Laura or
Loren. She gave me a quick smile as if to conserve her energy. A
little girl offered her a marshmallow, which she pulled gingerly off
the stick. "For the road," she said, dropping it into her mouth.

As I watched them mount their bikes, I felt lonely again and knew I should go before the feeling got the better of me. I retrieved my Tupperware bowl with its remaining pasta salad—it hadn't been a hit. After I said my obligatory good-byes, Mark Nicholson escorted me to the car. "So what did you decide about Michael?" he asked, opening the door for me.

"I agreed to be his supervisor—on a trial basis."

"Well, it should be interesting, if nothing else. Good luck tomorrow—sorry we gave you a large lecture course. Usually there's a grace period, but there's no one else who can teach European history. Remember, half of them don't really know where Europe is."

"I'll begin with a map."

"Don't assume they know much about World War Two either."

"I'll assume nothing."

"Always the best policy."

On the way home I passed the two bikes on a straight stretch along the Portage Canal. It only took a few seconds, but afterward I looked in my rearview mirror at their retreating lights, trying to recall what it felt like to ride at night with the wind in your face. Until Marcy was born, Sajit and I relied on bicycles for transportation, and some of our best moments were those spent riding along the canal in the evening down to Port Meadow, where we would cross over the Thames to the Perch pub for a drink. And then we would ride back along the river, past the lock and the old "nunnery" where Henry VIII kept his women. Even though I was the faster cyclist, Sajit would go first and hold the gates open for me. I didn't mind. I was carrying his baby and deserved those little acts of chivalry.

I rode my bike up to the day before I gave birth. I was so young, much younger than Laura or Loren. I thought a baby would fold easily into my life, but my labor took thirty-six hours and I hemorrhaged afterward. I remember watching them set up the bag of someone else's blood and wondering whose it was, which stranger's life force now inhabited me.

Lucy feels disoriented waking up in the house. Even though it's bigger, it seems more closed in than the cabin, and she misses the lake view. Hank left early for the Ironwood meeting, so there's not even his face to look at. She puts on her bathrobe and stumbles out to the kitchen. The coffeemaker is missing—she must have left it in the cabin. She couldn't concentrate very well on the moving with the Reverend helping her. He kept getting in the way with that big butt of his. She would have done better on her own.

That's always the way, isn't it? Someone comes to help and you end up helping them. Even before she made the bed, he wanted to have sex in this house too. She made him help her put on the sheets, and after he left she washed them with a cupful of bleach. It's a relief to have him gone for the weekend. Just too bad Diane's busy; she was looking forward to going to Marquette.

Instead, she'll have to go out to the cabin to fetch the coffeepot, either that or buy a new one. But why leave a perfectly decent one there for Nelson to spoil? She hates having Nelson living in the cabin. "He'll guard the place," Hank said, as if it needed guarding. She hopes the winter's hard and Nelson can't get his truck down the road. She hopes he turns around and drives south, away from here. The store is losing money since she left—what a surprise.

But Hank keeps saying not to worry, the Reverend will make it all work out. Hank's eyes go blurry when she shows him the numbers, and he gets up and pours himself a glass of milk.

She should get more milk today and something for herself to eat, maybe one of those frozen lasagna dinners.

She turns on the TV and then turns it off again. After a summer without it, the noise doesn't seem right; it's like having people you don't know suddenly jabbering all around you without listening to what you have to say. Rude, it just sounds plain rude.

She makes herself a piece of toast and sits at the table, looking out the picture window at some kids roller-blading up and down the street. She'd like to try that some time, she's still a good ice skater. Her nieces are impressed with the way she can jump and spin and skate backward. Diane was never as good, and now she's too fat anyway.

After breakfast she puts in a load of laundry, then decides to drive to the cabin to get the coffeemaker. There's fog in the low-lying areas, so she has to go slowly and put on her lights. She swerves to avoid a dead deer by the side of the road, surprised that no one's taken it away yet. Usually someone beats the highway department to it. No use wasting the venison.

When she reaches the cabin, she hurries out of the car and up the steps. She feels watched even though Nelson's in Ironwood. She turns the key in the lock and pushes open the door. His clothes are all over everywhere; he's a slob; she's not surprised. The sink is full of dirty dishes and the coffeepot has grounds in it. She washes it out and unplugs the machine.

She knows she should leave, but she doesn't want to. It's her cabin and Nelson shouldn't be living here. He shouldn't have a gun on the table. He shouldn't have taken her job at the store. She kicks one of his shirts off the carpet. Another week and the place will smell.

No Bible by the bedside either. She's always seen through him—there's no light of Jesus in his eyes. Instead there's a pamphlet, which she picks up and leafs through. It's from the International Aryan Covenant, with post office addresses in Chicago and Rostock, Germany. Building brotherhood across borders, it says, reuniting the tribe. Their logo is a cross with a swastika overlaying it.

CHAPTER 6

PINE CONES

I am a good lecturer. I know how to move across the stage, crack jokes, humiliate the smart-asses, and dispense history like holy water, a few droplets at a time. In my first large lecture at Keweenaw University, I managed to reach most of the class with the message that the map of Europe has changed over time. Maps change—that's a novel idea for a generation whose cartographic knowledge is limited to diagrams of the mall.

My father taught me to love maps. He collected antique atlases and globes, which he displayed in the den. That was his room, off-limits to my mother's monster vacuum cleaner that sucked the living innards from our house. As a young child I used to escape to the den and spin the globes, more attuned to colors than continents, but as I got older, my father and I played a game. I spun the globe with my eyes closed, then put my finger down on it. Wherever it landed, he'd say something about the place—even in the middle of the ocean—coming up with some obscure fact about nautical history, trade routes, or battles at sea. On the rare occasions he didn't know anything, we'd consult the *Encyclopedia Britannica.*

My father was a much-loved high school geography teacher. His memorial service was packed with former students who told my mother and me how much he had changed their lives, parting the curtains a crack so they could see that the world was more than driving a few exits down the interstate. Whatever gift I have for teaching, I got from him, though I don't have his energy. One lecture and I'm drained. So when I returned to my office after my first performance at Keweenaw, I prayed that no one had signed up to meet me.

But of course Michael was there waiting, this time holding a briefcase instead of a helmet and dressed respectably in khakis and a plaid shirt. An engineering student, I would have said, viewing him from the back. But then he turned and flashed that intense look of his, and I was locked into his need. It was almost lunchtime, so I suggested we go somewhere to eat. He told me about a quiet cafeteria in the forestry building and we headed over there.

It was a raw day, so windy we had to keep our heads down to keep dirt from blowing in our eyes. Rain spat at us, but an umbrella would have been no use. Still, the fresh air felt good and I climbed the steps to the forestry building as fast as he did. The cafeteria was on the second floor, with large windows overlooking a patch of carefully tended forest where all the trees bore markers with their names. I got a bowl of chili and a piece of corn bread and followed him to a table for two by the window.

After draping his brown leather jacket carefully on the back of his chair, he sat down and spread three little packets of mustard on his ham sandwich. I dipped my spoon into the chili—the beef was greasy but the sauce was OK. We ate in silence for a minute

or so, avoiding each other's eyes. I had the view, so I watched a
squirrel scurry up an oak tree to a nest precariously perched in the
high branches.

In unison we picked up our drinks, but neither of us seemed
very thirsty. "How was your first class?" he asked. When I told
him about the geography lesson, he admitted to having an addic-
tion to U.S. Geological Survey maps—one wall of his house was
covered with USGS maps of the Upper Peninsula. "I used them to
map out cross-country ski routes," he said. "I published the first
guide to trails up here, but it was a mistake."

"Why?"

"I let snowmobilers in on my secrets."

"They wreck the trails?"

"Sometimes. And sometimes they almost run you over, and
then you have the pleasure of breathing their exhaust for the rest
of your ski."

"Mark told me you used to own a ski shop," I remarked, stir-
ring the chili to disperse the grease.

"In a past life."

"And you were a competitive skier in college."

"He told you that too?"

I nodded. "What made you give it up?"

He shrugged, then wiped a spot of mustard from his chin. "I
went as far as I could with it. I pushed my body to the limit, and
then it didn't make sense anymore. I got tired of always training
for something. So I opened the ski shop and then I got fed up with
that because retail's all about anticipation too, what to order, how
many to keep in stock. And the sport changed. It got trendy and
everyone went for waxless skis. The art of it disappeared. I

shouldn't complain—the business kept growing, but then I had to become a manager, and I hated that the most. I don't like to manage other people. So I sold when the price was right."

"Do you still ski?"

"Have you ever cross-country skied?"

"A couple of times in New England."

"Well, it's not something you give up, especially if you live up here. I just do it differently. I don't force destinations on myself and I don't compete against my watch. I'll take you out when we get some snow. It really changes the way you look at winter."

"Thanks," I murmured, unsure whether to accept the offer or not.

He pushed his tray to the side, moving his gaze from me to the neighboring tables with a mechanical jerk of his neck, like a windup toy. He seemed nervous suddenly and reached around to see if his jacket was still on the chair. "Do you want to hear about the Sons of the Shepherd meeting in Ironwood?" he asked, lowering his voice. I nodded; there was a piece of corn bread in my mouth. He leaned forward, spreading his hands on the table. They were small and slender, out of proportion to the rest of him. No wedding band, just a silver and turquoise ring on his right hand.

"The rally, prayer meeting, pageant—I don't know what to call it—was held at a football stadium," he began. "There must have been over five thousand men there, because the bleachers were full, plus people were sitting on the ground even though it was muddy. It started with a marching band playing 'When the Saints Come Marching In'—they made a formation of the cross—and then we all rose to sing the 'Battle Hymn of the Republic.' That's when the big guys and their underlings entered like a football squad: a Reverend Walters from Idaho, a Reverend Thompson from Chicago, and a Reverend Ramsay, supposedly from around here. I never heard of him before.

"They spoke for about twenty minutes each. It was a strange combination of fire and brimstone and then repentance and love— every sinner finds a home in Jesus, that kind of thing. And then the sinners spoke. One guy was a wife batterer who mended his ways when he joined a shepherding circle, another was a reformed homosexual who was now happily married, and there was a young guy who confessed he was too weak to marry his pregnant girl-friend and so she murdered his baby in her womb. Then the reverend from Idaho came back up and said the lesson was that real men love their women and children and treat them well. They have to accept the responsibility of being masters of their families because—you'll love this—men were born to lead and women to follow. But while real men should be the masters in their own homes, they're servants in the house of the Lord. Shepherding circles teach men to be humble lambs of Jesus. He told us to turn around and look the man standing next to us in the eye and con-fess a sin and ask for forgiveness. Then hug each other and say, 'I forgive you, brother.' And the men did it—there were strangers weeping in each other's arms."

"What did you do?" I asked.

"I confessed a sin. I told the man next to me I was having sex with a woman I didn't love."

"And what did he confess to you?"

"What didn't he confess? The poor guy was so beset with guilt he couldn't stop talking. He even felt guilty about mistreating his dog. Finally, I just had to hug him and say it was all right, and he started crying. It was weird, I tell you. And then when the crying died down, we said a prayer and sang more hymns, and Reverend Ramsay exhorted all of us who weren't members of a circle to sign up outside at the tables. I left and went to look at the tables. I collected a lot of literature." He retrieved a stack of pamphlets from his briefcase and set them before me on the table. "I sorted through them last night. A lot is standard Born Again stuff, but there's political literature too."

He handed me a pamphlet with a picture of a bloody fetus and the message STOP THE EXECUTIONERS on the front. On the inside was a diatribe against abortion, Planned Parenthood, sex education, and women's lib, all apparently the work of the Devil. "Look at this one," he said, as he gave me a booklet on the New World Order. "This is the Black Helicopter stuff—the UN is trying to take over the United States, and there's an international financial conspiracy masterminded by the Jews. But this is the most interesting." It was a sheet of paper advertising a sporting goods store "with all the tools you need to survive the coming chaos." "I know that store," Michael said. "It's about three miles from here, on the road to Calumet. I used to buy bait there when Johnny and I went out fishing. I'm going to check it out."

"It could be they're just selling flashlights and batteries to survive power outages."

"Maybe. I also signed up for an introductory session about joining a shepherding circle."

"Where?"

"Hancock."

"They'll figure it out."

"Figure out what?"

"That you're not who you say you are."

"I'm not going to lie about who I am. I'm Michael Landis and I've been studying history, hoping to find the meaning of life, but I can't find it."

"It doesn't sound convincing."

"You'd be surprised. I'm a good actor when I have to be."

"And how will this help your thesis?"

"Don't they call it 'participant observation'?"

"Participant observers aren't supposed to lie," I rejoined.

"I'm not lying, I *am* still searching for the meaning of life." He paused, straightening the pile of pamphlets. "It's just a place to start."

"But these people may have nothing to do with guns and bombs and the Far Right. Or with Johnny's death."

"I didn't say they did," he replied defensively. "But you don't know what's connected and what isn't until you at least find an entry point. I go to a store, I go to a meeting, that's all."

"That won't be all."

"Look," he said, exasperated, "I went to see Johnny's brother after I got back from Ironwood. He's an alcoholic, but he's one of the most lucid men I know. He told me the local police aren't doing fuck-all about the investigation. Another dead Injun, what's the big deal, probably got involved in some illegal racket at the casino. An FBI agent's been around to see him, but he's based out of Milwaukee. There are no real leads.

"Johnny's brother took me to see their mother in the nursing home. She still thinks Johnny's alive, even though they keep telling her he's dead. She asked me when he was going to bring her a pine cone, and I said soon. And then she held on to my hand for the longest time and starting calling me Johnny. I didn't know what to do, so I started telling her stories about Johnny and me. About the first and only time we went hunting together and I was too scared to shoot the damn deer, and he refused to shoot it for me. 'It's yours, Michael,' he said, 'but only if you want it.' I didn't want it, but he never held it against me.

"Or the time we were both working at the Ojibwa marina and took out a bunch of guys from Detroit on a kayak tour. Turned out they were drunk, and when one of them rolled the kayak, he couldn't get out. The guy went nuts when Johnny tried to save him, almost punched him out. It took both of us to subdue him and get him back in the boat. When we got back to shore, he acted like John Wayne and swore Johnny out, calling him a dirty half-breed and all the other slurs he'd learned from Westerns. That night I saw his car parked outside a bar and I slit the tires. I never told Johnny that."

So, I wanted to say, so fucking what. I don't want to hear any more of these stories; don't play my emotions, it doesn't work. But an image of the old woman suddenly came into my mind and I saw her dead son too, lying in a pool of blood. I saw the face of the Turkish man contorted by grief, crying about his friend dying in the fire. I looked hurriedly at the face of my watch. Time was the great excuse: time to go here, time to go there, no time to dwell on pain, just carry it along with you. Give the old woman a pine cone to appease her, but no more stories, please. "I have to go," I announced abruptly. "I have a class in twenty minutes. E-mail me and we'll arrange a time to talk more later."

"OK," he said, casting a searching glance at me as if I were the one who needed help and not him.

Hank's mad. She can see it in the way he grips the kitchen counter with his knuckles all white and his face blotchy red. His chest is puffed out too, like a rooster's. But she's not scared of him anymore, because he won't hit her. And she doesn't need him, not for *that* anymore, though he still needs her.

"Nelson says you've been in the cabin," he says.

"So?" she replies. "I went over to get the coffeepot."

"He doesn't want you in there."

"It's my cabin, Hank." She pushes in a drawer with more force than is necessary.

"It belongs to the Lord, Lucy. Everything we own is His."

She laughs. Oh, how good it feels to laugh. Before, he'd hit her when she laughed like this, but the Reverend's got him on a tight leash and his neck's straining like a dog that wants to chase a rabbit. "Does He own this?" she asks, picking up a dirty plate. "Does He own your socks and shoes? And tell me, if the Lord owns the cabin, then why does Nelson have a claim on it? What business is it of his to tell me not to go in?"

"The Reverend says—"

"So it's the Reverend who owns the cabin?"

"Listen to me, Lucy!" Hank shouts.

Dog barking, rabbit dancing, she feels so light that she could float, but she wants the cabin back. It's hers, not Nelson's or the Reverend's or the Lord's, not even Hank's. Her father left it to her in her name and it stayed that way; she made sure of that.

"The Reverend's hired somebody to change the locks," he says, and she can't tell whether he's happy about it or not.

"He can't do that."

"He's done it already. Your key doesn't fit anymore."

"It's my property, Hank. You all just can't do this."

"It was the Reverend's decision. I told him you wouldn't like it, but he said it's just until Nelson finds another place to live. Through the winter, that's all. Nelson needs his privacy. How would you like it if someone kept coming in here without you knowing about it?"

"I went over there exactly once, to get the coffeepot."

"Once is enough, I guess."

"For Nelson."

Hank nods, and she senses he's not mad anymore. He probably agrees with her because he doesn't really like Nelson, she can tell by the way he comes home at night after working with him all day in the store. He doesn't talk, just hands the accounts to her and turns on the TV. And he eats less for dinner too. Maybe the Reverend's ordered him to go on a diet. Why not? He orders everything else; he orders up her body like fast food. She's supposed to be cooking dinner now, but she doesn't want to. The ground beef's frozen, so she'd have to put it in the microwave. "Can we go out, Hank?" she asks, letting some sweetness into her voice.

"Where?"

"Anywhere. We haven't been out to eat in a long time."

"I guess so."

"Maybe Papa Gino's?"

"OK."

She goes to the bedroom to get a sweater and brush her hair. It's getting dark earlier now, so she has to turn on the light to see her face in the mirror. She's not pretty and never has been, but she has fewer wrinkles than Diane, who smokes almost as much as their mom did, smoking her way into the grave. She puts on a little eyeliner and mascara for herself since Hank won't notice. But they're going out, that's good. And somehow she'll get hold of the new key to the cabin. After all, she has some power over the Reverend; he can't do without her now. Hank can't do without her either. You don't need a pretty face to have that power over men. That's the mistake a lot of women make. It's not the face. She puts a hand to her belly, wondering if anything is growing there.

After I taught my last class, I swung by the house to pick up Marcy. We went to the mall to buy her jeans and some turtlenecks. I never know how these shopping trips will go; sometimes they exhaust me because we bicker so much. The jeans are too tight, I say, or too long, or too expensive, and she pouts until we both realize the only resolution is at the checkout counter. This time went better, though I'm not sure why. Maybe because we poked fun at the small collection of stores, or she insisted I buy something for myself too, or because we were both feeling like strangers in a strange land and in J. C. Penney's we found comfort in predictability.

We carried the mood with us to dinner at Papa Gino's. The pizza was passable, though the Caesar salad wasn't. Next to us a couple ate dinner so silently I thought they were deaf, but they didn't use sign language either. The woman kept looking over at us. That's not unusual when I'm with Marcy. Her exotic looks attract attention, typically with a hint of disapproval. But I didn't sense that from the woman. I sensed longing, and it made me appreciate the moment more. I had something other people wanted, a beautiful daughter.

That night I dreamed of sex with Michael. I didn't want to dream that, some part of my mind kept telling me not to, but my body was desperate for climax—I meet my needs in dreams. I got up early, before Marcy, and logged on to my e-mail. There was another message from Sajit, asking again how everything was: How did Marcy like school, how was my department? Nothing about himself, but I could tell he was lonely. And then a bulletin from the list I subscribe to that monitors neo-Nazi activity in Germany. Good news: Antifascist protesters outnumbered skinheads by a ratio of ten to one at a rally in Bremen. Bad news: The offices of a progressive newspaper were bombed in Rostock and all their files destroyed. Could people please send any information they had about groups in the area so they could rebuild their files? I jotted down the address since I had a thick file on Rostock in my office. Nice to be of some use, I thought, as I went into the kitchen to pour myself another cup of coffee.

CHAPTER 7

CLIFF WALK

My peace with Marcy was short-lived. The next night at dinner we fought yet again about Sajit. Why couldn't I just make a decision and either stay with him or leave permanently? Living in limbo was the worst. "And don't use me as an excuse," she demanded. "You always say it's for my sake, but you know it's not. It's driving me crazy, and it's driving both of you crazy too. Why are you two like this?"

Without any good answers I couldn't really engage in battle, and that made her even angrier. I couldn't tell her what bound us together, because I thought she was too young to understand. Maybe I was wrong and she had a right to our history. I kept shielding her from it, rationalizing that she already had too much to deal with. I gave much more weight to her epilepsy than she did. She had learned to live with it. I hadn't.

She stormed to her room and I did the dishes, turning on NPR and then turning it off again because I couldn't take the announcer's self-satisfied tone. If I strained my ears, I could just make out Marcy talking on the phone—to Evan, probably, to punish me. When the phone bill came, I'd be able to see how many times she called him and for how many minutes they spoke. Evan already had a police record for stealing car stereos. In a few years I reckoned he'd be put away for pushing heroin, safer under lock and key.

I scrubbed the tea kettle even though it didn't need scrubbing and swept the floor even though there were hardly any crumbs. What was next? I could always look over my lecture notes or, better, get out of the house and walk along dark streets that mirrored my mood more closely than the bright-flowered wallpaper above the sink. In a few weeks I'd have the interior of the house stripped and painted; maybe I'd even spring for new carpet, light blue or beige. I left Marcy a note, then grabbed a flashlight from my room.

At the end of the neighborhood I headed downhill on the road that leads to town. The fight with Marcy had revived memories of Sajit, and now, walking in the dark, I recalled my first fateful trip to Devon.

I traveled there on the day of the winter solstice, when evening fell in mid-afternoon. The bus let me off in a tiny village with lanes so narrow the hedgerows brushed the bus windows on either side. The pub was closed at this hour, but there was a small café where I ordered a scone and a cup of tea. I showed the waitress the map Sajit had drawn me as an addendum to his love letter. She was old enough to be my grandmother and had to go back to the kitchen to fetch her glasses. When she sat down next to me, I didn't want her to get up. I wanted her to say in a grandmotherly way that I'd best catch the next bus back.

"Oh, the Tunstill cottage," she said, looking at the map. "That's where you're going. An Indian gentleman's staying there, is that right?" I detected a hint of disapproval in her voice and nodded my head, embarrassed. "It's about a half-mile down on the cliff path toward Hartland Quay. The path starts in back of the church, at the end of the road here. You have a good torch?" I nodded again. "Be careful, now. It's easy to slip on the path in the dark, and you don't want to go falling off into the sea."

I thanked her and left a good tip and went outside, where it was starting to drizzle. I lifted my backpack onto my shoulders and set off for the church. From the churchyard the path turned left, passing along the edge of a pasture, then wound right, hugging the cliff. Maybe it was good it was dark so I couldn't see a hundred yards below to the sea wildly crashing against the shale. I could hear it, though, and the sound seemed to get louder and louder, as though I were falling toward it.

Why hadn't the waitress told me to turn back?

Why did I need someone else to tell me?

I was riding high on impulse and I wasn't used to it. Blindly, I'd spun the globe and put my finger down here on the edge of nowhere, but there was no daddy to tell me where I'd landed or to give me permission to spin again. A therapist would probably say I was attracted to Sajit because he was older, replacing the father I had just lost, et cetera, et cetera, but that wasn't the reason. I was going to see Sajit because it was the first rash thing I'd done in my life except for swallowing a penny when I was three. I wanted to see what it was like.

So far it was damp, dark, and lonely, and I walked slowly so I wouldn't topple into the sea. I walked toward the small bright circles cast by the flashlight, one after another, step by step.

How boldly I strode now under the streetlamps of Houghton, the flashlight in my pocket. Nowhere to fall here. To trip, yes, but that would only be a matter of scraping a hand or knee.

I had wondered how Sajit would receive me. We were both capable of great awkwardness, a kiss almost unimaginable, and then worse—the unbearable act of stripping naked for bed. It was not my own sexual passion that drove me forward, though maybe it was his, pulling me toward him. Or maybe it was something else, his need for a confessor. How could I ever tell Marcy this? Maybe I would have to take her there someday, stand her on the side of the cliff, and say, *Listen, listen to how your father called for me. You can hear it between the waves, but only if you listen hard enough.*

I had to climb down a steep side path to get to the cottage. It stood at the neck of a sheltered cove by a freshwater stream that spilled into the sea. Lantern light illuminated several of the windows. I knocked on the door, but no one answered. It was unlocked, so I went in. "Sajit," I called, but got no response. I put my backpack down and entered the kitchen, where a pot of lentils simmered on a coal-burning stove. On the table by the lantern was a note.

> Dear Gillian,
> If by any chance or miracle you have come, I am down
> by the water. You will find the steps outside just past
> the kitchen door. Or you can wait until I return.

I left the cottage and found him standing close to the water, so deep in thought he didn't notice my approach. "I'm here," I said.

He turned, and I noticed he was crying. He hugged me for comfort, crying into my shoulder.

"I've forgiven my father," he told me when he recovered himself. "I haven't been able to write since I left Oxford, and I finally realized I could write five hundred books and I'd never really understand why he defected to the Japanese. My words can't exonerate him—all that's left for me to do is to forgive him. And so I did, right now, right before you came."

Our lovemaking that night was excruciatingly gentle, as if we were two feathers or tufted milkweed seeds touching lightly in the wind. In the morning he woke early and brought me tea, and we made love again, harder this time, and in the gray light I watched in fascination as my white breasts brushed against his dark torso. I teased him with my nipples and he teased me with his tongue, and afterward we slept again, limbs bound so tightly around each other that there was no chance of escape.

I didn't want to escape. Not from the quaint stone cottage where we sat wrapped in blankets by the coal stove reading each other poetry. He read Tagore in Bengali; I read the English translation. Or from the walks along the shore where we threw rocks into the sea and screamed at the gulls and chased each other like schoolchildren. Or the evening visits to the pub where we drank pints of bitter and ate plates of greasy chips, oblivious to the censure of the scandalized locals—we were mixed race, mixed age, and, worst of all, just the gleam in our eyes flaunted our sexuality. I was so crazy, so drunk, so young that for the first time in my life I dared myself to make love without protection. He didn't know my diaphragm wasn't in place.

So I guess you could say it was my fault.

My fault too, several months later, when I decided against an abortion and accepted his marriage proposal.

My fault now that I was walking down this pathetic little street and not safely ensconced in an Oxford life where for most people like myself the little amenities—vintage port, witty repartee, and a daily dose of Gothic magnificence—make up for any defects in one's marriage. We would probably do all right now, Sajit and I. We would probably manage to make love once every two weeks, and he would put up with my little affairs on the side because I put up with his manuscripts. My husband is nothing if not prolific.

Maybe it was because I *could* go back that I couldn't make the decision Marcy wanted me to make. When you have a safety net, why destroy it when you know you may find yourself standing on a window ledge with flames licking at your feet? It was for my sake, not hers, that I kept Sajit as a backup. And he kept me because he needed an excuse not to engage deeply with another woman. He had tried once and failed and was too scared to try again.

How could I explain this to her: Your father and I are equally incapable of living together or apart? How can you explain that to a teenager who believes passionately in the power of passion?

It was getting colder out, so I walked briskly to keep warm and found myself in the center of town after only twenty minutes. At this hour Houghton seemed populated mainly by students, many of whom were drunk, and I wished I hadn't come. I hoped none of them would recognize me. The movies were letting out and I got caught in the flow from the theater, forced to walk along the curb. Behind me someone said my name. I turned and saw Michael, his arm draped around Loren. She was wearing a jacket with fake fur around the collar. Tacky, I thought unkindly. We walked together until the crowd thinned. "We're going to get a drink," he said. "Want to join us?"

"Thanks," I replied, "but I have to get home." Loren didn't look displeased.

"I went to that store this afternoon," he said. "If you have any time tomorrow, I'd like to stop by to tell you about it."

"I'm free until ten."

"I'll come at nine-thirty, then."

His hand had slipped off Loren's shoulder, but she linked her arm in his and smiled confidently as if advertising her ownership. We said good-bye and I turned around, retracing my steps to the house, where I hoped Marcy would be off the phone by now, safely doing her homework.

The rest of the evening I sat in the living room reading through my Rostock file to see if any of my papers might be of use to the newspaper that had been bombed there. I had visited Rostock three years ago when I received a summer grant to study the neo-Nazi movement in the Mecklenburg–western Pomeranian region of eastern Germany. I parked Marcy with her father in Oxford and traveled alone for several weeks.

It was a strange trip, not so much because of the strange people I was studying—I have interviewed so many fascists in my day that they almost seem "normal"—but because of the transition taking place in that part of Germany. From one block to the next, even from one house to another, I encountered startling juxtapositions—old gray buildings with crumbling facades giving way to tastefully refurbished medieval gabled houses, more charming, some say, than those in the tourist towns of the west.

Before the war, the Mecklenburg region was largely agricultural and semifeudal, and the Communists did little to develop it aside from collectivizing the farms. The towns were left more or less to decay, but that spared them the bulldozer and the blight of Stalinist architecture. So they are capable of being restored, at least in an aesthetic sense. Economically, the region is still poor and many of its young people unemployed.

Rostock is one of the largest cities in the region, a port and ship-building center on the Baltic Sea, which since the end of the Cold War has experienced something of a revival. Its central avenue is lined with stores selling the latest consumer fashions, but on the outskirts are neighborhoods where the only things freshly painted are the swastikas on the walls.

My guide was a professor from the university who found it useful to have a visiting American interview the people he would rather not meet face-to-face. He gave me a list of right-wing groups and arranged a car and driver. Some people refused to meet me, but most agreed. I've discovered that most homo sapiens like to be interviewed no matter what their political persuasion. I call it the blabber gene, and it's very handy in my line of work.

As I looked through my files, faces came back to me. A young punk with bleached blond hair and a skull and crossbones tattooed on his shoulder; an old fat guy who didn't stand a chance of outrunning the police; his wife, who silently served me coffee but then, as I stood to leave, started to rant and rave. Their words were all a variation on the same theme: hate foreigners, hate democracy, hate yourself, though they would never say that. They were nervous in my presence, unsure of what kind of enemy this was who gave you a hearing. And despite everything they professed, they probably were intimidated by my class, by my expensive linen suit, and by the way I crossed my legs so demurely and nodded noncommittally and smiled and thanked them for their time.

Who else thanked them for their time? They had far too much of it.

There was one exception—Karl Gruhl—a man whose face I would never forget, because he frightened me. There are very few people who truly frighten me when I meet them one-on-one. The individual skinhead may be nasty, but he only becomes threatening as part of a larger group. Gustaf Schmidt, the eco-guru, seduced me, but he didn't frighten me; I frightened myself. But Karl Gruhl wore his cruelty like an expensive aftershave, a luxury he was entitled to because he was rich and smart and slick. I knew I was in the presence of real power.

According to a colleague at Rostock University, rumor was that Gruhl had been a well-paid informer for the Stasi in the late seventies and eighties. He ran a state-owned freight forwarding business that had become his own. No one could prove it, but anyone who had been his business associate and professed any democratic sympathies had been interrogated and detained. In any case, he had prospered under communism and was amassing a fortune under capitalism, so why was he a neofascist? I asked.

My colleague shrugged. "Maybe because his father was a Nazi officer," he said. "Maybe because he's bored or impotent." He blushed at this point, then quickly went on. "Or he's sadistic and enjoys destroying people. There are so many possible reasons. You ask him. See what he says."

I met Gruhl in his office on the tenth floor of a building that overlooked the port. His secretary ushered me into his meeting room, saying he would be a few minutes late because of an important phone call. She suggested I take a look at the antique nautical maps that hung in gilt frames on the wall. "These have just come back from Hamburg," she told me. "Herr Gruhl lent them for a museum exhibition."

I was looking at one of them, trying to decipher the date, when he came in. "That map is over three hundred years old," he told me. "I bought it for almost nothing at a used bookstore. Under the Communists people had no idea of the value of these things." He reached out his hand, and I shook it. "I'm quite honored that you've come to see me. I've read your book."

The idea that he knew my work threw me off guard, and I remained that way the rest of the interview. I sat across from him at the opposite end of a long wooden table. My chair was straight-backed, his was leather-cushioned. He had very soft pale skin that seemed resistant to wrinkles, though I knew he was in his early sixties. His silver hair was thick too, but it could have been a toupee. He inhabited his body adeptly, exuding so much alpha-male confidence he didn't even need to draw on his sexuality. When he smiled, his face hardly creased, and his eyes stayed fixed on you. They were the hard eyes of someone who has never drunk the milk of human kindness. I could believe he had worked with the Stasi.

He turned every question around, trying to find out more information from me than I could get from him. Only at the end of the interview did he provide me with an oblique statement of his faith. "I'm not a fascist," he asserted. "I'm not even a German nationalist. I'm an internationalist. Look," he said, pointing to the view of the port from his window. "Every day I look out at this river, and I follow it in my mind to the Baltic Sea. I'm a man of commerce, Dr. Grace; I send freight on the ships of many foreign nations. But commerce requires order, and out there in the world there are enemies and there are friends. I know how to identify my friends, that's all."

"Who are your friends?" I asked.

"Oh, I have too many to even begin to tell you. Maybe another time. You will come back, I hope?"

I thought about Karl Gruhl again the next day as I sat in my office, waiting for Michael. I wondered if he had anything to do with the bomb at the newspaper office or if he left that kind of messy action to the skinheads. Michael arrived late, some problem with a bicycle chain, he claimed, but I suspected he'd slept late with Loren. I was irritated since I only had fifteen minutes until class. I sat behind my desk and he sat in front, my computer between us like an electronic fence. I was even more irritated when he started giving me orders. "I want you to go to that store yourself," he declared, "and see the kind of literature they have on their shelves. You know this stuff better than me."

"Did they have the *Turner Diaries*?" I asked, and he nodded. "What else?"

"A guide on how to make your own explosives."

"Nice."

"Yeah, real nice. There were two guys behind the counter, and one of them really gave me the creeps."

"Why?"

"He kept looking at me and never cracked a smile."

"Did he say anything?"

"No, he let the older guy do the talking. He's the one I remember working there before; he knows a lot about fishing tackle. Here"—he handed me a sheet of paper—"I've drawn a map of how to get there. Maybe this weekend you could drop by."

Maybe I don't have the time, I felt like saying, but it wasn't true. I had nothing scheduled. "I'll see," I said.

"I'm going to the shepherding circle Sunday afternoon."

"Are you really sure you want to do that?"

"Absolutely. Can I meet with you on Monday?"

"The sign-up sheet is on the door."

As he rose to leave, he put a hand on my desk and I noticed his fingers were black with bicycle grease. I felt childishly relieved that he hadn't slept in late with Loren.

Lucy always feels strange when she dusts the crucifix. Face-to-face with Christ, feather duster brushing his loincloth, the red-paint blood not quite real enough, reminding her that someone made this, pouring plaster into a mold like her mother used to do. She made ceramic bunnies and dwarfs, which she glazed and put out in the garden, where they got covered with mildew and bird shit. Every fall she took them in, washed them off, and stored them above the dryer.

Lucy volunteered to clean the church this week because she wanted an excuse to be close to the Reverend. He's in the office now, writing a sermon. If he doesn't come to her, she'll go to him because she has a plan. She turns on the vacuum cleaner and runs it over the shabby gray-green carpet, picking up a few dry bread crumbs from the last communion. She knelt at the altar too, received his blessing.

"Lucy," he calls at last, and she switches off the vacuum. "Do you want to have a cup of coffee with me?" She runs her hand through her hair, pulls her blouse down over her skirt. It's black and stretchy, a little too tight. She wore it on purpose.

In the office he swivels around in his desk chair to greet her. "Have you finished your sermon yet?" she asks.

"Not yet. I think I need a break."

"I think you do too, Reverend."

She wills herself to do it, focusing her mind's eye on the lake in front of the cabin. It's June and she's watching the dawn creep across it. She kneels down in front of him and unzips his fly. She doesn't want to do this, but she knows he won't notice what her other hand takes from his pocket. He's surprised and grateful and keeps thanking her, thanking her. . . .

Afterward she tells him she has her period and he says he's sorry, he knows the Lord wants her to conceive. "We'll keep trying," he says, and she murmurs yes; she tells him she's going out to buy some flowers for the altar. "That's nice of you," he says. "I'll finish my sermon, and when you come back we'll have that cup of coffee."

She smiles and kisses him, his keys forming a weight in her pocket now.

She drives fast to town, where she has copies made at the hardware store and then buys a big bouquet of roses and carnations from the florist. She can't afford it, but it doesn't matter. One of the keys will fit the cabin, that's all that counts. Hank told her the Reverend kept a copy. Maybe she won't even use it, but she'll have it, the key to her own home.

Back in his office, she pretends to discover the keys on the floor. "You dropped these, Reverend," she says, handing them to him.

"I wondered where they were," he replies, but he suspects nothing; he's still feeling grateful.

She pours him a cup of coffee and stands over him, reading the last page of the sermon. She notices his spelling is bad, but she doesn't correct it. Instead, she massages his shoulders, and he closes his eyes and sighs.

On Saturday morning the drawbridge went up just as Marcy and I were going to cross over the Portage Canal to Hancock. Mark Nicholson and his wife had invited us to have lunch at their lakeshore cabin near Copper Harbor at the end of the Keweenaw Peninsula. As we sat waiting for the boat to pass through, I looked again at the map Michael had drawn me. The store he wanted me to check out was only a short detour, so I'd decided to stop there on the way.

Finally over the bridge, we wound our way through Hancock and merged onto the two-lane highway to Calumet. On the right was the abandoned Quincy mine-hoist-turned-tourist-attraction, perched on the hillside like a gigantic aluminum funnel, visible for miles around. Next to it were several sturdy outbuildings constructed of reddish sandstone erratically streaked with white. Someone at the university had told me we should go on a tour of the old mine before it closed for the season. "Not for me," I'd said. "I get claustrophobic."

A few miles short of Calumet, I turned right after a shack advertising fresh Lake Superior trout. The store was only a hundred feet farther on the left. Marcy asked why we were stopping as we pulled into a gravel parking lot that sprouted a healthy crop of weeds. "Someone told me it was a good place to get outdoor equipment," I lied.

"Since when do you need outdoor equipment, Mom?"

"Well, I just thought they might have good deals on hiking boots."

"It doesn't look like that kind of place."

She was right. It looked like the kind of place that only men frequent, and not to get shoes but things that protrude—like fishing poles and rifles and the accessories that go along with them. LIVE BAIT, a sign said in the window. The paint was peeling from the ledge and the letters above the front door were fading, so I could just make out the name: Harbinger Sporting Goods. I considered turning away, but already a man had spotted us from the window.

What were we looking for? A warm wool shirt for my father. I had no father. For Marcy, then. "I want to buy you a wool shirt," I told her.

"Why?"

"It'll come in handy."

The man opened the door for us. He looked harmless enough, short and paunchy with a buck-teethy smile and ears that stuck out too much. He was wearing a baseball cap advertising a brand of animal feed. "What can I do for you, ladies?" he asked, trying not to look too hard at Marcy, who was wearing a tight purple-and-black striped sweater that rode several inches above the waist of her low-slung jeans. If he looked a little farther, he'd notice her belly button was pierced. "I was wondering if you carried any wool shirts," I asked.

"I'm still waiting for the new stock to come in," he said, "but we've got a few left over from last year."

He led us to a shelf where the shirts were stacked so haphazardly that Marcy had to rummage through all of them to find her size. "See what you like," I told her. "I'm going to take a look around."

The bookshelf was over in the opposite corner. Sure enough, in between the fishing guides and maps were several familiar right-wing tracts, though there was one I hadn't seen before. *Sea Change*, it was called, *Navigating the New World Order*. I picked it up and read the blurb on the back:

> Communism has not collapsed. Like a mutating germ, it assumes new forms and spreads new deadly diseases. Its goal is worldwide domination of transport lanes and cyberspace so that differences between peoples and nations are erased and we all become slaves to one master, one Super Computer. The only true unity is between the Aryan peoples. How do we create our own world communications systems and build brotherhood beyond our borders? How do we fight back against the Global New World Order?

The publisher was Time to Act Press, location: Chicago, Illinois, and Rostock, Germany. I read it again to make sure: Rostock, Germany. I tried to look nonchalant as I took it to the counter along with a guide to the Lake Superior shore and the shirt Marcy had chosen.

Just then another customer entered the store, an old man clad in tall green rubber fishing boots and chewing either a big wad of gum or tobacco. "Got some good bait for me, Hank?" he asked.

"Be right there, Bill. Nelson"—Hank pushed open a door to a back office or storeroom—"can you ring these ladies up?"

The man named Nelson didn't hesitate to look my daughter over. He was younger, maybe in his early thirties, with a buzz cut and a nose that ended too fast and flat. He was wearing army fatigues and had a day's growth of beard. Not my favorite kind of guy, but I tried to smile pleasantly as he rang up the book. As he put it in a bag, he stared long and hard at me. "Thanks," I said, and he grunted something in reply. As we left, he walked over to the window and watched us get into our car.

On the way to the Nicholsons, Marcy opened the bag and pulled out the book. "So that's why we went there," she said. "You could have told me what you were doing."

"One of my students told me they sell right-wing literature there, but I wasn't sure," I replied. "Besides, I wanted to get you a shirt."

"Yeah, right."

"Don't you like it?"

"It's not about liking it or not, Mom. You should just tell me when you're going to do something like that."

"So you can wait in the car?"

"No, so I can help. I could have spent longer looking at the clothes."

"OK," I said, touched by her offer.

"I don't like those kind of people any more than you do, you know."

Sometimes I forgot her skin was dark, and by necessity she had to view the world through a different lens. "Paki, Paki," they had taunted her on the playground in Oxford, and in South Boston she told me some Irish toughs yelled *nigger* at her once. What would they say here? Had they said anything? I hadn't really considered that her revulsion at these things might be even stronger than mine, that she might feel the book in her hand was a weapon pointed directly at her. Because it was.

But who was doing the pointing?

Chicago and Rostock. I knew there were connections across the Atlantic, but I hadn't expected to find them up here. The local drugstore sold a postcard with a picture of a road sign that read, END OF THE EARTH 1 MILE, HOUGHTON 2. Up here past the end of the earth I wasn't supposed to find Rostock on a right-wing tract, just simple home-grown fascism and paranoia, militias arming to defend their freedom to bear arms. Dangerous enough, yes, especially for people like Michael's friend Johnny, who represented the Big Bad Government and was murdered for it.

But was there more to the story?

I tried to look at the trees on the side of the road. Everyone had told me to look at the trees because it was peak color season and the leaves would fall fast. It was true, the reds were even more intense than those in New England, but I couldn't appreciate them. Chicago and Rostock kept running through my mind. What the hell was going on? And why was it falling on me to find out? I had enough problems already. I wanted space for more mundane thoughts: Would Marcy get along with the Nicholsons' son, Seth? He was probably a nerd, but at least by virtue of being a year older, he had seniority. Maybe he would introduce her to some nice kids for a change.

As it turned out, she did get along with him. He was into music, and so they began with CDs and ended up with him playing the blues guitar to her on the couch. I found myself fantasizing that he would replace Evan, although there was something in the way he moved, a slight swivel in the hips, that made me suspect he was gay. I wondered if his parents had noticed.

Mark and his wife, Anne, proudly showed me around the cabin before lunch. It had started out as a simple A-frame but now rambled to the back and sides with additions that didn't quite match, their stain and shingles a different vintage and shade. The view was beautiful, though—the triangular front window overlooked the lake and a private pebbled beach. The wind had picked up, so there were whitecaps and rapidly moving shadows of clouds that broke up the intense blue green of the water.

After lunch we took a walk along the shore. Anne was nice enough but mousy, and she laughed nervously at the wrong things. We had already exhausted our main topic of conversation, the local high school, so Mark and I talked about the department. He asked me how I was getting on with Michael, but I didn't tell him about our discoveries.

Mark was attracted to me, I could tell that, and even worse, I found it gratifying. I wanted to be attractive again so I might attract Michael. We were walking too close, leaving Anne several feet to the side, pretending to study the waves. Suddenly, she bent down and scooped up a handful of rocks. "You can find agates here," she told me, so I moved toward her and she gave me a grateful look. "Here's one," she said. "You can tell by the circles. Polish it up and it will look really nice. Here, take it." For the next ten minutes we all knelt down and sorted through the rocks to see if we could find any more agates, but that was the only one.

I never polished the agate, but I still keep it in my jewelry box. Perhaps Anne had a premonition that I needed a lucky stone.

CHAPTER 8

DROWNING LIKE A PIECE OF GLASS

The rest of September passed by in a blur. In my lectures I marched the students, or dragged them, through the dark passages of modern European history. Someday I'd like to teach a course where you start from the present and go backward, because the present is what they know, what they're capable of feeling. I'd like to unravel it bit by bit until they don't know what time is anymore and they're as lost as the rest of us.

I survived my first faculty meetings, struggling to decipher a new set of signals. On the surface, upper-Midwest polite was quite different from the Boston University bite, but I knew hidden ego wars were raging around me and I'd better learn fast how to stay out of the cross fire. For the moment I let Mark Nicholson protect and patronize me. I played the good girl and crossed my legs, only occasionally stealing a glance out the window at some dead leaf drifting by.

At home Marcy was unhappy, but that was nothing new. She kept feigning a stomachache so she wouldn't have to go to school, and I kept forcing her out, until one day she got back at me by throwing up in biology class while she was dissecting a frog. In between my classes, I had to drive to the high school to retrieve her. Most afternoons she shut herself in her room and did all her homework, so I had nothing to bug her about. She even brought home an A on an English paper.

Meanwhile Sajit was sending me strange stream-of-consciousness e-mails, depressing rants about the bleak state of England and the world. I worried about him, but not enough to ask what was really going on. He also sent me a book by a nihilist London poet, whose photo on the back had all the polish of a police mug shot. Marcy took the book from me and said she liked it, especially the poem about drowning like a piece of glass.

Michael was half crazed too, totally caught up in his subterfuge in the shepherding circle. He came into my office on a regular basis to give long, detailed accounts of his supposed submission to Jesus. One day he acted it out, kneeling on the floor and pretending to pray and weep. "Then the other men lift me up," he told me, "and the Reverend blesses me, saying Jesus is calling me to the flock."

"What else does he say?"

He stretched back in his chair, looking a little too pleased with himself. "We've been working on my relationship with Loren. They tell me we're living in sin and I need to ask her to marry me. And I tell them I'm not the problem, she is; she wants her independence. And then they give me this long song and dance about how women are meant to obey, but they can only obey once men accept the responsibility of being the true master. They think I haven't accepted that responsibility yet, and that's why Loren won't marry me."

"But is there a political connection?" I asked, uncomfortable with the mention of Loren. "Anything to do with that store?"

"The guy named Nelson is up to something, I think. He watches us all like a hawk, and I noticed that after the meeting he and the Reverend stay in church after the others leave. The rest of the men seem pretty harmless, kind of sad, really—a lot of them are heavy drinkers who are just trying to fix up their lives. But they're vulnerable and I don't know what the larger plan is."

"If there is a plan."

"Oh, there's a plan, all right."

I bristled at the certitude in his voice. "How do you know that?"

"You went into that store."

"But the books in there are not necessarily connected with the shepherding circle."

"Nelson is, and the owner, Hank."

"Maybe, but you can't just jump to conclusions."

"I'm not jumping to conclusions," he argued, his eyes wandering to the bookshelf. He walked over to it and grabbed my book, *The Fourth Reich? Neofascism in Contemporary Germany.* "I'm just making connections. I've read your book, and that's what you advise: Trace the connections. Right here," he said, opening it and pointing at a passage. "In the second paragraph of the introduction. That's all I'm doing."

"I never lied, Michael. I never pretended to be someone I wasn't. How long can you keep up this act?" I heard the anxiety in my voice, felt my fingernails dig into my palm.

He laughed but not convincingly. "As long as I need to. It turns out I'm a good actor."

I wasn't sure he was, and it started to worry me that I'd encouraged, or at least hadn't stopped, his unconventional research. If there really was a connection between the shepherding circle and

Time to Act Press, he could get in big trouble. I could get in big trouble too. Was that why I was so worried? I'd written to my contacts in Rostock to see if they knew anything about the press, but so far they'd come up short. Maybe there was someone in Chicago at the NAACP or Anti-Defamation League who would know something. That was the kind of research I liked, straightforward, no playacting. Not like Michael falling on his knees and praying.

A few nights later he broke all the rules by appearing at my house unannounced at ten o'clock. I should have been angry with him, but he apologized before I could say anything. I made him tea and we sat in the kitchen, where the new wallpaper was too bright for the dark walnut-stained cabinets. Now I would have to change them too, I thought inanely.

He was high on information. I recognized the symptoms: adrenaline-bright eyes, sweaty forehead, shaking hands, and a reluctance to start because then it would be over too quickly, like a premature ejaculation. I watched him stir his tea even though there was no sugar in it and wondered if Marcy was listening from her room. Finally, he put down the spoon and began.

After the shepherding circle ended, he had pretended to leave, then returned to the church, hoping to spy on the Reverend and Nelson. They moved into the Reverend's office, and he hid behind a bush and watched them through a window. "Five minutes later a blue pickup with Illinois plates pulled into the parking lot and a guy got out, tall, with a long ponytail. He knocked on the back door and Nelson got up, holding a gun. But he let him in and they all sat around the table together looking at a map."

"What kind of map?"

"I couldn't tell exactly, but it was about the size of a USGS map and it looked detailed. Somehow I'm going to get into the Reverend's office and find out what it was."

"Breaking and entering is against the law, Michael," I reminded him.

"So is shooting a forest ranger."

"You have absolutely no proof."

"That's why I need to get it."

"Michael, I can't go along with this. You're getting carried away."

"So don't then," he declared angrily. "Drop me from your roster. Pretend I haven't told you anything."

"It doesn't work that way."

"Oh, sure, it works that way. Out of sight, out of mind."

"It doesn't work that way with me."

"Then how does it work with you?"

"I'll tell you how it works," I said, summoning up all the authority I could muster. "We start by doing some investigative work in Chicago about the press. I pursue my contacts in Rostock. And then we think about the next step. Meanwhile you leave the shepherding circle, because you won't be able to keep up the charade much longer. Maybe you've already blown it by hanging around and spying on them. If these men are who you think they are, you have to start being careful; you can't go breaking and entering, because they'll shoot you in the back of the head just like they shot your friend Johnny. And then you'll be off the roster permanently, of no use to anyone. You have to be careful, Michael. That's the nature of the work, and that's the only way you find out anything. It's not just some big macho game."

"Do you think that's how I see it?"

I paused and looked him in the eye. "Yes."

He pushed his chair away from the table and got up and walked to the front door. Maybe he hesitated a moment before opening it, I don't know, maybe he wanted me to tell him to wait. But I didn't say anything, just watched him leave. Then I walked by Marcy's room. Her stereo was on, thank God; hopefully she'd missed the conversation. I knocked on the door. "Time to go to bed," I said.

She turned down the music as I entered. "Who was that guy?"

"One of my graduate students," I replied. "At least he used to be."

"He's quitting?"

I nodded.

"He looked pretty strung out."

I nodded again. "Go to bed now. I want you to get over that stomach bug."

"OK, Mom," she said sleepily.

"Want me to turn off the light?"

"All right."

When I logged on e-mail the next morning, there was a message from Michael. "You win," he wrote. "I'll play by your rules."

"All right," I wrote back, "but it's not a game between you and me either."

She doesn't like having them in her kitchen. She has to lean over both Hank and the Reverend to put the platter on the table, and she feels like her breasts are exposed even though she's wearing a heavy sweater. She doesn't like the idea of Nelson eating her food either. He's already taken her cabin away; now he wants her to serve him, but he isn't worth serving. He eats like a pig—that's where the expression comes from, men like Nelson who don't even know how to cut right with a knife and fork. Next time she'll set the table with a shovel. Shovel it in, Nelson. Free food, my job, my cabin. Take it all, pig.

She doesn't want to sit down with them, but they expect her to. The Reverend says something about how much he loves mashed potatoes. She feels like saying she knows what he loves even more than that. There's a rumor he was married before, left a wife and two kids in Kansas somewhere. She bets *they* left *him* and are laughing about it now, sitting down to dinner without him and enjoying every bite.

Why don't they all just leave her alone? She likes to eat alone, always has. She likes to sit at the table for a long time and pretend she's being waited on. *Can I get you something else, ma'am? she hears the waitress saying.*

"Can I serve you some peas?" she asks the Reverend. Nelson and Hank have already helped themselves.

"Well, thank you, Lucy," he says, handing her his plate, and maybe he winks; she hopes not. She reaches behind her and touches the radiator. Too cold in here. Hank keeps turning the thermostat down. He's worried about money and ought to be. The store's not doing well; Nelson has a way of driving customers out. Another month and Hank will want her back in there again. Maybe he does already but is too timid to say it. Just one more month of having sex with the Reverend—that's about all she can take.

The Reverend has better manners than Nelson, but there's something about the way he wipes his mouth with his napkin, just using one edge at a time, that drives her nuts. When he's finished eating, he lays it flat on the table as if it's never been used.

She takes a bite of pot roast. Not bad. She got it right this time.

The Reverend says something about having a Satan in our midst. She doesn't see it that way; she thinks there's a little bit of Satan inside each of us and it depends whether you activate him or not, kind of like one of those battery-operated trucks her nephews have. Do you press GO or not?

This particular Satan is a woman, the Reverend says, and she has an accomplice, a man named Michael who's infiltrated the shepherding circle. He says her name. Dr. Gillian Grace. "She just moved here to teach at the university. Her name is on the list."

"What list?" she asks.

He smiles at her like she's a child. "Just a list we have, Lucy."

"Who's Michael?" she asks next.

"Her student," the Reverend replies. "A local boy."

"What's his last name?"

"I don't think you need to know that yet."

She looks to Hank for support, but he's got his head down, staring at his food. Underneath the table the Reverend moves one of his hands to her thigh and presses down. When she stiffens, he releases the pressure but still keeps his hand there. She feels like screaming out but takes a sip of water instead. Hank's still not looking up. She wishes he knew about the hand and would hit the Reverend in a fit of jealousy, send his head banging into the radiator. *Don't fuck my wife.*

"We have a favor to ask of you, Lucy."

Another favor? How many favors has she already given him? *Don't fuck my wife,* Hank should be saying. The Reverend out stone cold, blood pouring out of his nose. How she'd like to see that. "What is it?" she asks.

"A very important favor." Nelson's staring at her now, and the Reverend's hand presses hard again, soft again. With the other hand he lifts some potato on his fork. "We have a friend in the phone company who's going to put a tap on Gillian's line so we know what she's up to."

"But that's against the law."

"Against whose law, Lucy? Is it against God's law to watch out for Satan? It's just a little transmitter. We'll listen, that's all. And we want you to do the listening. We'll give you the tapes and you can tell us if there's anything important on them."

"But Reverend—"

He's gripping her so tight now it hurts. "We're in a war, Lucy, and we need your help. You know how the mud people want to take over everything we have—our land, our houses, our schools—and the Jews are helping them do it. The Jews are buying up everything, and then they'll hand it over to the mud people when the time is right."

"Is this woman Jewish?"

"Yes. And she sleeps with black men. She has a black daughter. From the womb of the Jewess come mud people. Tell me we're not in a war, Lucy."

She says yes to get his hand off her and because maybe he's right about the Jews. The Jews from Chicago are buying up all the property in the Keweenaw. They want her cabin; next thing they'll want this house too. Everything.

Later, when she's doing the dishes, Nelson comes into the kitchen and stands behind her and whispers in her ear. He threatens that if she tells anyone about the phone tapping, he'll tell Hank and the whole congregation how she throws herself on the Reverend like a bitch in heat, even in the church, even when he's writing a sermon, and he has to push her away with all his strength.

Friday I was exhausted and decided to work at home, grading the first round of papers from my students. Among them were a few deep thinkers and a few semi-illiterates, with most inhabiting the gray middle of middle-American education, which is to say they knew how to put down a complete sentence but not a coherent thought. I kept getting up from my chair and putting things away because it was easier to tidy the house than tidy their prose.

Finally, I found myself outside the door of Marcy's room. I knew I shouldn't go in, but I convinced myself her trash needed emptying. And so I entered the forbidden territory uninvited.

In Oxford when Marcy was little and off at school, I sometimes went into her room and lay on the bed, trying to remember what it was like to sleep with such a magic clutter of stuffed animals and dolls. Then I'd try to feel what it must be like to be different, to have your brain slip into seizures and to wake up with worried parents or teachers hovering over you. To feel watched all the time, as I was watching her now because they told me to watch her, first when she got epilepsy and then again when the high school psychologist declared she was "at risk." They told me I needed to be home more. I was at home, but I was at the computer, trying to get tenure. They implied I treated her like a footnote to my work, but it wasn't true. Every day as I stared at the monitor, all my senses strained to know what she was doing, feeling, thinking, imbibing—oh, no, they can't accuse me of neglect. Sajit, maybe, but not me.

I lay down on her bed now. There were still a few stuffed animals but no dolls. On the walls were posters of male rock groups and a collage of male models, all with bare overdeveloped chests stripped of hair. Androgynous, almost. The androgynous, anorexic generation. "At least Marcy doesn't have an eating disorder," one of my friends in Boston told me. "You can be grateful for that." But I was starting to wonder. She had hardly eaten anything the past two weeks.

What did she think about when she lay on this bed? What were the things she couldn't tell me?

I'd never been very close to my own mother. I looked down on her because my father seemed so much smarter and more worldly. And he knew how to gather me effortlessly into his lap, while her hugs were awkward, too tight. Now that she's a widow, I see that she has more savvy than I gave her credit for. She manages her limited finances well, even affording a cruise every once in a while, and she manages her love life so she gets what she needs. In that respect she does much better than I do.

The lonely professor, lying on her daughter's bed. At least Marcy can lie down and daydream of Evan, I thought. I'm not allowed to daydream of Michael, because he's my student, lover of Loren and a maniac. I wondered about his chest—how much hair?

It was wrong to think about sex, or the lack of it, on my daughter's bed. I got up to empty the trash.

As I spilled the contents into a plastic bag, I noticed a small cardboard box ripped into pieces. I retrieved them and spread them on the dresser, fitting them back together like a puzzle. It was a pregnancy testing kit. I felt myself drowning like a piece of glass.

CHAPTER 9

RECKONING

Lucy wishes she were listening to her parents' old tape recorder with the wide gray ribbon that curled like a snake and hissed when it reached the end. The Walkman she's using now lets her move from room to room, but it makes it seem like the Satan woman and her daughter are right there with her, talking in her ear, and it gives her the creeps.

She dusts the hall table, then wanders into the living room, where she sits down on the rocker and listens to Gillian talking to someone at Reynold's garage about getting the oil changed on her car. The phone clicks. Now she's talking to someone at the photo store. Wants to know if her pictures are in yet. They aren't. Hardly seems like Satan's business.

She considers pretending to the Reverend that she listened to the tapes and found nothing, but what if he checks up on her and there's something important? What if Nelson goes around telling people she's a whore? And besides, what else does she have to do? She likes the daughter's conversations the best, the ones with her boyfriend in Boston, where she cries and carries on about how much she misses him and he answers in grunts. Just like Hank's grunts; you'd think no one had taught them to talk. Hank hardly speaks these days, and she's noticed his willpower is slipping. When he came back from the grocery store the other day, a bottle of Jack Daniel's was on the receipt. She doesn't know whether to be mad or glad. Was it really any worse when he sat around in bars and drank with his buddies? At least they had friends back then. Now they just have the Reverend and Nelson, and you can't call them friends.

She wonders if Gillian has any friends. She never calls anyone.

The Reverend told her he was coming over this afternoon. She hopes he cancels, because it's getting harder to have sex with him. After Nelson's threat, she's dried up down there because it makes her sick thinking about how the Reverend must have boasted to him, saying she throws herself on him like a bitch in heat. Just like the boys in high school who couldn't keep their mouths shut after you did it with them in the back of a car. Except for Hank. He didn't tell anyone, because he wanted it to be their little romantic secret. He was sweet back then, gave her chocolates on Valentine's Day, and took her out every Saturday night to dinner and a movie even though he didn't have much money.

Another call. Gillian's voice is louder now, more anxious. She's trying to make a doctor's appointment for her daughter, but the receptionist claims that no one at the medical center has any room until next week. "I need one right away," she says. "It's urgent."

"You can go to the emergency room," the receptionist replies.

"It's not that kind of emergency."

"If you could tell me the nature of the problem, Mrs.—"

"Grace," she says, "Gillian Grace. And I'd rather talk to a doctor directly."

"Then in that case I might be able to recommend another medical group in Calumet."

"But you're the only one on the insurance list."

"Well, then, the best I can do is give your daughter an appointment next week with Dr. Glover and call you if anything opens up sooner."

"All right." Gillian sighs. "But please call me right away if there's a cancellation."

"I'll pencil her in for next Thursday at four. What did you say her name was?"

"Marcy Mukherjee."

"What?"

"Mukherjee."

"Can you spell that please?"

And so Gillian spells it slowly, too slowly—in the silences between the letters Lucy can tell how agitated she is—and hangs up. Lucy imagines her walking over to the window, staring out at the street like she does herself sometimes, hoping a car will come by just to provide a flash of movement, color, something for her eye to follow.

Gillian Grace and Marcy Mukherjee. Funny names. Hard to get used to.

In the next call there's panic in Gillian's voice; she's talking to Planned Parenthood downstate, wanting to know where the nearest abortion clinic is. Green Bay, Wisconsin, the lady on the other end of the line tells her.

"Wisconsin? Isn't there one closer to Houghton than that?"

"I'm afraid not. They're getting fewer and farther between every year. Here's the number. I'd call soon to schedule an appointment—the doctor only comes once or twice a week, and sometimes it's hard to get in. How far advanced is she?"

"I'm not sure."

"Well, you better find that out first before you call."

"I'm trying to, believe me."

There's a pause, and then the receptionist wishes her good luck, letting a little warmth creep into her voice. "Call us again if you need to. We could find you a place in Detroit if it doesn't work out in Green Bay."

"Thanks," Gillian says, and the tape switches off.

The devil woman has a daughter with a baby growing inside her. Lucy puts her hand on her belly even though she knows there's nothing growing there. She has the crazy idea of asking Marcy for her baby, but it would be a dark baby and everyone would stare at her and know it wasn't hers. The Reverend would call it a mud baby. Still, it's wrong to have an abortion, just plain wrong, whatever color the baby is.

She rewinds the tape and listens to the conversation again. How can the Planned Parenthood woman talk so matter-of-factly about something like that? Where is God in all this?

Her God protects children. He's not as mean as the Reverend's God. He protects more than He punishes. Life punishes you enough already.

She wants to call Marcy and tell her not to have the abortion, but then Marcy will wonder how she knows. She'll pray, though, pray for the souls of the mother and the child. She closes her eyes and goes to that place in her head where it's quiet and she receives instruction. The Voice tells her she should follow Marcy, but at a distance, until there's a sign that it's time to save her.

She hears the doorbell ringing and hesitates for a moment; she could pretend she isn't home, but her car's in the driveway. Better to get it over with. Maybe she can retreat to the quiet place again while she's having sex with the Reverend; he would never know.

It turns out he doesn't have much time and wants to hear about the tapes first. So she draws out her report, telling him all the details she can remember, and even makes some up. "But is there anything important, Lucy?" he asks, starting to sound exasperated. He's sitting in the rocking chair now but isn't rocking. He's still as a statue.

She'd like to freeze him into a statue and put him out in the rain to rust and get covered with bird droppings. "Well," she says, holding the image in her mind as long as she can, "she's trying to get her daughter an abortion."

"Where?" he asks, suddenly sitting forward. The chair moves with him.

"Green Bay, maybe. I'll know more when I get the next tape."

"I'll get it tonight," he says, so excited his cheeks turn red. "Listen to every detail and write it down. You're doing a great job, Lucy." She smiles, pretending to be pleased at the compliment. He rises and takes her hand, leading her to the bedroom.

He thinks he's rewarding her when they have sex; he thinks she likes it. In the quiet place she prays for herself this time, asking for a baby as the Reverend enters and spills his seed. He gets up fast because he has an appointment, and she stays in bed with her legs up like some of the books tell you to do.

Later she drives over to Gillian's house and parks down the

street, watching for the school bus. She has to wait twenty minutes, but it's worth it because she sees Marcy get off. She's seen her before somewhere, you don't forget a girl like that, pretty in the way dark people can be pretty, catching the light so their skin and hair gleam. Marcy has long hair, almost down to her waist. Lucy watches her fetch the mail and let herself in the front door. She's still so thin no one would know she was pregnant. It feels like a secret between them.

It was a painful week, though you can't really predict in advance how you will feel pain, with a knotted stomach or urge to cry or a dull blurring of the senses. Those were my usual responses, but this time was different. This time pain was deep icy water I had to swim through, and I kept changing strokes, hoping one would be faster than the last. But no matter how fast I swam, the shoreline kept receding.

Now I floated on my back in bed, hopelessly awake, replaying the scenes between Marcy and me. I'd left the pieces of the pregnancy testing kit on her dresser, waiting for her to come to me, but she hadn't. She pretended nothing had happened, so I had to ask. We were eating dinner, canned spaghetti sauce on undercooked tortellini, al dente but not on purpose. I poured myself a big glass of wine that I hardly touched. I planned to ease into the subject, but how can you ease into something like that? "Are you pregnant, Marcy?" I asked.

"Yes," she answered calmly, looking down at her plate. "I was going to tell you—you didn't have to sort through my garbage."

"I was just emptying it."

"Sure you were."

Her voice was starting to rise; mine would too if I let it and we would be back in familiar territory. But I wasn't sure I wanted to be there for something as serious as this. So I controlled myself. "What are we going to do about it?"

"You mean what am I going to do about it?"

"What are you going to do about it, then?"

She gave me a defiant look. "I want to keep the baby."

I pretended not to be shocked. "I don't think that's a good idea," I replied, as if discussing the proposed subject of a student paper.

"You decided to keep me."

"Yes," I said, "but I was older."

"Only four years."

"There's a big difference between sixteen and twenty. Besides, the circumstances were different. Your father was older, ready to settle down."

"I want my baby just like you wanted me."

"But wanting is only part of it."

"What's the other part?"

I took a sip of wine now to buy time. How could I explain the other part to her without sounding patronizing? "It changes your life profoundly," I started.

"In my case, that wouldn't be such a bad thing."

"It's much easier if there's a father."

"Is it?"

I ignored the question. "Who's the father, Marcy? Is it Evan?"

"You don't need to know."

"I do need to know. Because you know if you have the baby, I'll end up raising it so you can finish high school."

"I don't need to finish high school."

"Oh, yes, you do."

"Face the facts, Mom. I'm dumb, so dumb I even got pregnant."

"You're not dumb."

"Oh, yes, I am. You just can't accept it because you and Dad are so smart—how can you have a dumb daughter?"

"You're not dumb, Marcy," I said again, starting to cry. "You are not dumb. Until you realize that, you shouldn't have a baby."

"Never, then?"

"Until you figure out who you are."

"I know who I am, Mom."

With that she stomped off, leaving me to cry into my miserable dinner. She didn't talk to me all weekend. We passed in silence on the way to the bathroom and ate meals at different times. Saturday night she went out with the Nicholsons' son and some of his friends. I should have been happy—finally, she was connecting with some local kids—but instead I worried about her and she didn't come back until late, after I'd gone to bed. Except I hadn't. I was lying there fully clothed, blaming myself for everything.

All week she tortured me and she knew it. I let myself be tortured because I felt it was the only way for something between us to end, something nebulous but persistent, a faint background noise that started the day I separated from her father, even though we pretended that I was moving to Boston just for the job. Sajit saw us off at Heathrow and told her he wouldn't change a thing in her room—it would be just the same when we came back at Christmas. It was true. He didn't change it, but what neither of us had reckoned on was how much *she* would change in the few months between. Her old room seemed to belong to another child—or, rather, she had left childhood behind.

And now, just as dramatically, she wanted to leave adolescence, but I couldn't let her. Not yet. I scheduled an appointment at the Green Bay abortion clinic and told her she should think hard about her decision.

In the end it was nothing that I did or didn't do that changed her mind. I was home the afternoon it happened, standing by the kitchen window to watch her get off the school bus. I noticed a woman standing a few feet from our mailbox and a car parked farther down the road. I wondered if it was another Seventh Day Adventist—they had come to the house once already. When Marcy got off the bus, the woman approached her with an envelope in hand. Even though the weather was fair, she was wearing a long raincoat and scarf, so it was hard to make out what she looked like. She gave Marcy the envelope, touched her briefly on the arm, and turned back toward the car. It was too far away to see the license plate. "Who was that?" I said, as Marcy came in.

"I don't know. She gave me this envelope and said she was praying for me to keep my baby." I watched as she opened it. Inside was a brochure from a crisis pregnancy counseling center in Hancock, providing "the support every young mother needs so she can bring a healthy, happy baby to term." The center gave information on government benefits and adoption as well as free diapers and baby clothing to women in need. I knew about such centers—their unstated goal was to prevent women from having abortions. "How did she know I was pregnant?" Marcy asked.

"I have no idea. There must be a leak somewhere—maybe the doctor's office. I didn't like that receptionist."

"It creeps me out. The way she touched me too. She had tears in her eyes."

It made Marcy angry that someone else knew her personal business, and it made me angry too. I called the doctor and complained, but he said his receptionist had been working with him for twenty years and was staunchly pro-choice. I called the clinic too, but they claimed all their personnel were carefully vetted. Maybe the leak was from a medical lab, they said. They had heard of that kind of thing happening before.

Whatever the case, it turned out to be a blessing in disguise. "I decided to have the abortion last night," Marcy announced the next morning, as she slung her backpack over her shoulder. "I don't like those fanatics. No one's going to tell me what to do."

I took the day off from work to drive to Green Bay. We left right before dawn, but the morning only brought a slight brightening of the sky, like skim milk in black coffee. It was mid-October and the colors had already passed. Leaves blew across the empty road and caught in the windshield wipers, smearing the drizzle. Near the turnoff to the Ojibwa marina we caught a glimpse of the bronze statue of Bishop Baraga, the Catholic priest who had spread the Word among the natives. He held a Bible in one hand, a snowshoe in the other. Mist rose from the lake, making it difficult to see the surface of the water.

There was a long stretch of nothing as we proceeded south on Route 141. Near the town of Iron Mountain, the forest gave way to derelict supper clubs and evangelical churches that looked more like storerooms than houses of God. Over the border in Wisconsin the roadside sprouted even more messages from Jesus, as well as signs proclaiming the right to bear arms. No bloody fetuses though, thank goodness. I tried to talk to Marcy about the abortion procedure, but she wouldn't respond. "I read the information," was all she said.

I thought about a lot of things on that trip, from the mundane to the existential. What should I make for dinner that would be easy for Marcy to digest? Would I have had an abortion if I hadn't been so far from home? Thank God I hadn't had one, because I loved her so much. Why couldn't I express my love better now? Should I stop for gas? Did I have enough room to pass that logging truck? Would the procedure be painful? How was Michael doing? I'd sent him off on a fact-finding mission to Chicago. He was obeying me now like a soldier his commanding officer. What would he find out?

The land grew more agricultural as we approached Green Bay, with dairy farms and fields of dried corn husks stretching to the horizon. We merged onto a proper highway, and before I knew it we were a few exits short of our turnoff. The bay lay off to our left, the same austere color as the sky.

In an expressionless voice, Marcy read me the directions to the clinic. She was sitting very still now, her way of showing nerves. I didn't want to worry her unnecessarily, but I warned her the clinic had told me that sometimes there were a few protesters outside holding placards. They weren't too aggressive—the new clinic protection laws had helped to calm things down, and the police were more helpful since the bombings and shootings elsewhere. Unfortunately, the presence of protesters was just a normal part of the abortion experience in the United States.

But when we turned onto the street leading to the clinic, there were more than just a few protesters, there were at least a hundred. I told Marcy to duck and cover her head. The police had set up a cordon, but the protesters pushed against it, taunting us with pictures of bloody fetuses and screaming that we were sinners, baby killers, murderers, executioners. Their faces were as full of hate as the neo-Nazis I'd seen marching in Germany, but ironically some held placards comparing abortion to the Holocaust. A few mothers had brought their children, boys and girls who couldn't have been older than ten. There was hate in their eyes too.

To ward off the fear, I concentrated on driving, my hands gripping the steering wheel so hard my fingers ached. A cop gestured me toward an electronic gate in the ten-foot fence surrounding the clinic, and it opened as I approached. Before I was safely through, a man hurled a plastic bag full of ketchup that splattered across my windshield. Inside the compound, an armed guard opened the car door and ushered Marcy and me to the clinic entrance. "I'll take care of the ketchup," he said blandly, as if he were a gas station attendant whose job it was to wipe our windshield.

The clinic director came out of her office and put her arm around Marcy. This was the worst demonstration in a long time, she said, she was so sorry it had to happen today. She had heard recently that antiabortion activity was heating up in the state, but she was under the impression the clinic in Madison had been selected as the target. "I guess it's us instead." She shrugged. "Don't worry—we're all used to working under adversity."

Marcy didn't want me there during the procedure, so I waited in the reception room, listening to classical music that was turned up high to cover the shouting outside. I was in such a state of heightened awareness that I felt the cold stainless steel cannula entering my daughter. She wouldn't feel much pain, they had assured me, but I felt it and I had to stop myself from crying out. When the pain was gone, fear returned, fear of the mob outside, fear of the men who had killed Johnny, fear of myself.

Lucy is so angry she can't speak. The Reverend's driving and Nelson's up front with him; she's in back with the dog, whose tongue hangs out too far. Hank didn't come to Green Bay. Someone had to stay at the store.

She's mad about how pleased they are with themselves because of all the people who came to the clinic, and the ketchup someone threw at Gillian's car. But ketchup can be washed off and the baby's dead. They don't really care that the baby's dead. She wants to tell them you don't stop abortions by shouting at people and calling them names. You pray for them; the Reverend should know that. She prayed, oh, she prayed so hard, but she needed other people praying too. She couldn't stop it all by herself, though she tried. She touched the girl's arm, but it wasn't enough. She needed more time with her.

It's late afternoon, getting dark already, and she lets herself doze so she won't have to talk to them. She bundles her jacket into a pillow and rests her head against the door. Her mouth is dry and her eyes sting from being out in the cold wind. She hung back from the crowd, leaning against a tree, wondering what it would feel like to just leave, walk away. She could get lost in a place like Green Bay.

You can get lost anywhere if you want to. Even here in this car, you can get so lost no one will find you.

She sleeps for maybe an hour, but wakes up when Nelson tells the Reverend that both bitches are sound asleep in the back. She keeps her eyes closed and her body slack.

"Keep your voice down," the Reverend answers. "We need her."

"You need her." Nelson laughs.

"You need her too."

"Hank and her are so fucking stupid it gets to me sometimes."

"It's good they're stupid."

"So you can fuck her all you want?"

"I didn't mean that. You know what I mean."

"I'd like to fuck the girl."

"Don't go there, Nelson."

"Ever fucked a black girl, Reverend?"

"Don't go there."

They lower their voices so she can hardly hear them. They're talking about something else now, some shipment they're waiting for. Got to get here before the lakes freeze. It will, the Reverend says, but we need to get the place ready first. That's the priority now, to get the place ready. And to get them out of the way, Nelson says. Yes, says the Reverend, but not in the way you're accustomed to. We don't want to draw that kind of heat, we've made that mistake once already. There are other ways, like today. Did you see Gillian's face? She was terrified.

Lucy sees Gillian's and Marcy's faces but not the baby's face, because the baby is dead.

CHAPTER 10

MIDTERM

I didn't sleep well for several nights after Marcy's abortion. I craved adult company, but all I had was a bottle of scotch and I'm not a very good drinker. I thought of calling Sajit, but Marcy didn't want him to know, and he wouldn't have been much help anyway. I wished I weren't such a loner. I wished I were one of those women who have a network of friends as dense as the wires in a telephone exchange. People would call me to ask how I was. "Fine," I'd reply, and they would know me well enough to say, "Gillian, something's wrong. I can hear it in your voice."

As it turned out, Michael was the only person who called. It was Saturday night after my second scotch. He had a lot of things to tell me about his trip to Chicago and wondered if I'd like to go for an excursion with him tomorrow to the Porcupine Mountains. The weather forecast was for an Indian Summer day, and it made more sense to talk outside than in. A little drunk and a lot desperate, I agreed.

He picked me up around ten. Marcy was still asleep—sleep seemed to be her way of coping with the ordeal. He asked me how

I was and I said fine, and he studied me for a moment. "You look exhausted," he commented.

The car rendered us more equal because he was in charge behind the wheel. I didn't have the energy to wear the professor's hat that day anyway, and even if I had, maybe I would have let the wind blow it off my head and straight out the window. Truth was I needed to feel a man's strength beside me, to watch his hand effortlessly work the gearshift as he took me somewhere, anywhere, outside my own head.

The Porcupines were about an hour and a half southwest of Houghton, giving Michael plenty of time to tell me about his trip as we drove through seemingly endless tracts of national forest. He told me he found a lot of information on Sons of the Shepherd in the offices of the antihate groups, but nothing about a link to Time to Act Press. In fact, no one had ever heard of it and urged him to share whatever he found out. The head researcher at the NAACP had recommended he talk to a journalist at a black newspaper who knew more than anybody in the city about skinheads and Nazis. The journalist's name was Chris Rollins.

I could tell Michael had been nervous about driving to the South Side of Chicago. It was probably his first time in the guts of a city, so different from the soft tourist underbelly of seductive skyscrapers and museums with marble floors. The newspaper offices, or rather office, was one room above a bar, and the stairway reeked of piss. That detail had obviously impressed him. Rollins was the only person there—he seemed to be chief editor, reporter, and layout man all wrapped into one. Michael described him as a little guy in his early thirties, wiry and nervous, always looking behind his back. It turned out he had been put away for several years for selling a few ounces of pot to an undercover policeman. He was politically active and believed the local cops had it in for him.

In prison they had had it in for him too. He was targeted by racist thugs, beaten up so badly he almost died. The guards looked the other way, so he had to seek protection elsewhere. He made friends with a black boxer and small-time drug dealer, Tony Logan, who was in for life because of the three-strikes-and-you're-out policy. Rollins started writing a newspaper column from prison in which he argued Logan's case. This got the boxer a hot-shot lawyer pro bono, and he became a bit of a cause célebrè among Chicago's liberal elite. He ended up doing life in prison anyway because he was stabbed to death while working in the laundry room. Rollins was next on the hit list, he told Michael, so the prison authorities paroled him early to avoid any more bad publicity.

"I asked him if he knew who Logan's murderers were," Michael continued, "and he said he was pretty sure. It turns out Sons of the Shepherd were organizing in the prison. At first Rollins thought they were pretty harmless, like the Muslims except for being white people, just helping men get their act back together. But a couple of them had another agenda. They started a neo-Nazi cell, though it was unclear what organization they were affiliated with. The ringleader was a guy named Driscoll." Michael paused here. "Skinny, with a long ponytail. Rollins thinks Driscoll and his friends killed Logan. He's been monitoring Driscoll's activities ever since he got released."

"Where's Driscoll?"

"Chicago."

"Any connection with Time to Act Press?"

"Rollins saw one of their pamphlets in prison. The post office where the press has a box is in Driscoll's neighborhood. I asked him about the Reverend and Nelson, but he couldn't place them offhand. He gave me Driscoll's address and I drove by the house. There was a blue pickup in the driveway, the same one I saw outside the church that night."

"Interesting," I said, but the word was lame. "Did Rollins know of any connection to Germany?"

"No. He wants to talk to you, though, thinks you and I may be on to something. I told him I'd give you his number."

We sat in silence for a few moments. I debated whether to tell him about Marcy's abortion and the menacing crowd that had met us, but I didn't want to violate her privacy. "Maybe it's time to go to the FBI with this," I said.

Michael shook his head. "Rollins told me not to. He says they're infiltrated by white supremacists."

"That sounds paranoid."

"His uncle was shot by Hoover's agents when they stormed a Black Panther house."

"That was a long time ago."

"I know, but Rollins said the Chicago bureau has been slow to change, very slow. They spend all their time watching people like him, not white guys."

"I don't know, Michael. Can you really trust this guy Rollins?"

"Call him. See for yourself."

"I will."

I looked out the window, hoping to recover the sense of a lovely fall day, as if I'd ever had it. We were climbing a steep hill, where stands of white birch broke the evergreen monotony like sun rays on dark water. We were in the Porcupines now—or Porkies, as the locals called them—hardly real mountains, but that didn't matter. I was used to these lesser versions, the Scottish Highlands, the Green Mountains in Vermont, the Poconos, where my parents took me in the summer. Not high enough to awe you but easier to traverse, so you had the sense that they might become familiar if you let them, if you only had the time.

Would this become familiar to me? Would I stay here long enough?

At the top of the hill was a picnic area. Michael pulled over. "Time for lunch," he announced. "I brought some sandwiches and coffee." We sat at a table overlooking Lake Superior, which met the horizon so sharply you could almost believe the earth was flat. The water was a Mediterranean blue today and I could make out a big boat in the distance: a freighter, Michael told me. There were a few left, though here as elsewhere most commerce had shifted to the roads.

The turkey sandwich was basic, the coffee tasted better. I warmed my hands on the cup, wanting to talk about something other than the grim subject that brought us together, so I asked him about his background. His father was of Finnish descent, he told me, his mother Swedish. His grandfather had emigrated to work in the copper mines and became a labor organizer with the Western Federation of Miners. His mother's family was on the other side of the line—the Swedes were the mine provisioners, part of the labor aristocracy.

When the mines shut down during the Depression, Michael's grandfather bought a dairy farm outside of Houghton with his wife's inheritance. He was never a very successful farmer, so his children were sent to work early. Michael's father worked at a gas station, which he took over when the owner retired.

"Is your father still alive?" I asked.

"No, he died in his early fifties of stomach cancer."

"And your mother?"

"She's still going strong—she teaches third grade in Calumet."

He looked down and I thought of volunteering something about my own family, but he started up again before I could. "I went to see Johnny's mother yesterday," he told me, "but this time she didn't think I was him. She said he'd come to visit her earlier that morning. Maybe he had. I've been thinking a lot about where his spirit is. It's funny, but even though we never talked much about religion, he's the only person I've ever felt religious with."

He paused, checking my expression to see if it was all right to proceed.

"He had this way of accepting silence, practicing it even, like a form of meditation. The first time I went out snowshoeing with him he was so quiet I thought he was mad at me. He'd point out animal tracks and say the name—squirrel, fox, deer—but nothing more. Once we canoed together all day without saying anything. I got so into the rhythm of paddling that the paddle became part of my body, and I wondered if that was why he was so quiet, so he could become totally one with whatever he was doing. For a long time I thought it must have something to do with his Ojibwa culture, but I don't think so. I think it was just the way Johnny was. At the funeral his uncle remarked on it too. He said Johnny was the only person he knew who was quiet enough to really listen. That was his gift."

"I wish I'd had the chance to know him," I said softly.

"Yes, he would have liked you. He never liked Loren."

Embarrassed by the comparison, I gathered up the picnic trash and carried it over to a garbage bin, where I had to unfasten a chain in order to lift the heavy metal top.

"There's lots of bears around here," he explained. "A bear stole my food once when I was camping, even though I tied it on a high branch. I had to hike twelve miles out on an empty stomach."

"Sounds fun."

"It was the first day that spring the blackflies came out. I was covered with bites. That's why I like fall and winter better—no bugs." He poured the coffee dregs on the ground and fastened the thermos lid. "We can take a short hike from here," he suggested, "but then I want to take you to another place I think you should see."

"Where?"

"You'll see when we get there."

We hiked about a mile along the ridge top, keeping the lake in view except during small dips the trail made into the forest. The path was narrow, so I walked behind him, conscious of how much longer his stride was than mine. I was more winded than I should have been, a reminder of the exercise I hadn't been doing. In Boston I went to a private gym, where I worked out on a treadmill like a caged rat. I hated it, hated all the rat machines and the false sense of accomplishment you got afterward as you preened in front of the locker room mirror. I'd vowed to seek more organic exercise in Houghton, but I hadn't. So Michael had to wait up for me.

He leaned against a tree trunk, his eyes monitoring my approach. I wondered how he saw me. I wondered how I would see him if I really let myself. As a vessel of possibility, like an urn standing at the far edge of an ornamental garden? In the forest he looked beautiful, blond boy from the north, the Aryan dream incarnate. Only that dream was what we were both fighting. This was no time for dreams, no time for possibility.

We turned around shortly after that and retraced our steps to the car. I looked down at the leaves I crunched underfoot, trying to distinguish one from another, but most had already lost their color and shape and blended into the forest floor. I wondered where Loren was, whether she knew I was out with her man. I knew without his telling me that he didn't share information about our work with her. She wasn't smart enough to keep a secret. Maybe she wasn't smart enough to keep him either.

But you can be too smart too, I reminded myself. Like Sajit and me, constantly coming up with brilliant new rationales to justify our estrangement, to render it normal. Our daughter thought she was dumb, but she was the only one astute enough to notice.

Back in the car, Michael retrieved a USGS map from the glove compartment and studied it for several minutes before we departed. "Would you mind holding it open?" he asked. It was a close-up of an area west of the Porcupines, a dense maze of brown contour lines broken by a few black dashes indicating trails or logging roads. He had marked a route with a yellow highlighter, but the destination was unclear.

On the other side of the mountain we turned off the highway onto a National Forest Service access road. It was paved for a few miles, then turned to dirt. Michael's car took the ruts badly, and he had to slow down when our heads almost hit the ceiling. The forest was ugly here, a mixture of scrawny pine plantations and swampland, where the trees were either stunted or dying, their cast-off limbs like old bones on a battlefield. A sense of claustro-phobia came over me, and I wondered what would happen if we broke down, how long it would take for someone to find us.

We drove for over an hour, and around three o'clock I started worrying about Marcy. I'd told her I'd be back before dark, but evening fell early these days. "Only a few more miles," Michael assured me, sensing my anxiety. He seemed calm but artificially so, as if he were steeling himself against something.

He had me keep a lookout for Forest Road Number 17, which I almost missed since the sign was obscured by brush. We traveled down it a few miles, then took a left on an old logging road, which we followed until we reached a pull-over. "We're here," Michael announced, taking the key from the ignition.

I thought he was leading me to a special spot, a stand of virgin timber or a gorge with a waterfall, but there was nothing to sepa-rate this place from the rest of the forest except our presence. I unbuckled my seat belt and asked him why we'd come.

"Johnny was shot here," he answered.

He didn't wait for my response but got out of the car and started walking into the forest. I hesitated and then followed him, not wanting to be left alone.

In a few minutes we reached a clearing. He stood in the center of it, studying the ground in every direction as if he expected to find a clue somewhere in the dead leaves. Then he looked up at me. "At least he died outside, not in a prison laundry room. He would have wanted to die outside." From his pocket he took a leather pouch. "Johnny gave me this," he said, pulling the turquoise ring off his finger. "I'm going to bury it here in this pouch. If we find the killers, I'll come back and get it."

He picked a spot midway between two pine trees, measuring the exact distance with a tape measure. He swept the pine needles away with his foot, knelt down, and loosened the earth with a camping spade from his backpack. He put the pouch about six inches deep, replaced the soil, and very slowly patted it down, as if he didn't want the task to end. When he finally lifted his hands from the ground, he covered his face and began to cry.

I stood for a few moments watching him, trying not to feel my own sadnesses, to reserve the moment for Johnny and him. And then as if by instinct, as if he were a hurt child, I knelt down beside him and put my arms around his shoulders. His back was tight. My touch seemed to make it tighter, but he didn't push me away.

Lucy wakes in the middle of the night for no apparent reason. She doesn't need to go to the bathroom, she's not thirsty, Hank's not snoring, and she doesn't think she's had a bad dream, although there are plenty of things to have bad dreams about these days. She listens hard and hears a faint cry. Is it the cry of Marcy's lost baby, the ghost baby? Does it need her?

She gets out of bed and wanders into the living room and sits in the rocker, cradling her arms in case the ghost baby wants to rest there. The warm spell is over and it's cold tonight, might even snow a little tomorrow. She shivers and thinks about how cold the baby must feel ripped from its mother's womb. Silently, she calls to it—is it a boy or a girl, or does it matter? Should she give it a name? She wishes she could talk to her sister about it, but the Reverend has sworn her to secrecy about everything.

Diane knows something's wrong, though. She came over today and told Lucy she was worried because she's keeping so much to herself. "The church takes all my time," Lucy lied. Actually, it wasn't a lie if you counted everything she did for the Reverend, though how could she tell Diane that?

"People say that church is strange," Diane said. "Kind of like a cult. Once you're in, you can't get out."

"They don't know what they're saying, then. I could leave tomorrow if I wanted."

"Why don't you? What's wrong with your old church, Lucy?"

"Hank likes this one."

"You and Hank could go to different churches."

She shook her head. "No, they need me there."

"They need you at our church too. They need someone to teach Sunday school to the younger kids. You used to like that so much, and the kids loved you."

"I need to be with Hank."

"Has he stopped drinking?"

"More or less."

"I hope he hasn't been hitting you again." Her sister hasn't trusted Hank ever since the time Lucy fled to her house with a bruised cheek and a black eye.

"He doesn't do that anymore, not since he joined the Sons."

"Glad there's something good about it."

"There's a lot good," Lucy lied again.

"Well, come over sometime, will you? You haven't seen the kids for ages. Doug's got a new bike."

"I will," Lucy assured her. She followed Diane to her van, waving as she pulled out of the driveway, then went back inside and put on another tape.

She wants to finish it now. She wants to hear the loss in Marcy's voice so she can pray for her and the baby. Maybe the soul of the baby will be born inside another body; maybe it will come through her own womb so she can protect it this time. Was it wrong to believe that could happen?

She takes the tape recorder from the table and turns it on. Gillian is calling someone named Chris Rollins. He has a funny voice, high but raspy—after every sentence he rests as if he's out of breath. She tells him Michael told her to call. Lucy knows Michael's voice too, he invited Gillian out on Sunday. "Oh, yes," Chris Rollins says, "I've been wanting to talk to you." He pauses and clears his throat. "I think it would be best to talk in person. Any chance you'll be coming to Chicago sometime soon?"

"I wasn't planning on it," Gillian says.

"Then maybe I'll drive up to see you. I can do some work in Green Bay on the way. Do you have any time next week?"

"I don't teach on Fridays."

"I'll drive up Thursday night then. Meet you in your office?"

They set a time and she gives him directions. "I'll see you then," he says, "unless something comes up. I'll give a call if there's any problem. You should take my home phone number too in case you need to get in touch."

Lucy makes a mental note of his name and telephone number to tell the Reverend. Maybe it's important, maybe it isn't, but the Reverend's hungry for information, and feeding that hunger is easier than feeding the other thing. And the more she tells him about Gillian, the less he asks about Marcy. She wants to keep the girl to herself.

She hears her voice next. She's talking to a boy, but it's not her boyfriend in Boston. It's someone named Seth, who goes to the high school. He talks about how stoned he is and Marcy laughs. It's the first time Lucy has heard her laugh.

Marcy says she wishes she were stoned too. "I'll play you a song," he offers. "Hang on."

After a few minutes Lucy hears his guitar. She doesn't recognize the song, it's slow, maybe sad; she can't tell because he doesn't sing along. She imagines Marcy lying on her bed, listening. Does she feel any remorse that her baby's dead? Or does she need someone to show her the path to remorse? "That's beautiful," Marcy tells Seth when he's done. "Really beautiful."

"I wish you were here," Seth says. "I wish you were smoking this joint with me."

Lucy switches off the tape and closes her eyes. She won't tell the Reverend about the marijuana; she doesn't want the girl to get in trouble. She's tired now, but she doesn't want to go back to bed. Lying next to Hank makes her feel bad, because he still doesn't have a clue about the Reverend. He trusts him, he even trusts Nelson, though she knows from doing the accounts that a few things from the store are missing. This week she'll go check out the cabin when he isn't there and see if she can find them. More evidence—as if she needs it.

She goes to the place in her head and listens for instruction. But all the Voice says is to keep listening, because by listening she'll find out how to show Marcy the right path. "You're a good listener, Lucy," the Voice says. She knows that. She wishes she could talk as well as she can listen.

"Lucy," Hank calls from the bedroom. "Where are you?"

"I'm here," she shouts back. "I just woke up hungry and went to get something to eat."

"It's the middle of the night."

"I know. I'm coming back to bed."

"I had a bad dream," Hanks says, as he nestles up close to her. "It was snowing and I couldn't find my boots, so I went outside barefoot. I was looking for you, but I can't remember why. I had to find you though, I knew that. So I walked around until my feet got colder and colder and I couldn't stand it anymore. And then I woke up and you weren't here."

"I was hungry," she says.

"Do you think it means anything?"

"The dream?"

"No, the fact that you were hungry."

"No, I don't think so, Hank."

"The Reverend says we'll be blessed with a child before the winter's through."

"How does he know that?"

"He just knows, like he knows other things."

Hank's hard against her. He wants to make love, he probably thinks he'll be able to give her a baby now. It's been a long time since they've had sex. He hasn't asked and she hasn't given, but she should probably give now. She lets him pull up her flannel nightgown and fumble with her breasts in the dark. She tries to go back to the Voice, but she hears the boy's guitar instead, slow, patient, resigned about something. She makes love from memory, trying to go back to the time when they didn't fall away from each other so fast, when the snuggling was almost as good as the sex.

But he can't comfort her anymore, and she can't comfort him. When they're done, she kisses him good night and rolls over onto the cold side of the bed. The ghost baby cries again, but only Lucy can hear it.

Luck had it that our first lead from Rostock came a few days before Rollins's visit. My friends in the anti-Nazi movement had a contact in Karl Gruhl's shipping warehouse who had reported seeing a box of copies of *Sea Change* there, the book I bought in the sporting goods store. The tie with Gruhl was intriguing, and I started to feel that maybe we were really on to something. I e-mailed Michael and told him to prepare a detailed file on everything we'd learned so far.

I also had him check out Rollins's story about Tony Logan. For a month or so Logan's murder had made the front section of the *Chicago Tribune*. A police investigation claimed the murder was the result of a drug gang vendetta, while black groups shouted cover-up and a few liberal columnists wrote about the need for prison reform. Then Logan faded from public view.

I read *Sea Change* again, compulsively this time, searching for things that might have eluded me before. The racist language had blinded me on the first reading. I'd reacted too viscerally, not seeing the forest for the trees. This forest was well planted. The book was by someone with a sophisticated grasp of navigation and information systems. The author, I. M. Truth, argued that whoever ruled the waves, literally and figuratively, would determine who ruled the world, and it wasn't the U.S. Navy or government Mr. Truth had in mind. Or their German counterparts, for that matter.

Liberal democracies had already fallen prey to the curse of the mud people, he wrote. The mud people were procreating faster than whites and invading our borders. "One man, one vote" was a recipe for disaster, for a slow, silent Communist takeover. "The Reds don't need to wage violent revolution anymore," he asserted. "They have won the demographic one. They just need the brown and black and yellow vote." The response should be the building of not one single Aryan nation but a confederacy of states, an international alliance of the pure-blooded.

It was hard to teach that week because I was so eager to meet Rollins. I spoke too fast and was impatient with the students who stopped by my office, hoping to glean some information about the upcoming midterm. Mark Nicholson took me to lunch on Thursday, supposedly to find out how my teaching was going, but really he wanted to talk about his son. He and Anne were so happy that Seth and Marcy were becoming friends, he told me. I could tell they wanted more than that; they wanted Seth to have a real girlfriend. He stopped short of telling me he was worried Seth was gay, so I didn't press him on it. I didn't want to know his secrets because then he might want to know mine.

I had too many of them at the moment, but they fueled me, gave me a sense of mission, involved me with Michael, because I did look forward to seeing him now. That day in the woods something brittle between us had snapped, and we stepped a little more easily around each other.

Friday he came to my office a half-hour before we were supposed to meet Rollins, dressed for the occasion in corduroy slacks, a black turtleneck, and a tweed jacket with sleeves a little too short for his long arms. Still, he looked good; better yet, he looked older, almost my age.

"So what do we really want from Rollins?" I quizzed him. I was standing by the window, too nervous to sit.

"Maybe we want to work with him. He could keep an eye on Driscoll."

"And what does he want from us?"

Michael shrugged. "Justice. Revenge. A good story."

"What if we can't give them to him?"

"What if he can't give them to us?"

Rollins was supposed to come at ten-thirty, but by eleven he hadn't arrived. I went to the faculty lounge to get some coffee, certain he'd be there when I got back. He wasn't. Eleven-thirty came and went. I tried calling his office in Chicago, but no one answered. Then I remembered he'd given me his home number.

I dialed it, but it was busy. I kept trying for fifteen minutes until finally a woman answered. I asked for Chris Rollins. "Who are you?" she asked suspiciously.

"Dr. Gillian Grace," I replied. "I'm a professor at Keweenaw University in Houghton. Mr. Rollins had an appointment to see me this morning, and he hasn't shown up."

"He's dead," the woman said.

"*What?*"

"According to the police, he died of a heroin overdose in the Holiday Inn in Green Bay last night. His mama says he's never touched hard drugs. The police say his briefcase was full of heroin—he was up there to do a deal. His mama doesn't believe it. I don't either. People been after him ever since he got out of jail. Don't like what he writes."

"Are you a relative?" I asked.

"I take care of his mama. She's got Parkinson's and can't get around too good."

"I'm sorry," I said. "Please give my regrets to the family."

"There's only his mama, and she's taking it hard."

I thanked her and hung up. "What happened?" Michael asked.

"He died last night from an overdose of heroin."

"*What?*"

Just then there was a knock on the door. I went to open it, hoping somehow the information was wrong and Rollins would be there, apologizing for being late. But it was only a student, a boy named Daniel, who spent most of his time chewing gum or sleeping in the back row. "I know you don't have office hours now, Dr. Grace," he began, "but I saw you in the coffee room and I wanted to stop by to see if I could arrange a makeup time for the midterm. I'm going to be away that day—I'm on the hockey team."

"I can't do it now," I replied.

"Oh, I'm not ready to take it now. I was thinking sometime next week."

"I mean I'm busy right now. E-mail me and we'll schedule a time."

I saw him look at Michael strangely. He was staring at the ground, seemingly unaware of the kid's presence. "OK," Daniel remarked. "Sorry to bother you. Have a good weekend."

"You too," I said by rote, and closed the door and leaned against it. "They found him in the Holiday Inn in Green Bay with a brief-case full of drugs."

"It was a setup," Michael asserted.

"Maybe. That's what his mother's helper implied on the phone. She claimed he never did heroin. But we don't know. He could have been dealing drugs on the side."

"I don't think so. I think they held him down and injected him with heroin and then took the papers from his briefcase and sub-stituted drugs."

"That's pure supposition, Michael."

He shrugged. "Look, I met the guy. He didn't strike me as an addict, and he knew things no one else knows."

"Maybe you're right. In any case he's dead."

"Like Johnny," he said.

CHAPTER 11

ALMOST SNOW

The day after Rollins's death I received two letters in the mail, one from him and one from Sajit. I opened Rollins's first.

November 20, 1999

Dear Dr. Grace:

I decided to send you this in case I couldn't meet with you in person. I didn't want to call again because I am beginning to suspect my phone is tapped. I've heard strange clicking noises, the work of an amateur. Perhaps your phone is tapped too. Yesterday I had the feeling I was being followed, and one thing I learned in prison is the need to plan for contingencies. So if you've already met with me, please disregard this letter.

I wanted to pass on some information that may or may not be of use. Based on my conversation with your colleague (student?) Michael Landis, I searched my memory for any evidence of a link between the men I knew in prison and groups in Germany. Besides the Time to Act

Press, the only other thing that came to mind was the fact that these men, especially Alan Driscoll, had a lot of money at their disposal. They regularly bribed the prison guards and always seemed to have a supply of spare cash for friends, which was one of the main reasons they had a following.

In the prison library, I worked with a man named Brian Oakley, who was serving a year for minor credit card fraud. When he first arrived in prison, he was a cell mate of Driscoll's but later asked for a transfer. He was white, but not a racist. His wife was Jewish, though he only told me that much later. We got along pretty well; we both liked to read and we discussed books as we worked. Brian was the one who told me about Driscoll's neo-Nazi cell and his obsession with everything about the Third Reich. Driscoll even had a swastika tattooed on his shoulder.

Anyway, last week I decided to see if I could locate Brian. I found his address on the Internet and showed up at his house unannounced. He wasn't keen to talk to me, but he owed me a favor. One of Tony Logan's friends had wanted him as his pretty boy, and I'd told Logan to make the guy lay off.

I asked Brian if he remembered anything that would connect Driscoll with Germany besides all the Third Reich memorabilia. He told me that Driscoll had boasted in front of him once about having important friends in Germany. At first he didn't believe him, but then he started wondering if that was where all the money was coming from. He said that once a week a minister would come to

see Driscoll, and after that he was always in a good mood,
passing out favors. The guards were in a good mood too. I
asked him if he ever saw this minister and he said no.
Maybe this minister is the same man as your Reverend up
there—just a guess but worth considering.

Hope I manage to tell you this in person. If not, you'll
have to carry the torch without me. Be careful.

Sincerely yours,
Chris Rollins

He had a fastidious signature, the kind of perfect cursive one
only learns in Catholic school, where nuns hover over the desk,
ready to whack you with a ruler if you forget to dot your *i*'s and
cross your *t*'s. But he was dead now. Kind of him to anticipate
that contingency and send the letter. Would I have had such
presence of mind?

Michael was right, they must have killed him. Should I expect
to be killed too? Was my phone tapped as he suggested? It
would explain how that woman knew about Marcy's abortion,
and maybe that's how they had caught on to Rollins. Did that
make me somehow responsible for his death? Academic life
lured you into thinking you could do this work and still stay
safe. That illusion was shattered, but what did it mean in practical terms: a bulletproof vest, a state-of-the-art alarm system,
sending Marcy away?

I avoided the question by opening Sajit's letter. It was written on
a note card of the Oxford botanical garden, one of my favorite
places in the city. During the first dark winters we shared together,
we made frequent forays to the greenhouses there, gazing up at

the banana trees with Marcy in her stroller, making believe we were in the tropics.

In the letter Sajit told me his depression had finally become so bad he went to see a psychiatrist, who put him on antidepressants. They seemed to work; he couldn't believe he had waited so long to try them. He wanted us to come to Oxford for Christmas and would pay for the tickets.

I would agree, I knew, not because it was his turn to host us, even though it was, or because he was getting help at last. I would go because it was a chance to get away. And after Christmas I would leave Marcy with him for a few days while I went to Rostock. I had to go there, it was clear, if only to carry the torch for Rollins's sake.

I e-mailed Michael and told him not to phone me, because the line might be tapped, but that I needed to see him right away. Then I went to Marcy's room to see if she was awake. It was Saturday, ten-thirty already, and I'd promised to take her shopping for a winter coat before she met Seth for lunch and a movie. I knocked on her door. "What?" she called drowsily.

"It's ten-thirty."

"So?"

"You wanted to go shopping."

"Wake me up in ten minutes."

Next time I opened the door, walked over to her bed, and tapped her on the shoulder. "Time to get up," I declared more forcefully. She rolled over to face me. Her eyes were open and surprisingly alert.

"What's the matter?" she asked.

"What do you mean what's the matter?"

"You were worried about something last night."

"I got a letter from your father today," I replied, avoiding her question. "He wants us to come to Oxford for Christmas."

"Oxford? I thought we were going back to Boston."

"We don't have an invitation there."

"I want to see my friends, Mom."

"Maybe we could stop there on the way back," I offered.

She sat up in bed, brushing her hair from her face, preparing herself for battle. "Nicole said I could stay with her the whole vacation."

"Your father wants to see you."

"So why doesn't he come here some other time?"

"It's our turn to go there."

"I want to go to Boston, Mom. You just don't want me to see Evan."

"Evan has nothing to do with it."

"Oh, yeah, right. You expect me to believe that?"

"Yes." I paused, unsure of what to say next. "Your father's finally getting help," I told her.

"What does that mean?"

"He's being treated for depression."

"So you want to reward him with a visit?"

"It's our turn to go, Marcy. Don't you want to see him?"

"I want to see *him*, not the two of you together."

I turned away from her then so she wouldn't see she'd hurt me. "Just tell me when you're ready to go shopping," I said curtly, as I left the room.

I went into the kitchen and poured myself another cup of coffee. I tried to read the paper, but it was no use. I kept thinking about

Rollins's letter. Should I tell Marcy about it, urge her not to use the phone? But that would worry her and give her another reason to want to leave Houghton. But maybe she should. I knew she would refuse to live with Sajit in Oxford, but she would be delighted to be shipped off to Boston for a few months. But wasn't Evan a greater danger? He would seduce her with drugs and get her pregnant again and God knows what would happen with her epilepsy. I wouldn't be there to watch out for her. At least here we were together.

I resolved to tell her just a little, enough to make her more cautious on the phone, but nothing about Rollins's death. She didn't need to know about that.

The phone rang a few minutes later, startling me. I picked up the receiver with trepidation, holding it a few inches from my ear as if it might reach out and grab me. It was Mark Nicholson, inviting us to an impromptu party that afternoon at their lake house. They were firing up the sauna for the first time. "Can I bring anything?" I asked.

"Oh, Anne's got it all under control. Bring a bottle of wine if you want."

I thanked him and hung up the phone. Marcy was in the shower now, angry but safe. Safe was all that mattered. I got the phone directory and looked up alarm systems in the yellow pages.

It feels like the right time to go out to the cabin. Hank, Nelson, and the Reverend left for Chicago yesterday afternoon for a Sons of the Shepherd meeting, and they aren't supposed to be back until after ten tonight. Lucy makes herself a sandwich and eats it standing by the kitchen window. Then she retrieves her copies of the Reverend's keys from their hiding place in a Tampax box.

She warms up the car for a few minutes, then backs it out the driveway with a strong shot of gas. Once outside of Houghton, she drives faster than usual. There's a football game at Keweenaw U today, and most of the cops will either be there or listening to the game on the radio. They'll leave the back roads alone.

She inserts a tape in the cassette player. She's heard it before, but she likes listening to Marcy and Seth talking. She doesn't like Evan, the boy from Boston, the one who got Marcy pregnant, though her mother doesn't know that for sure. Evan keeps telling her he needs to see her, he wants her to run away. She says no, she can't do that, and Evan asks why. "You shouldn't let your epilepsy make you scared," he says.

"It's not that," Marcy replies.

"Then what is it?"

"It would totally freak my mother out."

"What do you owe her? She took you away from here."

Seth is much nicer. Marcy's voice is more relaxed with him, and she laughs at his jokes. She's laughing now. Lucy wishes someone could make her laugh like that.

It starts to sprinkle just as she reaches the turnoff to the cabin. The paper said rain in the evening, but it's only a little past one. At this time of year a hard rain makes the road to the cabin impassable unless you have four-wheel drive. She considers going back but decides against it. How often are Nelson and the Reverend both out of town? She'll just have to move fast in the cabin.

She turns off the tape and concentrates on driving, ticking off the familiar sights along the way, like the charred trunk of the tall pine that got hit by lightning last summer, split in half as if God whacked an ax through it. The ruts are well worn—in addition to

Nelson, hunters are probably using the road, which goes on a mile or so beyond the cabin to another camp. The rain starts to fall in slow, heavy drops, almost snow, almost winter. She sees the lake ahead and remembers the last time she swam in it. It was at the end of August, just before the Reverend came to see her and everything began to change.

She parks beyond the cabin so that if Nelson happens to look, he'll think the tire tracks are from a hunter's car. She zips up her jacket, but her face is exposed and the cold rain stings her eyes. She walks on the grass on the side of the road so she won't leave footprints in the mud. By the front steps she takes off her shoes and climbs sock-footed to the door. She has five keys. The second one works.

She closes the door behind her and stands for a minute, surveying the room, but for what? Merchandise he's stolen from the store? What if he comes back suddenly, what will she say? She hasn't thought of that. The cabin's even dirtier than the last time she was there—a week's worth of dishes in the sink, clothes strewn everywhere, an odor of stale sweat and garbage. She checks an impulse to turn around and flee.

First she searches the obvious places, the cabinets and drawers and under the furniture cushions, but finds nothing there. Then she remembers how you can hide a lot under a mess. She doesn't want to touch Nelson's clothes, but maybe she has to. Carefully, she lifts a jacket from the couch, then the shirt beneath it, to reveal a couple of porno magazines. Figures, she thinks, and lets the clothes fall back on top of the naked cover girls.

There's another pile of clothes in the bedroom, by the window. She tries to lift the jeans, but they're too heavy; something's stuck in the pant leg. She looks inside—it's a semiautomatic rifle she recognizes from the store. The type that was banned a couple of months ago and Hank was supposed to send back to the manufacturer. She wonders whether he gave it to Nelson or Nelson stole it. It's worth a lot of money.

She fights back a cough, maybe from the dust in the cabin. The rain is heavier on the roof. She knows she should leave soon, but she wants something else. The gun didn't surprise her. Nelson loves guns, fondles them like they're Playboy bunnies. What else is she looking for?

Proof. But proof of what?

Lately, Hank's been staying out late, coming back all dirty and sweaty, showering before he comes to bed. When she asks him what he's doing, he lies and says he's doing some repairs inside the church. But he smells damp and mossy like the outdoors, and his boots are muddy. He's so tired he falls asleep in thirty seconds, and there's no whiskey on his breath. He could be hunting, but she doubts it. He'd tell her that; he'd bring something home to put in the freezer.

Where else should she look? She closes her eyes, trying to make her way to the Voice, but at first all she hears is the rain. Then the Voice reminds her that this is her cabin and she knows it better than anyone. She knows the place where her father used to hide his extra money, the loose floorboard under the dresser. But how would Nelson know that, unless Hank knows? Maybe she told Hank; maybe Hank told Nelson.

It takes all her strength to push the dresser aside. She should have removed the drawers first, but it's raining harder; the road will be impassable soon. She pries the floorboard loose and reaches under it. There's a plastic bag with some papers rolled up inside. She unfastens the rubber band and unrolls the papers, but she can't read them because they're in German. How does Nelson know German? She scans them to see if there are any words she can recognize. Only one: Ontonagon. She puts them back under the floorboard and moves the dresser back, but this time it makes a scratch on the floor. She buffs it with her foot, hoping he won't notice. It's pelting now. She has to go.

She's soaked by the time she reaches the car. She starts the engine and tears off her jacket, throwing it in the back seat. She feels sick; her heart is racing. The rain is so hard she can't see the lake as she passes by. A couple of miles short of the main road, her left rear tire sinks into a muddy rut. She tries low gear, then reverse, but the wheel just keeps spinning, working its way deeper into the mud. Finally, she gets out and pushes, but one person's not enough. She puts a piece of bark under the tire and starts the car again. It moves an inch, then starts to spin. She'll have to walk out to the main road and hail a car, but Nelson might be back by then.

Suddenly, there are lights coming toward her. It's a pickup, but she can't make out what color it is; it could be Nelson's. She wants to run, but she's too tired and wet, and if she runs he'll know she has something to hide. He might shoot her in the back; she wouldn't put that past him. She tries to make up a good story about why she's here, but nothing comes to her mind. She grasps the steering wheel and prays to the Voice.

Marcy and I got a ride to the party with Bart Swenson from the environmental studies department and his wife, Judy. They lived a few blocks away and were serious about curbing energy consumption. When we pulled into the Nicholsons' driveway, I recognized Michael's car and was relieved since I hadn't heard back from him. I carried a bottle of wine, Marcy a pink cyclamen I'd picked up at the florist's that morning. A mean sky spit icy rain on its petals.

Someone I didn't recognize slid open the glass door for us. I spotted Anne at the dining room table, laying out a plate of crackers and smoked salmon. I moved toward her, holding the wine in front of me like a candle to light my way. Her face lit up when Marcy gave her the plant, and she placed it incongruously in the centerpiece of knobby gourds and Indian corn. She told Marcy that Seth was in the study and directed me to the drinks after explaining that Mark was outside, stoking the sauna stove.

Michael came up to me as I was pouring myself a glass of wine. "Did you get my e-mail message?" I asked.

He looked over my head at something or someone against the wall. "I was gone all day—it was my mother's birthday. Loren called me there and told me about the party, so I picked her up and came straight here."

"I got a letter from Rollins."

"What?"

"Sent before he died. I'll tell you about it later." I noticed Loren approaching from the rear. We smiled at each other, but it was a clean miss, or not so clean really, clouded by our claims on the man. I felt ashamed of myself for comparing our appearances. Today I came out on top, only because I had taken the time to blow-dry my hair, put on a little makeup (she had used too much), and select clothes—a purple chenille tunic and black pants—that hid my thickening waist. She wore a tight red sweater and short pleated skirt that made her look like an aging cheer-leader. We exchanged a few words, but then she pulled Michael away to meet someone. I could tell he wasn't pleased.

I stood alone for a few minutes, drinking my wine and debating the best course of action, to mingle or go help Anne in the kitchen. I spotted Ed O'Connor from the political science depart-ment giving me the eye; word was probably getting around that my marriage was a sham and I might be available. He was single, on the make, and moderately good-looking but too pedantic, the kind of man who takes you from point A to point B in a hundred steps when, with a little intuition, you can leapfrog it in three. I shuddered to think what he was like in bed and almost retreated to the safety zone of the kitchen, but the prospect of slicing bread and cheese didn't appeal to me either.

I thought, *Here I am in my late thirties still playing these games.* That drove me to finish my wine and pour another glass. And then I thought, *There are no safety zones. Rollins is dead.* For a moment I felt crazy, caught between two worlds: this normal party and the abnormal men I was tracking. Only Michael would understand this craziness, maybe experience it himself. He was looking at me now and I let him. I met his eye and held his gaze until Loren noticed us looking at each other and tugged at his arm again. Tugboat Loren, I thought; chug-a-lug Gillian, finishing her second glass of wine. I realized I'd already made the decision to get a little drunk since I didn't have to drive. Evidently, so had a lot of other people.

Like a current that gets stronger with a heavy rain, the party, whetted by alcohol, finally forced me to circulate, sweeping me along from group to group, where I engaged in mundane conversations. Many involved the weather, because it was starting to snow outside, big sticky flakes that fell thicker and thicker until the A-frame window was completely covered and you couldn't see out. Bart Swenson regaled me with stories of blizzards, wind-chill factors of forty below, and newcomers whose roofs caved in because they didn't know you have to shovel them off after the first one hundred inches.

Around five o'clock Mark Nicholson came in, stamping his feet on the mat. His hair and beard were coated with the white stuff, and his nose was Rudolph red. When he announced that the sauna was ready, a cheer went up around the room. "Coed?" I asked Bart's wife, Judy.

She nodded nonchalantly. "Most everyone goes naked—it's a Finnish thing. But you can wrap a towel around you if you want." As the first batch of people took off for the sauna, I decided I wasn't going to partake at all, not even wrapped tightly. Finnish custom or not, it didn't seem appropriate to sit squeezed between male colleagues and grad students with dangling genitalia, especially with my daughter around. But the pressure mounted—an outdoor sauna was part of the ritual initiation to the Copper Country—and in the end I felt forced to go along.

At least Anne was kind enough to lend me a terry-cloth robe. I followed her to the sauna, which was about fifty yards away from the house, not far from the beach, but the distance seemed longer because the snow was already a few inches deep. In the anteroom people shed their shoes and most their towels, but I stayed in the robe. We crowded into the hot room, where I found a seat on a bottom bench as far as one could get from the stove. It didn't matter. It was so hot that for a moment I thought I couldn't breathe. Some of the people around me had their eyes closed and were breathing so deeply I thought they were asleep. I can breathe like that too, I told myself.

Loren was sitting across from me in late-twenties naked splendor; Michael was above her, seemingly oblivious to how Ed O'Connor was gazing at her breasts. At least she was a decoy—as long as she was there Ed wouldn't look at me. I looked at Michael because I had to; I had to acknowledge him. His chest was more slender than I anticipated, almost hairless, but the muscles on his shoulders and arms advertised his strength. His hair was damp with sweat and he'd slicked it back. I pushed mine back too. I let my robe fall open just a little to let in some air.

Loren noticed the connection between us and looked hurt. Then, as if to punish Michael, she returned Ed's gaze, smiling drunkenly and accepting his compliments. Mark Nicholson was starting to look at me, so I closed my eyes.

I don't know how long it was, maybe ten minutes or twenty, before Anne announced that we should all take a break and go down to the beach. The alcohol and the heat had made me so light-headed that when I stood up I fell back dizzily on the bench. "I'll get her some water," Michael announced, and brought me a glass from the anteroom. I drank it and he helped me up, holding on to my arm.

The snow felt wonderful against my burning skin. We walked down to the beach, and he told me to take off my robe and roll on the ground. "That will wake you up in a hurry," he claimed. All around us people were rolling in the snow, laughing crazily, and he joined them. I watched them until something else caught my eye. Ed and Loren were throwing snowballs at each other, running toward the woods.

"Your turn now," Michael urged, standing up and brushing the snow from his naked body. "Come on, I'll hold your robe."

I did what he told me. I became as crazy as everyone else, opening my pores to ice crystals, forgetting where the ground ended and the sky began because everything was white. I rolled toward the water and the sound of waves breaking, wanting to be even drunker and dizzier than this, to be in the moment instead of studying it. But soon the cold reached my consciousness and I saw Michael's hand, ready to help me up. Maybe he looked at my breasts, I don't know, I think he was trying hard not to. "Time to go back to the sauna," he said.

It was intentional, the way I looked in the direction they had run. Because once you looked, you could hear Loren's laughter and then you could see, if you strained your eyes hard enough, that between the white birches two figures were locked in some kind of embrace. "I need to read Rollins's letter," Michael remarked abruptly. "Maybe I could come over tonight after I drop off Loren. Would that be all right?"

It was something in the way he said *after* that made me know he'd seen what I saw. And back in the sauna, not jealously but almost with relief, he watched Ed and Loren fuck each other with their eyes.

Lucy sits by the wood stove, wearing a pair of the man's jeans and a flannel shirt while her wet clothes tumble in the dryer. Outside, the rain has turned to snow, and she watches it through a crack in the curtains. He's making a hot toddy for her, swears it's the best way to ward off a cold. She's prepared to believe anything he says, because he's not Nelson, he's a guardian angel who pulled her car out of the mud and now wants to send her home in comfort. He was on his way to hunt deer down by the lake when he found her. He was glad for the excuse to get out of the rain, he told her, not a good day for hunting. She told him she'd made a wrong turn.

He's Paul and Donna Saleski's son. They passed away a couple of months ago within a few days of each other, and he's trying to sort out the house and convenience store they own on the main road. Doesn't know whether to sell or not. He just got laid off at a GM plant downstate, and he's wondering whether it's a sign to move back up here. "It's quieter here," he tells her. "Not so crazy." But he has an ex-wife and two children in Detroit and he doesn't want to be too far from the kids. She doesn't tell him she knew his parents, used to buy milk and lottery tickets from them. She lies about her name too, just in case he happens to meet Nelson sometime.

She's doing everything wrong. You shouldn't accept a strange man's hospitality like this. At least his parents weren't strangers, but they're dead now and even the knickknacks on the shelf look sad. The china boy with a fish on the end of his pole is only grinning because he's supposed to; he feels bad about killing the fish.

The man's sad too; she can tell. He hands her a hot toddy and sits down in the rocker beside her. They both stare at the stove for a while and let the hot toddy spread fire down their throats.

She lets him talk to her about his ex-wife. They were too young when they married, he says, and she got restless after the second kid—started having an affair with one of his best friends, so he lost them both. He wanted to keep the kids, but the judge gave her custody. Now he gets them every other weekend and during holidays. The boy's five, the girl's eight. "They're doing OK," he says, "but she still hasn't settled down. How about you? Are you married?"

"Yes," she says, and nothing else.

"Have any kids?" She shakes her head and looks down. "Do you want some?"

"Yes," she says again, "but I can't seem to have any."

After a little while she hears the dryer stop and gets up and tells him it's time for her to go home. He invites her to stay for dinner—he's got a pot of soup he can heat up real fast. She declines, says her husband's due back soon from Chicago, and besides, she doesn't want to get caught in the snow. "Maybe you can come again sometime," he replies.

She goes into the bedroom to change back into her clothes. She doesn't want to take off his flannel shirt, it's so soft, and she likes his smell. She unbuttons it but leaves it on. And then the Voice comes to her before she even thinks of summoning it. It tells her to go to him.

She opens the bedroom door and stands there before him, the shirt just open enough so he can see the edges of her breasts. "I'm not ready to go home," she says.

He spends a long time with his hand between her legs. He's not rushed, so she tries not to be, to remember what it's like to want more time, not less, to feel pleasure coming her way. She's so hot she kicks the comforter off and lets the cold air run up and down the back of her leg like another hand. So many hands on her. His other hand is on her breast. She closes around the hands, lets them lift her up until she closes again.

He has no condoms, he says, so maybe he shouldn't come in. She lies that she's infertile. But for safety? he asks. She doesn't answer, just guides him inside her with her hand and he lets her because her will is stronger than his. He comes fast, but it doesn't matter because she's satisfied enough.

Afterward he gives her his phone number and tells her to call whenever she can. She asks him if she can keep his shirt. "Of course," he says, "as long as you wear it like that again." He walks her to the car and brushes the snow from the windows with his glove. "Drive safely," he tells her, and kisses her before she gets in.

CHAPTER 12

RECURRENCE

Sometimes I look back at that night as a beginning, sometimes as a midpoint, sometimes as an end.

Marcy and I got back from the Nicholsons' party around eight, but Michael didn't come over until eleven. Dropping off Loren meant dropping Loren, though he didn't tell me that at first. He sat on the couch, pale and visibly agitated, his fingers in need of something to occupy them, like knitting needles or a cigarette. I handed him Rollins's letter while I went into the kitchen to make some tea.

Marcy was standing by the open refrigerator, staring blankly at the shelves. "Do you want something?" I asked.

"Maybe some juice," she replied, then reached for it in a kind of slow motion that meant one of two things or a combination of both. Alcohol and dope. She was medically indicated to stay away from them, but I didn't say anything. All the parenting books I read said mistrust was worse than letting your kid get away with an occasional minor infringement. I hoped it was minor. I hoped she hadn't drunk as much I had.

"You'd better get to bed," I said. "You look tired." She glanced at Michael in the living room. "I have a letter related to his research," I explained. She looked at me suspiciously, then poured herself a glass of juice and retreated to her room.

I put a tea cozy on the teapot and carried it on a tray to the living room along with two matching mugs. Proper, quaint, slightly ridiculous. He didn't even notice. He was rereading Rollins's letter, holding it so tightly I thought the paper might rip. "We should be careful," I said, setting down the tray.

He looked up at me strangely. "What do you mean by that?"

I started to pour the tea, though it was still too weak. "I think we may be in danger."

"Of course we're in danger. We're in danger of a lot of things." He paused, watching me as I passed a mug toward him. "I broke up with Loren tonight," he announced.

I asked him why because it was the only thing I could think of saying.

"Because I had to. I had to clear the decks. I was starting to hurt her—that's why she went off with Ed tonight. She's not very smart, and she could get in trouble because of me. You could get in trouble too."

"I already am."

"Do you want to be?"

"No one ever wants to be, Michael," I said, with a conviction that had a bitter aftertaste.

"I don't know about that. Look at Rollins. Look at me. I could have passed Johnny's murder off as a freak occurrence. Look at you. You study this—you've made it your career."

I deliberated for a moment, searching for the right words. "Some people see the patterns in things," I finally began, "and some don't. Once you see them, you have to make a choice. Do you paint the picture or not? Do you let other people see what you see? Because it's a burden. Once you paint the picture, it becomes your responsibility. But it's also a burden if you *don't* do it. If you keep the knowledge to yourself."

I don't know if he really heard me; he looked too intent on what he was going to say next. "I want you to make the decision about whether or not to go ahead with this," he stated, sitting forward as if the couch were a straight-backed chair. "You don't owe me anything—it's gone way past your being my professor. And I don't want—" He stumbled here, reaching for a spoon. "I don't want to confuse one picture with another. I don't want to confuse my attraction to you—"

I would have liked to draw out the hearing of that phrase, let it dissolve slowly like a hard candy, taste the sweetness for more than just a second. But he was right, so right. We couldn't afford to act on the attraction, because then we wouldn't be able to judge when it was time to draw away from the other, clearer danger, though maybe it was the danger itself that was turning up the sexual heat.

"Let's proceed on the assumption that I'm still your professor, Michael," I said, allowing myself to meet his eye. And then I lied. "I'm sorry you had to break up with Loren."

"It was time anyway. We never really got along."

Somehow we got back on track; somewhere between the first

and second cup of tea our tone became brisk and businesslike. We discussed Rollins's letter with the dispassion of police officers, and then Michael told me he had a plan. He was going to break into the church and look for the maps the men had been studying that night, photograph them with a special camera. I told him he was crazy—if they caught him, they might kill him. "They won't catch me," he asserted. "I'll make sure of that."

"How?" I asked, but he didn't have an answer.

I tried hard to dissuade him, but somewhere along the way I had lost my authority. I was a pretend professor, not a real one. No one was in charge now. It frightened me and made me feel older, not younger. I got up and parted the curtains of the living room window, ostensibly to see if it was still snowing, but subconsciously I expected to see a face there, watching. We would probably be watched now, as Rollins had been watched. Never mind the snow. Never mind the comforting sound of the furnace turning on and off.

Just as I was about to sit back down, I heard the groan: the groan I was always listening for, anticipating, the groan that governed my life. I rushed toward it, but Marcy's door was locked. "Oh, God!" I cried out.

Michael was behind me. "What's the matter?"

"She's having an epileptic fit and the door's locked. I've got to get it open." I tried the knob again, then thrust my body against the door, trying to break it open.

"Here, let me try." He grabbed a pen from his pocket and inserted the point in the hole in the doorknob. I could hear the button on the other side spring loose. I opened the door and ran in. She was on the floor, but thank God she hadn't hit anything as she fell. Her eyes were rolled upward, her jaw clenched, and her lips had already turned blue. It was a tonic-clonic seizure; her last one had been five years ago.

I put a pillow under her head, unbuttoned the top of her shirt, and waited through the shaking and jerking of her limbs. "Should I call nine-one-one?" Michael asked.

"No, it will pass," I told him. I knew that, yet I didn't really believe it. I always believed it would go on forever, that I would lose her and never look into her eyes again. I felt unbearably cold all of a sudden and started to shake. He draped a blanket over my shoulders.

It only took a minute, maybe two, before her body began to relax and she started to breathe more normally, but it felt so much longer. As gently as I could, I turned her on her stomach, guiding her face to one side.

"I didn't know she had epilepsy," he said. "What do you do now?"

"Wait for her to wake up."

"Do you want me to stay?"

"She'll be OK."

"Are you sure?"

I nodded.

"Are *you* OK?" I clearly wasn't; I was still shaking. "I want to stay," he said. "I can sleep on the couch."

I remembered that it was still snowing, that the roads were probably bad, that it would do no harm to have someone else keep vigil with me. In the end I gave him my bed and shared Marcy's. I didn't need to; she would be all right, but I wanted to sleep close to her. I wanted to sleep close to him.

Lucy keeps the flannel shirt in the cedar chest underneath a pile of wool blankets she inherited from her parents. Hank's allergic to wool, but she can't bear to throw them out. At least once a day she looks at the shirt and sometimes even puts it on. She remembers him then, thinks about his loneliness and the way he touched her. But then she forces herself to backtrack, to the car stuck in the mud, the cabin, the papers under the floorboard. Ontonagon. Her father came from that town. He used to boast about how important Ontonagon was as a port during the copper boom, but now it was run down, nothing going on. Why would Germans be interested in it? Why would Nelson need to hide those papers?

She doesn't want to think about Nelson, she wants to think about *him*. She opens the cedar chest, lifts the blankets, and runs her fingers over the flannel shirt. The Reverend is coming at eleven. It's getting so much harder to pretend.

She waits for him in the living room, thumbing through a catalog of clothes she can't afford. Why does the company send it to her, to make her feel bad? At least when she worked at the store she felt she had a right to some of the money. But now she doesn't like to ask Hank for anything extra. She knows from the books there's nothing extra to give.

It's almost eleven-thirty when the doorbell finally rings. She's hungry already, kind of dizzy. She's only seen the Reverend twice since he got back from Chicago. The first time, he dropped off another tape and brought her a red frilly nightgown that made her look like a slut. But she was relieved—he didn't say anything about someone's being in the cabin. The second time, he picked up the tape and left after only a few minutes. She told him there was nothing important on it because she wanted to guard Marcy and Seth's secrets.

She opens the door to find Nelson there too. She wants to close it in his face, but she has to be careful. Maybe he's found something; maybe he noticed how the dresser leg scuffed the floor. She smiles, welcoming them, but they don't smile back. The Reverend marches into the living room as if it's his own house. "You lied to us, Lucy," he says, sitting down on the couch. He still has his coat on. Nelson stands near the doorway, blocking her exit.

She's scared but she doesn't show it; she's always been good at hiding fear. She plays dumb, easing herself into the rocker. "What do you mean?" She still hasn't thought of a good reason why she should have been in the cabin. Looking for something, but for what?

"You didn't tell me everything that was on that tape."

So it's not the cabin, it's the tape. He listened to the tape, checked up on her. "What do you mean?" she says again.

"You didn't tell me that boy confessed he's a homosexual and the girl told him she's got epilepsy and wants to run away. That's important information, Lucy."

"Why, Reverend?" she asks, trying to put on the coy look she wears in bed with him sometimes.

"Because these are sinful people, Lucy, and every detail counts."

"Even personal details like that?"

"You bet. That was extremely important information. Can I still trust you to listen to the tapes?"

She nods vigorously. "Of course, Reverend."

"I want every detail. You hear me?"

She nods again, then looks down at her lap, feigning shame, but really she's watching a shower of dust particles settle on the rug. Will they leave now? Leave her alone? The Reverend gets up and says he needs to use the bathroom. Nelson is staring at her, she can feel it. She hears him move.

Suddenly, he's standing behind her chair. Without saying anything, he places his hands on her shoulders and she freezes. Then he puts his fingers around her neck, pushing up on her chin so she's forced to look back at him. He's bending over her; she can smell his breath. "I want to know everything about that girl," he says. "Everything." She tries to nod, but his fingers prevent it. Only when the toilet flushes does he release his grip. She coughs and struggles for breath.

Marcy swore she had only one drink at the Nicholsons' party and she didn't smoke any dope. I didn't know which role to play, disciplinarian or sympathetic mother. Shit happens; a fit happens for no apparent reason.

Later that week we made our first visit to the epilepsy specialist in Marquette. It had snowed five inches the night before, but the roads were clear and I drove fast. "No need to try new medication yet," the doctor told me, "but I'll up her dose a bit. I'd like to do a blood test in a few weeks—you can get it done in Houghton and have them send the results to me." She was young and a little too keen, but I sensed her competence was real. When we left, I shook her hand, grateful that someone else was involved in this struggle besides me.

On the hundred-mile drive back to Houghton, Marcy and I spoke only a few times. When I asked her if she was being careful about what she said on the phone, she scoffed at me. "Do you really think those right-wing lunatics are interested in what I say to my friends? Aren't you being a little paranoid, Mom?"

"I hope I am," I told her. I tried to interest her in the topic of Christmas, but she wouldn't bite. The fit had depressed her; she carried her body around like a sack of rotten potatoes she wanted to dump somewhere. She was so inside her head she couldn't get into mine. Maybe that was lucky, because my anxiety level was way above flood stage, spilling over into everything I did. Like the way I jerked the steering wheel too hard when I cut back into a lane, or delivered frenzied lectures as if any second the cavalry might charge. We were studying the Napoleonic Wars, and even the bored students in the back row chewed their gum with renewed intensity.

Boom, boom, went the emperor's cannons. Bang, bang, went the general's guns. Would they shoot Michael when they found him looking for their maps? Would it be my fault because I didn't stop him?

I had tried. I e-mailed him every day for four days, but he didn't respond. He didn't come to the office either. Maybe he was devastated by his breakup with Loren or she was devastated and hounding him. Maybe he was embarrassed about admitting his attraction to me.

Or maybe he was dead.

This last possibility consumed me on the drive back from the doctor's office. I dropped Marcy at home and told her I was going to my office for a meeting. Instead, I drove to Calumet.

I had already looked up Michael's address on a street map. He lived about a mile west of town near a cross-country ski area. I got lost a few times but finally got good directions from an old man walking a dog. The house was set back from the road, hidden behind a tall evergreen hedge that looked like it hadn't been pruned in years. The house was two stories, asphalt-shingled, nothing special except for the stained-glass birds hanging in almost every window. A woodpile extended from the front around to the back of the house and was at least five feet high. His car was in the driveway, and there was smoke coming out of the chimney. I knocked on the door.

He looked out the window to see who it was. I noticed he had a rifle in one hand—later, he told me it was a hunting rifle. Johnny's brother had given it to him after the murder in the woods.

"I wanted to see if you were still alive," I said, as he opened the door. "I've been trying to reach you."

He ushered me into the front hall and we stood by the stairs. He took my coat and hung it up but didn't invite me into the living room. He was wearing a baggy black sweater, sweat pants, and slippers on his feet. His face was unshaven and there were dark circles under his eyes, but the effect made him more handsome, not less. The athlete with the perfect posture was untouchable, but this was a man you might wake up next to in the morning. "I wanted to have everything done before I got in touch with you," he explained. "I've been working in the darkroom in the geology lab. One of my friends manages it."

"So you got pictures of the maps?"

"Yes," he replied tersely. "How's your daughter?"

"OK."

He didn't move except for putting one hand on the balustrade. "I didn't want to stress you out any more after that."

"Your silence stressed me out. I even thought you were dead."

A flicker of recognition passed over his face as if he finally realized who I was. "I'm sorry," he said, "I should have been in touch, but I knew you didn't want me to break into the church and I had to. And I didn't want to involve you in case something went wrong."

"I'm already involved, remember?" I paused, shifted a foot. "How did you break in?"

"I picked the lock on the basement door. My father taught me how—he was a volunteer fireman. I picked the lock on the Reverend's cabinet too."

"No one saw you?"

"No one saw me, and I didn't leave a trace."

We stood there for a few more minutes until he took me down to the basement to see the maps. The stairs opened onto a utility room with a washer and dryer and racks of ski and biking equipment. A table was set up for stained-glass work—he had never told me about that hobby. He unlocked the door to his office and turned on the light.

Three maps were tacked on the walls on top of other maps, probably the ones he used for cross-country skiing. The room was small, and I felt his breath on my neck as he stood behind me. Reluctantly, I reached into my purse for my glasses and then leaned forward to view the first map. "They just look like a maze of lines to me," I commented.

"Look closer," he instructed. "See that dot right there? Can you read the writing next to it?"

"Barely."

"It says Victoria. That's about fifteen miles south of Ontonagon. These three maps are close-up contour maps of that area; I matched them to the USGS one I have. That blue line there is the Ontonagon River."

"Why do you think they're interested in this area?"

"I'm not sure. All that's there now is an abandoned mine shaft and a lot of timber. I don't think they're prospecting for copper."

"So what are they prospecting for?"

"All I can think of is they need a place to hide."

"What? Themselves?"

He shrugged. "Your guess is as good as mine. Could be guns, bombs—they were messing with explosives when they killed Johnny."

"Could they use the old mine?"

"Maybe. They'd have to dig out the entrance. But it's safe—no one's going to go out there, especially in winter." He paused. He was next to me now and our arms brushed against each other, wool to wool. "Except for me."

"What do you mean, Michael?"

"I know the trails through there. I charted them for my ski guide, but they were too rough for the average skier so I left them out of the book. I'll wait for more snow and check it out."

"You're not going alone," I said.

"Yes, I am."

"I'm going with you." I sounded stubborn, even to myself. It was the same adolescent voice I used with my parents when they held me back.

"No, you're not, Gillian. You don't know how to ski."

"I've done it a couple of times, and you said you'd teach me."

"It's not like you're going to be on a groomed trail."

"It doesn't matter. You can teach me."

"Don't be crazy," he admonished. "You have a daughter to think of. What if someone's there?"

"So that's it—it's not the skiing that's the problem, you're afraid something's going to happen."

"It's both."

"You don't understand, Michael. I need to do this."

"Why?" He stared at me, studying me, and I studied him back. I didn't have an answer. The only answer I had would have meant breaking our rule, moving so close to him he would have had to embrace me. Probably if I'd done that—and God knows I wanted to—I would have handed over the right to protect me and he would have prevailed.

Instead, I used the sexual heat between us to bend him like molten metal, and he agreed to a compromise. He would give me skiing lessons starting tomorrow, and if I proved good enough I could accompany him out to the mine.

CHAPTER 13

LESSER DANGERS

Mark Nicholson invited me out to lunch on the last day of classes before winter break. I met him in his office, and he drove me the few blocks to the Lebanese deli in town. It was a clear, cold day after a night of blustery snow, and my boots squeaked on the sidewalk. The air was so clean it felt foreign to my lungs. The conditions would be excellent for my ski with Michael that afternoon.

After getting pitas and hummus at the counter, we took a booth in the back of the deli. Mark looked worn down, and I muttered something about the burden of his departmental responsibilities. He didn't take me up on it, lifting his Coke instead in a toast to my successful first semester at Keweenaw University. He told me he was getting lots of positive feedback about me from my students.

I thought of my father, wishing he were still alive so I could call him on the phone and tell him that the students liked me. But then I'd have to tell him all the rest too and he'd worry about me. He did the worrying in the family; when he died, I missed it. My mother fussed, but it wasn't the same thing.

"And how's it going with Michael?" Mark asked. "You beat the record by about a week, I think—you've lasted longer than any of his other supervisors."

My pita was poised in midair, so I took a bite, buying time. "We're surviving," I said, which was true but not in the way he would understand it. I changed the subject. "Have you had any time for your research?" I asked. "It must be hard, being the department chair."

"At least I teach less." A bit of hummus was stuck on his beard and he wiped it off and tucked the napkin under his plate. "I'm going back to something I worked on a long time ago," he continued. "I wrote my dissertation on ethnic conflict during the Michigan copper miners' strike in 1913 and 1914. That's what got me interested in this area—I made a lot of trips from Ann Arbor to Houghton to search in the archives. It's hard to believe now, but this was once a hotbed of labor activism. The entire Michigan National Guard was deployed up here to keep order. Nine workers were killed. The worst tragedy of all was the Italian Hall stampede. Have you heard of it?"

"No," I replied. "What happened?"

He told me how on Christmas Eve in 1913 the Western Federation of Miners organized a party for the strikers' children at the Italian Hall in Red Jacket, now part of Calumet. Families were hurting—after months without work, they could hardly afford anything extra for Christmas. The hall was up a flight of stairs and several women gave out candy and gifts to the children from the stage. It was pandemonium; the crowd kept pushing forward, and the curtain broke and came down so the children couldn't see the women on the stage. "Then someone yelled 'Fire!' and all hell broke loose," he said. "Seventy-four people were trampled to death in the stampede down the stairs, fifty-nine of them children. The door at the bottom of the stairs opened in, not out.

"No one ever identified the man who yelled fire. There were all kinds of rumors—a story is still circulating that whoever yelled fire released talcum powder into the air to look like smoke. The strikers said he was a union buster, the strike busters claimed he had to be a union man. And maybe it was just an accident; maybe someone thought the lights on the Christmas tree were starting a fire. We may never know the truth, but I want to take one more look at all the evidence. It's crazy, but the thing has been on my mind ever since graduate school. I need to lay the story to rest, at least for myself." He paused. "Am I crazy?"

"No," I replied, "you have to be obsessive to be an historian."

"How about a parent?"

"What do you mean?"

He leaned forward, his voice lower. "Sometimes I think it's harder to find out the truth about my own son than about the man who yelled fire."

"What do you mean?" I asked, more gently this time. His face was suddenly so vulnerable that I felt responsible for every nuance in my expression and voice.

"It's stupid, I know, but when Marcy and Seth started to become friends, I hoped they might get together. He's never had a real girlfriend." He blushed slightly and pushed the edge of a potato chip back on his plate. "Anne's convinced he's gay. She worries about it all the time now. I tell her that it doesn't really matter one way or the other, but she's scared for him. And maybe I'm scared for him too. I mean, I have nothing against being gay, but it doesn't make your life easy." He paused and swallowed hard. "Anne went through his backpack the other day. She shouldn't have, but she did. And she found an anonymous note someone had written him, calling him a dirty faggot and other offensive names. It's just not the kind of thing kids do around here. Sure, a lot of them are from conservative families, but people mind their own business."

"Kids have been doing this kind of thing for a long time, Mark. They did it in my high school."

"I guess you're right, but I don't like it."

"Maybe you should try to talk to Seth. He needs your support."

"Marcy hasn't said anything?"

I shook my head. "Unfortunately, she doesn't tell me very much."

"I just don't know how to deal with it. It's hard for me to accept the idea that he's gay."

"Why?"

"Oh, probably because I want him to be like me. Because he's our only kid. Because Anne wants grandchildren."

"It will take work," I said, "but you have to do it."

I considered confiding in return my own struggle to accept Marcy for who she was, but I had so many things to hide from him that I didn't want to open the door even a crack. He talked to me a little more about Seth and then asked about our Christmas plans. I told him Marcy was leaving on the eighteenth for Boston, and I would meet her there on the twenty-third to fly to London.

Mark went up to the counter to get us coffee and baklava. The latter was too sweet for my taste, so I spent the rest of the lunch pushing it around my plate as we made small talk about the department. When we rose to leave, I ventured a hand on his arm.

"Don't worry about Seth," I said. "He's going to be OK." He nodded, wanting to believe me, but there was doubt in his eyes.

Hank's sick in bed with a fever and a cough, but his chills aren't just regular chills. Lucy can tell he's scared about something. He burrows under the comforter and folds himself up in the fetal position so you'd never know he was such a big man. "Soup's on," she says, trying to sound cheerful as she carries a tray of food into his room. "You've got to sit up now."

"I'm not hungry." His muffled voice comes from under the covers.

"You should try to eat a little bit. It's just chicken broth and a few saltines."

He sits up slowly, collapsing back against the pillows she sets behind him. His face is splotchy, and his hair is oily from not taking a shower. He eats a couple of spoonfuls of soup but leaves the crackers alone. "Too dry," he says. "My throat hurts."

She puts her hand on his forehead. He's hotter than he was this morning; she should take his temperature again. "It's all those nights being out there in the cold," she scolds him. "What have you been doing?"

"We're fixing up the church, like I told you." His voice is too weak to be convincing.

"No, you aren't," she says. "I've been in the church, and nothing's changed. Your clothes are wet and dirty—I can tell you've been working outside. That's why you're sick. What have you been doing?"

"I can't tell you, Lucy."

"Why not?"

"Because it's God's work, secret work."

"Is that what the Reverend says?" He nods meekly. "I don't think God likes husbands to keep secrets from their wives."

"The Reverend told me not to tell anyone."

"I'm not anyone. Look at what the Reverend trusts me with. I listen to those tapes."

"Don't make me explain, Lucy."

"Hank, you need to talk to me. Something's on your mind."

She tells him to lie down again, then strokes his head because with Hank it's always best to wait. She feels a little sorry for him because he's trapped like her but doesn't know it. He doesn't realize the Reverend and Nelson are using him. Is it better to know or not know? He doesn't even know he's lost her, but how would he, since she's still here, stroking his head? "Hank, you're not going to get well until you tell me," she says. "God wants you to tell me."

He's shivering so hard she gets another comforter from the closet. The curtains are drawn and it's so dark you'd think it was nighttime, even though it's just a little past noon. "Tell me," she whispers, as she puts her hand back on his forehead. She rests it there lightly, just to ground him. "Tell me, Hank. Let's not have any secrets."

His eyes are closed and she's afraid he's gone to sleep, but then he opens them and looks at her. "You really want to know, Lucy?"

"Yes."

"We're digging out the old Plessey mine shaft."

"Why?" she asks, trying to sound casual.

"To store something important."

"What?"

"I don't know, Lucy, I really don't know. I'm only in the second circle of the Sons, so they don't tell me everything. But the Reverend says if I do this job well, I'll graduate into the first."

"Is Nelson in the first circle?" He nods his head. "Is Nelson doing this work with you?"

He nods again. "And a guy from Chicago. Don't tell them I told you, Lucy. I swore on the Bible."

"Why would I do that, Hank?"

"I think they're good people, Lucy, but I'm tired."

"You're sick, Hank. You've been working too hard."

"Maybe after we're done with this, you can come back to the store."

"That would be nice. We could be together again." She pauses, runs her fingers through his hair. "I'm going to go out to the pharmacy to pick up more cough medicine. You go to sleep. I'll be back soon."

"Don't stay out too long."

"I won't. Just get some sleep. It's the best thing you can do."

In the phone booth outside the pharmacy Lucy dials the number she keeps hidden in the side pocket of her purse. "Don," she says when he answers, "this is Sandra."

"I was beginning to give up hope you'd ever call."

"It's hard for me."

She hears something in the background—maybe a door opening. "I have a customer," he says. "Can I call you back?"

"No."

"When can I see you then?"

"In a few days, I hope. Will you be there?"

"I'm going downstate a week from Friday to see my kids."

"Before that. I'll call and we can arrange a time."

"I'm looking forward to it."

"Me too."

Reluctantly, she hangs up the phone, then looks around to see if anyone she knows has noticed her. But it wouldn't matter. How would they know her secret? She's just Lucy, on her way from the pharmacy to the convenience store and then back home again to nurse an ailing husband.

I was a quick study; I had to admit it. Cross-country skiing came easily to me, probably because the situation awakened old competitive instincts: I wanted to keep up, be as good as the boys. I bought an exercise bicycle and worked out at home in the evenings. I was getting so fit I had to yank my boots over my calves, and my shirts fit tightly around my muscular shoulders.

Michael was a good teacher, more patient than I'd expected, able to give instruction without being patronizing. There were a few tense moments when he could have extended a hand to help me up from a bad spill but chose to ski ahead, waiting for me somewhere farther up the trail. I reacted like a child, tired and abandoned, pouting until the next long, smooth hill brought so much delight that I forgave him. I was in love with him, and I was in love with the glistening and gliding and swishing sound of moving through the medium of snow, snow like I'd never seen before, so deep and perfect I took a perverse pleasure in puncturing it with my poles.

He kept a supply of dark chocolate in one pocket and a small silver flask of brandy in the other, and when he deemed the time was right, when I deserved a reward, we stopped and partook. Just a little, enough to warm our throats. "Johnny's trick," he told me. "He gave me the flask for my thirtieth birthday." Sometimes I thought he kept bringing up Johnny as a way to remind us of the larger purpose of these afternoons of ours. I wanted to forget that purpose; I wanted these times to belong only to ourselves.

That afternoon after my lunch with Mark, Michael moved me off the groomed trails into the backcountry. He selected a route outside of Hancock that started out flat on an old railroad bed but got tougher once we turned off onto an abandoned logging road. I fell so often going up a narrow hill I almost cried in frustration. He told me to take my skis off and walk up, but I was too proud. Instead, I followed close behind and studied his technique, trying to mimic his subtle shifts in weight and balance. I made it up the hill at last, but I was exhausted.

At the top of the ridge we were able to ski along with only a few obstacles, a tree fallen across the path, a patch of ice in a depression. "Speed is not our main aim here," he told me. "You have to temper it with caution. Better a slow ski than a broken ankle. We don't want a helicopter airlifting one of us out of Ontonagon." I was happy to go more slowly, though slow for him was still too fast for me. Whatever he might say, there was pressure to cover distance.

I concentrated hard on the rhythm of my glide, trying to fall into a kind of meditation, but my mind started to dwell on what Mark had confided in me. Why was there such a fear of difference? On the continuum of hate, a nasty homophobic note passed at school hardly rated, but I knew it had the power to devastate. I hoped Mark and Anne could find a way to talk to Seth. What were we so scared of as parents? Why could I face the much greater danger of going to the mine yet balk at speaking truthfully to my daughter?

As we began the descent, Michael let himself go too fast down a steep hill and encountered an unexpected stream at the bottom. I heard him cry out and arranged my skis in a wide snowplow, but even then I had to fall to avoid crashing into him. He was face down in the snow in an unseemly sprawl. "Are you all right?" I asked, struggling to get up. I was forced to take off my skis.

"Eating snow is not my favorite occupation," he said, as he turned over. "I'll have to add that stream to my map."

I offered him a hand once I was up. He hesitated but then agreed. As I tried to pull him up, I lost my balance leaning backward and ended up falling on top of him. For a moment I let his arms encircle me, and we lay there laughing until the cold forced us to get up. He brushed the snow from my back, and then as I turned around he pulled me toward him. "Just once, Gillian," he urged, "just once."

His tongue was so warm it heated my whole body. "We shouldn't," I said, as I finally willed myself to stop.

The rest of the ski was on more gentle terrain, and we fell into a shared silence. I say "shared" because I sensed he was thinking the same thoughts as I was, seeing the same things, wanting me like I wanted him. The sun was setting and the light filtering though the trees was the color of dying embers, the cross between gold and pink that is too hot to touch but cool to the eyes. A light wind brought a shower of snow from the hemlock branches. I followed his tracks faster than he could make them, and so I caught up with him and had to wait until he broke another stretch of trail.

Back at the cars, we kept our silence for a few extra minutes as we put the skis and poles on the rack. "I think you'll be ready to do the long ski by the nineteenth," he said finally, as he adjusted the tightness of one of the cords. "But you don't have to go."

"Of course I'm going, Michael. I've cleared the decks. That's why I'm letting Marcy go to Boston."

"It could be dangerous."

"We've had this conversation before."

"You have a daughter—"

"I'm aware of that."

He reached into his pocket for his car keys. "I'll let you come on one condition. You let me go to Rostock with you."

"How did you know I was going to Rostock?"

"I didn't, until now."

He'd trapped me, but I couldn't feel angry. "Why do you want to go to Rostock?"

"For the same reason you want to ski out to the mine shaft. I don't want you to be alone."

"If you're with me, we'll stick out that much more."

"In Rostock they already know what you look like. They won't know me."

"You'll hardly fade into the background. You don't speak German."

"I just want to watch your back."

"Be my bodyguard?"

"In a manner of speaking." He unlocked his car but didn't open the door. "I need to know your dates so I can book a ticket."

"Michael, this complicates everything. I'm not sure—"

"Certainty's not something we can afford, is it?"

"What do you mean by that?"

"We don't have the time. We have to trust our instincts. My instinct says I need to go to Rostock."

Reluctantly, I gave him the dates and unlocked my own car. He tried to kiss me again, but I wouldn't let him this time. "We can't," I said, but I let him have the last word.

"Not yet, you mean."

Hank's back at work, still coughing, but he claims he's better now. Lucy hopes he passes the bug on to Nelson. She'd like to see that man sick, though probably it would just make him nastier than he is already.

Don can see her early this afternoon since he closes the shop on Mondays. She's nervous about seeing him again, afraid someone might spot her car outside his place. Maybe she'll ask if she can put it in his garage. And what if they don't take so well to each other this time? What if it was just the fire and the brandy and her gratefulness for the rescue? What if he's cold or awkward or too hungry, like the Reverend?

She hasn't slept with the Reverend for over a week. He'll want to soon, but he wants the information from the tapes even more, though there's not much these days. Gillian never talks to Michael anymore. She told the Reverend this when he came over yesterday to see how Hank was doing. "Maybe they suspect something," he said, "but keep listening. The girl may say something important, you never know."

She's worried for the girl. She's going to see Evan in Boston even though her mother doesn't want her to. He might get her pregnant again, and Lucy can't bear the thought of another lost baby.

Once or twice the ghost baby has come to her late at night and she has sung to it, the same songs she used to teach the children in Sunday school. The baby is at peace then and so is she, because her arms are full.

She goes in the bedroom and puts on Don's flannel shirt over her only lacy bra. She brushes her hair until it shines, dabs her neck with cologne. This is wrong, she knows, but it's so much more right than being with the Reverend.

When she arrives at Don's, he's already cleared a space for her car in the garage. She notices he has a snowmobile in the back of his truck. "I like to snowmobile," she tells him.

"Well, maybe we can go sometime."

"I'd like that."

They sit by the wood stove again, only this time he holds her hand and they don't say much. Finally, he asks her if she's ready and she says yes. In the bedroom he unbuttons the flannel shirt and just looks at her for a minute. He tells her she's beautiful. Hank used to say that, the Reverend never has. Maybe Don's lying, but she lets herself believe it for a second that stretches to an hour. They stretch out the lovemaking this time, find the places they'll come back to again. Afterward he sets the alarm for three. "Sometimes I think the best thing about lovemaking is the sleep afterward," he says, as he nestles into her back.

She wakes before the alarm goes off and lies there listening to his breathing. She wants to fall back asleep, but she's too awake, and the risk she's taking being with him is fueling her desire to take another risk. She nudges him, then kisses him on the cheek and whispers into his ear. "Don, I have to go."

"Already?"

"I forgot, but my sister might be coming over."

He rolls over and pulls her toward him, pushing her hair gently away from her face. "Just so long as you come back soon, before I go downstate."

"I promise."

"We'll go snowmobiling if the weather's good." His hand is on her breast, fingers closing around her nipple, making her excited again. She closes her eyes, why not, why not? The ghost baby floats around her, demanding nothing except that she let him again. There are no walls now inside her; they crumble and melt with the friction of his pushing, which is not really pushing but reaching, reaching for what she wants too, more than pleasure, more than the sum of their two bodies, more than anything in the world. The ghost baby laughs, or is it she who is laughing? He cries out, then laughs along.

She hears the sound of that laugher all the way to Gillian's house. Her garage door is open, but there's no car inside. Lights are on in the living room. The girl chooses that moment to pass by the window, as if giving Lucy a sign. But she needs no sign. It is time, finally it is time. She parks down the street and walks quickly to the house. Gillian must not come home.

She rings the doorbell, her heart beating hard. Marcy opens the door a crack and at first doesn't recognize her. "Hello," she says. "Can I help you?" Her hair is down, covering the sides of her face, so that it's difficult for Lucy to look her in the eye.

"I've brought you the ghost of your baby," Lucy tells her, "but don't worry, it's at peace now. Its soul is ready to come through another body."

"What are you talking about? Who are you?"

Lucy sees the light of recognition in Marcy's eyes and then fear. "Don't be afraid," she says gently. "I'm watching out for you, praying for you."

"Please go away," Marcy begs, in a shaking voice.

"I'm praying for you," Lucy repeats, as Marcy closes the door.

CHAPTER 14

TRACKS

There were so many reasons I cried when I saw Marcy off at the airport. I cried because I was worried she might have a seizure or get pregnant again with Evan, because something might happen to me in the five days we were apart, because she was my daughter and I always cried at her arrivals and departures. I cried at my failures, our failures, and the sight of the little twin-engine plane disappearing into a thin fog of ice particles.

I also cried with relief. She would be away from Houghton for a while. She had been upset by the visit of the strange woman, and so had I. I told her not to open the door to strangers anymore, and I was debating whether to ask Sajit to keep her in Oxford until the investigation of Sons of the Shepherd was finished. But then I would have to admit my recklessness to him. In the back of my mind I worried about giving him cause for custody in case we ever went through with a divorce. The less he knew about my work, the better.

Back in the car, I turned on the ignition and her rock tape started playing again, heavy metal that sounded like a demolition derby. I switched it off, not wanting to understand the lyrics, which would be all about getting some, but only from the point of view of the man, or, rather, boy.

The silence was worse. It was all about *me* not getting any. My attraction to Michael was driving me crazy—the last few days my slumbering sexuality had woken with a vengeance. It was caffeinated and jittery, a nervous twitching pulse that competed with my heartbeat so I didn't know what rhythm I was moving to. I turned on NPR for some soothing classical music, but it was opera and the soprano's passion sounded too pure in comparison with mine.

When I got back from the airport, I drank a tall scotch and made myself an early dinner. I went to bed around nine, just after Marcy called to say she had arrived safely in Boston. As long as the weather cooperated, Michael and I were making the long ski to the mine tomorrow. The forecast was for light snow, perfect for covering up our tracks, but the wind chill was supposed to be brutal.

I didn't sleep well. My dreams were filled with so many bizarre images I woke up with that tired feeling you get from spending all day in a modern art museum. Michael called at seven to say the ski was on. He told me to stretch well and eat a big breakfast. He would be over around eight.

My nerves kicked in around seven-thirty, and I felt sick and scared and not sexual at all. I wrote a note to Marcy saying that if anything happened to me, she should remember how much I loved her. Then I tore it up. Michael came right on time. He barely greeted me before handing me a waist pack and balaclava. "Extra provisions," he said, "in case we get separated." Inside there was water, a few energy bars, a map, and a compass. "I have a gun," he added matter-of-factly, though I could see from his face that he too was nervous. His left eye twitched and he was incapable of a smile.

We hardly said anything on the drive. The snow was falling in a slant toward the windshield, and I watched the battle between the wiper blades and the flakes. No victory, just stalemate. How much more information did we need to collect before the story made sense, before there was a story? When you write academic papers, you can make up any story you want as long as you have enough footnotes, but this story was writing itself and I had lost control over it. He had a gun. I had a water bottle. And they—whoever they were—what did they have besides the power to summon a false god and kill their enemies?

We parked on a back road in a turnoff to an abandoned barn. I knew I should have paid more attention to the route, but I've never been a good map reader and I needed to trust that nothing would happen that would put me in charge. Michael was not so sanguine. Before we got out of the car, he made me show him on the map exactly how we got there, then handed me a spare set of keys. "I forgot to put these in your pack." He paused, pulling his jacket zipper up all the way so the collar covered his chin. "How do you feel?"

"Frightened," I said. "And you?"

He tried to look at me, but his eyes wandered to the window. "I don't know. We may find nothing, it may just be a long day of skiing. And so that's what I have to concentrate on—following the map, keeping the right pace. I can't afford to feel anything." He took my hand, but there was little for either of us to feel through

our thick mittens. We pulled on our balaclavas in the car, and I
ventured a weak laugh at our distorted faces.

First the snow, then the woods closed us in. The trees helped
to break the strongest gusts of wind, but it was always chasing
us, blasting us from the back, then the sides, then the front,
making sure each part of our body was equally frigid. A climb up
a steep hill helped to warm me, but then I was damp with sweat
and the cold seeped farther into my skin. Michael traveled at a
moderate pace and always waited for me to catch up, but I knew
standing still cost him—you had to move, you had to keep your
blood circulating. I kept my eyes down because of the snow and
because I needed to watch his skis. I was an ant following
another ant on a long white tablecloth, never sure of where the
edge would drop off.

We skied for over an hour until we came to the edge of a frozen
swamp where dead trees stuck out of the snow like totems from a
vanished tribe. "Day old, maybe," Michael said, as he pointed to a
snowmobile track running through the center. He pulled a map
from his pocket, laminated to withstand the snow, and held it
tightly in the wind. "We have a choice here. We can cut across the
swamp on that snowmobile trail, but then if anybody's watching,
we're sitting ducks. Or we take the more difficult trail I told you
about through the woods."

"I thought we already decided to go through the woods."

"I know, but it's longer and we have to keep breaking trail and
the wind's already slowing us down."

"The wind will be worse in the swamp."

"OK," he replied. "We'll stick to the original plan."

I knew he was worried I wouldn't be able to navigate the more difficult trail, but I preferred the idea of taking a few spills to having someone take a few shots at my back.

The trail was relatively easy at first, then narrowed as it approached a steep ravine. We skied down, but it was impossible to ski up the other side, so we had to take off our skis and trudge through heavy snow to the top. The rest of the way we dodged obstacles at every turn: a fallen pine, protruding rocks, streambeds that were not yet fully frozen. I almost lost the tip of my ski to a birch tree but managed to fall a few inches short.

I was exhausted but didn't tell him. I closed in on myself, harnessing every breath and thought to move my legs forward or force them to slow down. He made me stop to eat and drink along the way, and even though he was right, I resented the intrusion. I wanted to remain a slave to my own forward motion because there was too much to see if I looked back. Too much to lose. Maybe this is what it means to be high on danger.

When we came within a quarter-mile of the mine shaft, we stopped again and he grilled me on our agreed procedure. He would go first to check out the mine and would call for me if it was safe to join him. I had to give him ten minutes—measure it on your watch, he instructed—and if he hadn't called by then because someone was there or something had happened, I had to turn around and ski out for help. He made me study the map again.

We skied together to the edge of the clearing where the mine shaft was located. I hid behind a cluster of pine trees, which helped break the wind. I whispered good luck, but I don't know if he heard. Like a dab of invisible ink, he disappeared into the snow.

They drink from Don's flask before they get onto the snowmobile.

It's an important part of the ritual, but Lucy hopes Don's not one of those real heavy boozers who drive drunk and take too many risks and get their head chopped off by barbed wire. Hank was starting to drive like that not so long ago, so she quit going snowmobiling with him. It wasn't fun anymore. But she still has her helmet and snowsuit and she's ready, as ready as she'll ever be. Don believed her when she told him she heard there was a good trail over by the old Plessey mine shaft.

Hank and Nelson are at the store and the Reverend's in the church. No one should be at the mine. The wind's almost too cold to be out on a snowmobile, but she told Don she doesn't mind; they don't have many chances. He's leaving soon for downstate. His wife said he could come over on Christmas and watch the kids open their presents, but probably all they want for Christmas is for their parents to get back together. They'll be disappointed when he leaves at the end of the day. Lucy didn't tell him that; he probably knows already. She bought him a new flannel shirt as a present.

They climb into the snowmobile and pull the visors over their faces. She puts her arms around his middle. If it's cold, she doesn't feel it. She likes the feel of Don's waist, solid underneath the soft insulation of his suit, the place she holds onto when he's on top of her. They have made love already, fast but nice, anticipating the speed of the snowmobile. In high school she had always wanted to be one of those girls in the movies riding behind her boyfriend on a motorcycle. She smiles to herself. She likes the sound of the engine warming up, even the smell of gas. "Hold on," Don says, and they take off.

The snowmobile kicks up snow, making its own clouds to fly

through. She can hardly see, but it doesn't matter; maybe it's even better this way because she can pretend they've lifted off the ground like a plane. Her house, the church, the store are all just little dots beneath them, and Nelson, Hank, and the Reverend are even smaller, almost invisible. She left the Keweenaw once by plane, the time her sister bought her a ticket to Minneapolis to stay with their aunt. Hank was hitting Lucy then, and her sister wanted her to leave him. But she came back. Next time she won't. Next time she'll fly away for good.

I watched every second pass, every second of ten minutes, and with each one of them I grew colder and more desperate to move. My toes and fingertips hurt so badly I felt like crying, but I imagined how the tears would freeze and cut my face like shards of glass. Finally, I heard his shout. I followed his tracks, already fading in the snow, to the entrance of the mine shaft, where he was waiting for me. I took off my skis, which he hid along with his behind some old timbers. A miner's light was strapped to his head.

"What's in there?" I asked.

"Inside the shaft there's a narrow tunnel that's blocked off partway down with a door and a heavy combination lock. I can't pick it, and I think it would take a long time to get a hacksaw through. Maybe together we can kick down the door."

The mine entrance, once sealed off, had been blasted open, and I picked my way through a pile of rubble into a dark anteroom at the head of two tunnels. It was warmer underground, but the damp was unpleasant and the smell of mold threatened to make me cough. "As far as I can tell, there's nothing down the right tunnel," Michael said, "but a hundred yards down the left one you come to the door." The ground was wet and slippery, and it was hard to walk on the smooth soles of our ski boots. I kept stumbling, but there was nothing to grab onto along the stone walls. My adrenaline was starting to give out, replaced by fatigue and fear. I didn't want to die here. I didn't want to die at all. I'm crazy, I thought, so fucking crazy.

Up ahead, Michael's headlight caught the shape of something that looked like it could be a gun. "Just part of an old drill," he whispered. A few minutes later we came to the door and he shined the light on the padlock.

I heard the noise before him. At first I thought it was in my head, the dull thud of exhaustion. But it wasn't a thud, it was a persistent humming like a swarm of bees, growing louder and louder. Michael turned his head just as I was about to call out to him. "A snowmobile," he said. "Quick, we need to hide in the other tunnel."

He grabbed my hand as he passed, pulling me along the slippery floor behind him. As we came into the anteroom, he took the gun out of his pocket. The sound was louder now, but I couldn't tell whether it was because we were nearer to the mine opening or because the snowmobile was drawing closer.

The other tunnel had more water seepage, so we had to step through puddles and my boots got wet. Michael had to bend down to avoid the low ceiling, further slowing our progress. We stopped at an indentation along the wall and crouched there, hoping we were out of view of a flashlight beam. Michael turned off his light. In the darkness I wrestled with panic, forcing myself to take long deep breaths to stop the shivering that threatened to wrack my body like sobs. He was unnaturally still. I wanted that self-control from him, but it scared me because I realized we'd raised the stakes just about as high as they could go. He had the gun ready, but I wasn't ready to die.

"You have a daughter," he'd kept warning me. Why hadn't I listened?

Now I listened hard. Could it be there were two engines, two swarms of bees? I told him that, but he didn't say anything. I saw them in my mind, one following the other. They would park outside. Maybe the snow had stopped and they'd see our tracks; they'd find our skis and then enter the mine. Three or four men, three or four guns. They would know where to find us.

How many men had it taken to kill Johnny? To kill Rollins? At least their bodies had been found. Who would find us here in this abandoned mine? Who would tell Marcy?

Lucy doesn't know what she'll do when she gets to the mine. Make Don stop so she can look in? But he'll wonder why she wants to do that, and she doesn't want to tell him anything. She doesn't want to think about it but she has to, because the Reverend and Nelson are thinking too. She wiggles her toes. They're cold, but she tries not to notice. She can hardly see, there's so much snow on her visor. She just hopes Don can see the way ahead.

When he stops for a drink at the edge of the swamp, she hears another engine in the distance. She tells him, but he's not concerned; why should he be? He believed her lie that this was a much-used trail, so he doesn't think there's any danger. "Maybe we should turn back now," she says.

"What's the matter, getting cold?" She nods. "Here, have another taste of this." The whiskey burns her throat and makes her eyes water. "I reckon it's only a few miles till we get to the mine. We'll turn back then."

"OK," she says, but the engine's getting louder. What if it's the Reverend or Nelson? What if they recognize her?

They take off again, but this time it doesn't seem fast enough. She wants more speed, but he claims he's going as fast as he can and maybe he is. It's just that the other snowmobile is gaining on them. They go over a large bump and she comes down so hard on the seat it sends a sharp pain up her spine. Her teeth lock together. She wants him to stop so she can run into the woods where the snow might protect her, but it's too late. A shot rips the air.

"What the fuck!" Don yells. The other snowmobile is next to them now, trying to cut them off. Lucy sees the gun pointed at them.

"Stop!" the driver shouts.

Don kills the engine. The driver idles his and then gets off and walks toward them, still pointing the gun. Lucy has never seen him before—he's tall and has a long ponytail hanging over the back of a black leather jacket. "What are you doing here?" he barks at them.

"What do you think we're doing?" Don responds. He lifts his visor but she keeps hers down. "We're out for a ride, is there anything wrong with that? Why don't you drop that gun and have a drink. I've got a flask of whiskey."

"Don't reach for it," the man orders, directing the gun at Don's arm. "This is private land—no trespassing."

"I didn't see any signs."

"Well, now you know."

"I guess I do."

"You and your lady friend need to turn around and get out of here."

"All right," Don says. "I'm with you."

"I'm going to follow you."

"No shots, OK? It spoils the mood."

"Just get out of here."

Don starts the engine and they turn around. The wind slows them down, and every extra second means another chance for the man to shoot. She presses her face against Don's back, hating herself for bringing him here and for making Hank tell her they were hiding something at the mine. Why did she need to know?

Somehow they make it back to the road, where the man holds the gun on them while they load the snowmobile in the truck. "You can put that thing down now," Don tells him, but he won't listen. Somehow they drive away, somehow they're safe, but it feels temporary, like a good day when you're in the middle of a long sickness. Her mother had days like that; she'd call up and tell Lucy to come over because she wanted to go shopping or out to the movies. You couldn't say no on those days.

Don's silent until he asks for the flask. She opens it for him and watches him take a long swig. "That guy could have killed us," he says, as he wipes his mouth with his sleeve. "Maybe we should go to the police."

"Remember, I can't be seen with you," she replies, twisting the cap back on the flask. "He was just a little crazy, that's all. People get like that around here."

"I've never had anyone hold a gun on me like that, just for crossing their property."

"People are scared," she tells him.

"Of what?"

She shrugs; then she reopens the flask and takes a drink herself. "Each other, I guess."

Michael and I both flinched when we heard the shot. It was too far away to be directed at us, but what did it mean? What did it mean that one of the engines had stopped? It started again, but then it seemed that both snowmobiles had turned around; their noise was fading. "Come on," he said, "let's get out while we can." I didn't argue, I didn't care anymore what was behind the locked door.

The snow was even heavier when we got out. My feet were so cold they'd lost all flexibility, and I couldn't get my left one into the ski binding. "Lift up your heel and press your toes in," Michael said, holding the ski down for me. After a couple of tries, the binding finally snapped shut. I grasped the poles with frozen fingers.

The snow was so thick I could hardly see him in front of me. It seemed to take a long time to reach the woods, though probably it was only a few minutes. We took shelter again in the pine grove, where he made me eat an energy bar and drink a lot of water. He told me I was probably dehydrated. I didn't know what I was, but I wasn't convinced I was going to make it back. I was dizzy and desperate for rest. I understood then how people can give up and just lie down in the snow and die.

I did make it back, though I fell so many times I lost count. Sometimes I fell just going straight, because I lost my concentration and then my balance. Michael helped me up each time, though I noticed even his grip was getting weaker. We heard a

snowmobile off in the distance. Maybe it was returning to
the mine.

Just before dusk we reached the car. A snowplow had been
through once, but at least four more inches had accumulated
since then. Michael started the car and got out to brush off the
windows. I stood there useless, holding my poles like a cane. He
told me to get in and warm up, though the fan was still blowing
cold air.

It took us a long time to get out to the main highway—the tires
slipped and the headlights only illuminated a few feet ahead. The
roadsides blended into the fields; we were afloat on a treacherous
white ocean. We were so tired we couldn't speak, or maybe it was
just that the questions were too big and couldn't be answered.
What was behind that door? Who was on the snowmobiles, and
why did someone fire a shot? Why did they ride away? Did they
know now that we had been there or had the snow erased our
tracks?

I fell asleep on the highway and woke only when we pulled into
Michael's driveway. "You're staying here for the night," he told me.
"I don't want you to be home alone." I nodded, too tired to dis-
agree. Inside the house he gave me a change of clothes, a pair of
sweatpants and a fleece, and told me to get out of my skiing gear.
I sat on his bed while he examined my fingers and toes for signs
of frostbite. He didn't find any, but the chilblains on my feet were
red and painful. He rubbed my legs and made me wrap up in a
down comforter while he went to make some tea.

I felt like a child. I *was* a child; I was with my father on a
camping trip when I swam too long in a cold lake and he wrapped
me up in a sleeping bag and sat me by the fire. Michael was like

him in some ways; he had that same practical confidence-cum-competence that sustains the illusion of protection—which was of course dangerous, because he couldn't protect me. I saw that in the mine but I didn't want to see it now, because I was a child and when you're a child your judgment changes from one moment to the next. It's fickle, self-indulgent, seduced by simple things like duck feathers and warm tea.

Seduced by sleep.

I fell asleep on his bed and he joined me there. We huddled together for warmth because in truth he was as chilled as I was. It must have been midnight when I woke to his touch along my thigh and then the sides of my breasts. He was already naked, hard against me. I let him pull off my clothes and kneel over me, mapping me, preparing for another journey. His tongue played between my legs until I ceased to be the child and became the woman, the guide. I guided him inside and he followed me, and we traded one danger for another.

CHAPTER 15

FALLEN ANGELS

Like Rip Van Winkle, my body awoke after a long slumber. And for the next few days whatever I saw, felt, heard, touched, or tasted was for a precious moment liberated from memory, a sensation unto itself, almost hallucinogenic in its intensity. This is one of the benefits of prolonged abstinence, I guess—when you break it, everything breaks; all doors swing open.

Michael was stronger, but I was more devious. He was a master of endurance, staying in me for as long as I wanted, until the sheets were so wet I felt like we were making love on water. But I knew where to pause, turn us over, make him slow down and beg. Sex was a battle of equals.

What it wasn't was gentle, but that was Sajit; that was the past, the man who had suckled at my breast, the man I would see tomorrow.

I looked out the plane window, but the view of Michael on the ground was blocked by a stream of pink deicing fluid. We hadn't embraced, afraid that someone at the airport might recognize us.

I regretted that now. I worried he might do something foolhardy in my absence, like revisit the mine. He insisted he was planning to spend a quiet Christmas with his mother and would meet me in Rostock on the twenty-ninth. I didn't believe him, but there was nothing more I could say.

Now there was nothing more I could do. I fastened my seat belt and opened a book, but the words slipped past me like debris flowing in a swift current. The plane took off right on time, and in only a few seconds Houghton disappeared into a landscape of snow and trees, trees and snow. I accepted the offer of a piece of gum from the man sitting next to me. As I crumbled the silver wrapper into a ball, I began telling myself the story of Michael and me backward.

That history starts at the beginning and moves forward is an artifice designed for schoolchildren. In truth we start from the present so we can imbue the past with the fickle meanings of the moment. I worked myself back to the first time Michael came to my office, turning it into a Harlequin romance of love at first sight. Then, disgusted with myself, I spat out the gum and forced myself to think of what lay ahead. My daughter. My husband. A Christmas I wasn't prepared for. And Rostock. How could I prepare for that?

Lucy sits in the living room, surrounded by rolls of wrapping paper and ribbon. The Scotch tape is lost under one of them, and she rummages around until she finds it. She vows to keep it on her lap so she doesn't lose it again. She couldn't afford anything expensive for her sister's kids this year, so she bought them lots of little things at the Dollar Store: a butterfly key chain, a pen flashlight, barrettes that glow in the dark. She got Hank a sweater for half-price at Penney's.

He helped her set up the tree last night, but she hung all the ornaments. Most are hers, inherited from her mother. Hank's parents didn't believe in saving things and passing them down. They're dead now, and there's hardly a sign of them in the house except the rocker and some casserole dishes.

The thought makes her lonely. Don's gone downstate and even Gillian and Marcy have left town, so there are no tapes to listen to. Only the radio, and it keeps playing the same Christmas songs over and over again. If she hears "Jingle Bell Rock" one more time, she'll scream. The ads are the same too; everything's the same, even the headlines.

She tries to concentrate on making a nice crease in the wrapping paper. Ever since she was a little girl she's been good at wrapping presents—everyone in the family relied on her to curl the ribbon. She tried to teach Diane, but her sister just couldn't get it and still can't. She buys ready-made bows that fall off too easily.

There should be a child sitting on the floor watching her, a child she can teach how to curl ribbon and make Christmas cookies.

She hears the door open. "Hank," she calls, but there's no reply. It can't be the Reverend, because he always rings the bell. "Hank!" she calls out again. She wants to believe it's her sister delivering presents, but she knows now, by the tightness she feels around her neck, that it's Nelson. Two sets of footsteps. Nelson and someone else.

Nelson and the man with the ponytail she saw that day on the snowmobile. She tries to hide her recognition, smiling up at them dumbly, focusing her eyes on the angel at the top of the Christmas tree. "Hello, Nelson," she says. "Who's your friend?" He doesn't reply. "Want anything to drink?" Silently, he takes a red ball from the tree, then sits down on the couch, motioning for the other man to do the same. She doesn't know whether to stand up or stay sitting on the floor. "What do you want?" she asks more bluntly.

"You know what I want."

"No, I don't."

He twirls the ball in his hand, watching it catch the light, then lifts it and throws it against the wall. It's cheap and breaks easily; it's not one of her mother's. "Get me another one," he orders Lucy, "a silver one this time."

"Why?"

"Because I told you to." She hesitates, not knowing whether to obey him or not, what game he's playing. "I said get me one," he threatens.

The tape rolls off her lap as she stands. She steps over the wrapping paper and takes a silver ball from the tree: another cheap one, not her mother's. "Are you going to break this one too?" she asks, handing it to him.

"That depends."

"On what?"

"Whether you tell the truth or not."

The man in the ponytail is staring at her. One of his eyes is much smaller than the other and red around the edges like he's rubbed it. He takes a gun from his pocket and lays it on his lap. She notices he's wearing black jeans, but they're frayed to white thread around the knees. "When I count to ten, throw that ball up into the air," he tells Nelson. "One, two, three, four . . . "

At the count of ten he shoots the ball. The gun has a silencer, so the shot isn't loud. A shower of silver glass falls onto the rug.

I met Marcy as planned at the gate in Boston. She looked more beautiful than ever, her hair piled on the back of her head in a twist with just enough loose strands to suggest sensuous abandon. She had on a new turquoise shirt and jeans with a gold brocade border cut from a sari. She didn't seem very happy to see me, but I was prepared for that. I wished I could tell her how she had almost lost me in the mine—maybe then she'd show some relief or affection. Instead, she was caught up in her own teenage trauma: Evan, I suspected, but she didn't even mention his name. She cried off and on during the plane ride, using up several packets of tissues.

I was jealous. I wanted to cry about Michael, but I was too old and too tired and couldn't plausibly explain my tears, if Marcy wanted to know. I fell asleep once, but then the plane bounced and the movie flickered. Over the intercom the pilot assured us it was just ordinary turbulence, but I knew he was wrong. I knew a rough wind was following me all the way from Houghton to England.

We began our descent near dawn, and as I looked out the window at the lights of the London suburbs, I remembered the first time I landed at Heathrow. Delayed by my father's funeral, I had arrived a week later than the crop of other Wellesley girls; they received an orientation in London before they set off for their respective universities. I was disoriented by my father's death, and at passport control I couldn't find the letter from Oxford I needed for my student visa. In the end I found it, but not before emptying the contents of my purse in front of a disdainful official: used Kleenex, tampons, American change.

A penny for your thoughts, I felt like saying to Marcy. A nickel, a dime, a quarter, how much would it take to get you to confide in me?

It took me awhile to spot Sajit in the crowd outside of customs. He was standing toward the back, jumping up and down and waving his arms. As he pushed toward us, a familiar pain stabbed me in the chest and I gripped the bar of the luggage cart. How warmly should I embrace him? He hugged Marcy first, and then I kissed him lightly on the cheek as one might greet a distant relative. As we walked through the terminal, I noticed Marcy was taller than her father now and there were specks of gray in his hair. As always, he walked with his shoulders hunched slightly forward from too many hours at a desk. So unlike Michael, but that was unfair; why should I compare them?

Neither should I compare landscapes. From the car window I looked out at the fields on the side of the highway, still green, though the color was diminished by the dull December sun. The Chiltern Hills gave a brief hint of wild, but most everywhere was settled, accounted for, a copse instead of a forest, a village instead of a lone farmhouse. Even the cows had the look of household pets. But it was safer here, I reminded myself. For a few days I would be safe, never mind what emotional business needed transacting with Sajit.

I fell asleep about twenty miles outside of Oxford and woke only when Sajit pulled into the gravel drive. He made us tea and toast, and then both Marcy and I went to take a nap. He told me he'd set himself up in the study, which meant I could have the bedroom to myself.

"Don't let me sleep too long," I said, as I climbed the stairs to the second floor. On the bedside table there was a vase of six red roses.

She's next. The man with the ponytail points the gun at her head while Nelson shoots questions: That was her on the snowmobile, wasn't it? What was she doing there? What had Hank told her? Who was with her?

"What are you talking about?" she says. "I haven't been on a snowmobile in over a year."

"Hank admitted he told you," Nelson claims.

"Told me what?"

"You already know, so I don't need to tell you."

"Well, someone does. I have no idea what you're talking about." She stares down at a scrap of wrapping paper. Candy canes with bows. What if it's true about Hank's confession? What if they held a gun to his head too? But Nelson's unsure, she can hear it beneath the bravado. Just keep staring at the candy canes, she tells herself. Watch the red and white stripes blur together.

"See that angel on the top of the tree, Lucy? My friend's going to shoot it, and after he shoots it, he's going to shoot you—but not before we fuck you, because you're not an angel, Lucy, you're a slut. You'd do it with anybody; you probably did it with your friend on the snowmobile. You're going to die getting fucked. How does that sound, Lucy? Straight to hell."

"I don't know anything," she says again, but her voice is weaker this time.

The gun goes off. The dying angel sprinkles her with angel dust. One of her mother's ornaments. Dead now like her mother, her mother in heaven.

"The Lord is my shepherd," she recites. "I shall not want."

The man with the ponytail stands up, pressing the gun into the small of her back. "Into the bedroom," Nelson orders.

"He maketh me to lie down in green pastures. He . . . "

"Take off your clothes and lie down on the bed."

She slips the turtleneck off her head. The air is cold on her shoulders. "He leadeth me. . . ."

"Get the rest of your clothes off."

Naked, she lies down on the bed. The Voice is with her now, coming through her. "And yea, though I walk through the valley of the shadow of death . . . "

"One more chance," Nelson says. "Tell us what you know."

"Nothing," she whispers, but the whisper grows. "Nothing!" she shouts, and closes her eyes, at peace with something or someone she doesn't even know.

Sajit woke me a few minutes before noon and I stumbled into the shower, which was still a primitive affair, a hose and nozzle tacked on the wall. Although he'd turned up the heat in our honor, the house was still cold by American standards, and after my shower I dressed in my warmest sweater. Marcy was still sleeping, Sajit told me; he had tried to wake her up but to no avail. He suggested the two of us take a walk through the Port Meadow to the Perch in Binsey, where we could get some lunch.

We didn't say much to each other until we reached the meadow. It was my favorite spot in Oxford, this floodplain of the Thames that had stayed common land for centuries, defying the depredations of landlords and developers. Cows and horses still grazed here, children on bicycles plied the paths, ducks and swans swam the river. The dreaming spires of the university were distant enough that you could pretend you had escaped their discipline. You were free not to think, or to think about things that were nebulous, like the vapors rising from the river, like Sajit's and my relationship or lack thereof.

Sajit began, which was unusual. It had always fallen to me to announce the bad news, which was usually old news by the time I opened my mouth. Maybe it was the Wellington boots or the tweed jacket that was a little too big, hanging a few inches below his pants pockets, that gave him an eager, boyish look. Whatever it was, it was disconcerting. He looked happy for the first time in years.

In recent letters to me he had already acknowledged his treatment for depression. Now, refracted in that new light, in the soft glow of Prozac, he revisited our past. Maybe he had rehearsed the speech with his therapist, I don't know, but it was eloquent, almost poetic. He had a good memory for the minor events that became major turning points. "Remember," he said, "when I went to York to give a talk right near the end of your pregnancy, even when you begged me not to? And I came back a day late. I hated myself for that, but I never apologized." I nodded, though I'd long forgotten about it. "Or our first holiday with Marcy in Brighton, when I holed up in the hotel room to write a paper and left you to push the stroller alone all day?" I nodded again. That I remembered because the kindly old ladies who peered into the baby carriage suddenly grimaced when they noticed my baby was black. He went on to describe his withdrawal, first from love-making and then from conversation, as he was seduced by lone-liness. And of course the epilepsy, how at first he blamed it on my going away to Germany. How he had come so much to fear my going away again that he had driven me to it, driven away his wife and daughter. As some kind of self-punishment, he said, or to prove he was as weak as his father.

By its own internal logic the story made sense, but it painted me too much as the hapless victim. The truth was, I had been seduced by loneliness too; we had formed a ménage à trois with the Invisible Man. Only our daughter had been able to see him lurking in the shadows. She became scared of dark places—closets, corners, underneath the stairs.

When we reached the Thames, we stood for a while on the bridge, watching a man lower a scull and oars into the water. On the railing Sajit placed one hand on top of mine, while with the other he fiddled nervously with the end of his scarf. I thought his speech was over and he was waiting for me to respond, but then he turned his face toward me so our eyes were only a few inches apart. "I've been having an affair," he said. "Not anything serious—someone I met at a conference in London. But it's brought me back into my body."

I hesitated but then told him I had someone too.

"Is it serious?"

"I don't know."

"Does Marcy know about him?"

I shook my head. "But it's getting harder to hide things from her. She wants something decisive to happen between the two of us."

His fingertips stroked the spaces between mine. "I want you to come back," he said, before I even had time to consider whether to withdraw my hand.

When Lucy hears the doorbell, she knows it's all been staged. The Reverend has arrived, and they won't do anything to her until he gives permission. She breathes deeply, trying to calm the shivers that pass like a pulsating current through her body. He rings again, then opens the door. "What's going on?" he shouts, as he storms into the room. "Don't touch her!"

Only the gun barrel has touched her, pressed against the right side of her head. The man with the ponytail takes it away but she still feels the pressure. "We just wanted to see what she knows, Reverend," Nelson says apologetically. "A little friendly persuasion, nothing else. We were about to leave. She doesn't know anything."

"Get out!" the Reverend orders, as he pulls a blanket over her.

"Sorry, Reverend."

"Just get out. I'll deal with you later."

After they leave, he sits on the bed and takes her hand. "Were you on that snowmobile, Lucy? You can tell me, it's OK."

She starts to cry, real tears, but they're left over from the fear; they have nothing to do with him, but he doesn't need to know that. "No, Reverend," she lies, "I don't know what they're talking about. Why did they do that to me?"

"Poor Lucy," he says, stroking her hair. "You know Nelson—he can get carried away."

"They were going to rape me."

"No, they wouldn't do that."

"Reverend, I'm scared. What's going on? Is Hank all right?"

His hand pauses for a second and then resumes the stroking, but not so gently now. "Hank's gone to Chicago for a few days."

"Chicago? But tomorrow's Christmas!"

"He's on the Lord's business, Lucy. It's urgent. He told me to tell you not to worry."

"When's he coming back?"

"Might be a week or so—it depends. He wants you to run the store while he's away." He leans over and kisses her forehead. "We'll have more time to be together." His hand reaches under the blanket to find a breast. She wants to hit him then like Hank used to hit her; she wants to see the look of surprise on his face as he falls backward. Instead, she reaches up and pulls him toward her, because she has no choice. She needs to survive.

Christmas was nice, too nice. Sajit and I succeeded in being "parents," in the plural, and Marcy was happy to be doted on, if only for a day. Sajit bought us both cashmere sweaters, and we wore them and looked lovely and soft as we sat together on the couch. Mine was blue to match my eyes; hers was black. I was white-skinned and they weren't—suddenly the difference in our color seemed to have everything to do with the risks I was taking, the risks I hadn't told either of them about.

I couldn't get to sleep that night. Along with jet lag, I had a fine French-wine high that made my brain dance, and the sound of passing trains made me restless. And so I was awake when Sajit came into my room in the middle of the night. "I can't sleep," he said.

"Neither can I."

He stood by the window, looking out, though there was nothing to see but the dull glow of Oxford streetlamps. He wore the bathrobe I gave him for Christmas, but his feet were bare. It was a legacy of his childhood in Calcutta—he went barefoot around the house even in winter. "Are you in love with this man?" he asked, his face still toward the window.

"It's too early to tell," I replied.

"Who is he?" He paused. "No, don't tell me. I don't want to know."

"He's my student," I said anyway, more to hurt myself than him. "Except he isn't really; we've been working together on some political research. That's why I have to go to Germany."

"Will he be there?"

"Yes."

"And what's the research about?"

"I don't really know yet. We're exploring links between a group in the U.S. and one in Germany." I couldn't bring myself to tell him more. "And who is she?" I asked.

"She's a sales representative for Blackwell's. Like I said, it isn't serious. I think she collects men at conferences."

"But you've seen her more than once."

"A few times. She's nice, but there's not much to talk about afterward." He paused, then came over and sat on the chair by the bed. "I want to spend the summer with you and Marcy, either here or there, I don't care. One more try. Would you like that?"

"I'll have to think about it."

"Try not to think too long." He rose to leave, but when he reached the door he turned around. "Remember that Brecht play we read together, *The Jewish Wife*?"

"Yes," I said.

"Our discussion about the absence of passion?"

"Yes."

"Well, I read it again recently and it's not really about that; it's about how people make choices. If they let circumstances sweep them along or not. She takes action, but he doesn't. You take action, I don't."

"It's not that simple, Sajit."

"I didn't say it was simple, did I? I just want to try one more time. If it doesn't work, we get a divorce—do something decisive like Marcy wants."

"I don't know. . . . "

As I watched him walk back over to my bed, I knew I would let him in even though I could have said no, just like I could have said no to Michael. I was the one who let circumstances sweep me along. I too was back in my body and I felt open enough for both of them. And so I made love to both of them that night. Sajit's mouth was Michael's mouth was Sajit's mouth; my pleasure was so intense I had to keep myself from crying out and waking Marcy. The Invisible Man had vanished, if only for a night.

The Voice comes through her dreams, waking her, telling her Hank is in danger, maybe even dead like the angel, with a bullet though his head. Pray for him, it tells her, pray for his deliverance.

CHAPTER 16

CAP ARCONA

M ichael and I met in the Hamburg airport and took an afternoon train to Rostock. He was tired from missing a night's sleep on the plane but overexcited too. Except for a few fishing excursions to Canada, this was his first trip out of the United States. He was too eager, too young, and I felt embarrassed by his arm around my shoulder and the fact that he turned my face toward him and kissed me on the train just as the conductor came down the aisle. "*Fahrkarten, bitte.*" Tickets, please. A ticket to where? Where was I going? From an old man to a young man, the lady professor and her pretty boy.

That's what I tried to tell myself anyway. I tried to hate myself on that train, but in the end it felt too self-indulgent. When Michael fell asleep, I focused on the work ahead and in the process worked my way back to him because he, we, were indistinguishable from the mission.

I stared out the window, but it was already dark by four and the lights of the little German towns were like silver jacks tossed by a child. I stared at a sleeping Michael and recalled a sleeping Sajit in my mind's eye. Then I did what I had to do. I compartmentalized. I arranged the jacks in discrete clusters, imposing my own logic on the random throw. Michael here, Sajit there. "*Fahrkarten, bitte*," the conductor called again.

Johan Kranz, my main contact in Rostock, picked us up at the train station. He had aged since I last saw him; he was nearly bald and his beard had turned from reddish gold to white. His trench coat was wet and in one hand he held a dripping umbrella. After greeting us, he whispered in German that he had been followed since yesterday and the same car was now parked beside his. I looked behind him but didn't see anyone watching. "What should we do?" I asked.

"We go by boat instead."

"Boat?"

He told me that a friend had a summer cottage on the island of Poel and that it was best if we stayed there, outside the city. "Come," he urged." He's waiting around the corner to take us to the harbor." I explained the situation to Michael as we followed Johan out of the station and hurried into the backseat of his friend's car.

As we sped away, Johan looked out the rear window, but there were no lights behind us. "The secret police were much more efficient under the Communists," he said. "Now many have lost their state jobs and work for private employers like Karl Gruhl. But their discipline has broken down. Probably the man sitting in the car next to mine is drinking vodka right now. He hasn't noticed that the train has come and gone."

"So you think it's Gruhl who hired him?" I inquired.

"He's the only one with enough money."

"How did he know we were coming?"

"They have ways of knowing—perhaps an informer in our group. That hasn't changed since 1989."

We passed through the city and then drove along the water until we reached a marina at the edge of the harbor. The buildings were all boarded up, and it was deserted except for a few boats that hadn't been removed for the winter. The rest of us stayed in the car while Johan's friend loaded our luggage onto a small cabin cruiser. I asked Johan who he was. "He'd rather you didn't know. He's got a lot to lose, but he's very reliable, don't worry. And he knows the sea."

It was a good thing he knew the sea, because it was a brutal trip to Poel. The waves were high and choppy and the wind blew at a sharp angle, driving the rain like bullets into the flimsy plexiglass of the upper cabin. I lay down below on a mattress, covering myself with a moldy woolen blanket and fighting off seasickness.

We docked in a village and walked several blocks through empty streets to the cottage. It was a simple three-room bungalow with a living room, kitchen, and bedroom and no central heating. We dried ourselves and our luggage around the gas fire in the living room while Johan and his friend prepared some food. Above the mantel I noticed an abstract painting, a zigzag of red, yellow, and blue lines that matched the colors of the fire. I tried to read the name on the bottom, wondering if the artist was Johan's friend, but the signature was as inscrutable as the image.

We had bread, sausage, and cheese for supper, washed down with schnapps that Johan's friend poured generously. I liked his face; it had that hard, ruddy quality of someone who spends a lot of time in salt air, but his eyes were gentle and wry and I suspected that in different circumstances he probably would display quite a wit. There was paint around his fingernails—maybe he *was* the artist. I decided I trusted him, as much as I could trust anyone these days.

We spoke English for Michael's sake but lapsed periodically into German. I told them what we had found out so far in Houghton and our suspicions about the mine. Johan had news about Karl Gruhl. "We hear he has new business associates," he remarked, his voice slightly slurred by the schnapps. "Several Russians and a gentleman from South Africa, an Afrikaner doctor—we don't know his name."

"How did you find out about them?"

He explained they had a contact in Gruhl's warehouse, the same contact who had found the books there published by Time to Act Press. He was a nervous man, paranoid almost. "He has agreed to meet you," he said, "but he won't come to the cottage. He's afraid every room he enters may be bugged. He'll meet you on the beach at one o'clock tonight. Only you. Michael must stay here." When Michael told him no, he had to come, Johan shook his head. "He won't talk if you're there—he wants as few people as possible to hear his voice and see his face." Then he turned to me. "You're not even supposed to tell me what he tells you."

He paused, picking up a piece of dark bread, which he tore in half.

"One o'clock on the beach; there's a short path from here I'll show you. My friend and I will return to Rostock soon, and he'll come back to get you tomorrow evening. We've brought enough food so that you can stay inside the cottage all day tomorrow. Keep the curtains closed and the lights off as much as possible."

"I was hoping to go through your files in Rostock tomorrow," I said.

He shook his head again. "There's nothing there you don't know already, and it's not worth the risk. Whatever you're doing, Gruhl doesn't like it. They'll follow me again tomorrow, but I'll lead them only to the university and back." He paused again, reaching for a knife to butter his bread.

Lucy refolds the turtlenecks and arranges them by size. In the four months since she left the store, order has all but broken down and she finds something hopeful in the act of restoring it. Otherwise there's little cause for hope. They watch her constantly now. The man with the ponytail—they call him Al—sleeps in her house and uses her car, and the Reverend takes her back and forth to the store. She deals with customers, while the men sit in the back office scheming about something. They prefer the store to the church now. Every day new shipments of guns and ammunition arrive, every day there are faxes from companies she's never heard of.

There's no word from Hank. The Reverend says he's still in Chicago, but she doesn't believe him. Diane doesn't believe it either. On Christmas she asked Lucy whether they were breaking up, but she said no, everything was fine; the Lord's business had called him down to Chicago. "What kind of Lord's business makes your husband miss Christmas?" Diane retorted. Lucy wanted to cry and tell her everything, but then Diane would go to the police and they'd kill Hank if they found out.

But maybe Hank's already dead, she thinks now, as she folds another shirt. Maybe she should run out the door and flag down a car and go to the police and it will all be over. Whatever they're doing will stop. She doesn't care anymore whether it's the Lord's business or not.

Quietly, she slips on her coat. She opens the door, remembering too late that there's a little bell attached to alert them of customers. She almost slips as she goes quickly down icy steps; Hank would have put salt on them. She runs through the parking lot and reaches the roadside, where she can see headlights in the distance. She walks into the road and lifts her hand. Headlights have saved her before; they will save her again.

But then the Reverend is next to her, his hand on her other arm, dragging her back. "Where are you going, Lucy?" he asks as the car slows down, then passes by.

"For a little walk, Reverend. I just wanted to get a breath of fresh air."

"Then why were you standing in the middle of the road?"

"I don't know," she lies.

"You'd better come back inside." His voice is stern; she knows she needs to soften him.

"Reverend," she pleads, "I'm worried about Hank. You have to let me talk to him."

"Come inside, Lucy."

Al is standing by the door, holding a rifle.

"It's all right," the Reverend calls. "She's coming back."

I left the cottage a few minutes before one. Michael still wanted to come with me, but I told him he couldn't; the man might not talk.

"I can hide in the trees," he said.

"He'll know, Michael. There's no danger; just stay here."

The rain had let up, but it was still windy as I walked down the path to the beach. The sound of the wind and the waves alternately fought and blended with each other like jazz percussion. The thin point of a pen flashlight guided my way, but it wasn't bright enough and I stumbled several times on stones and roots. On the beach the damp sand felt like mud, except it didn't stick to my boots.

I stood where Johan had told me to stand, staring out at the sea and an invisible Denmark that lay somewhere to the north. I'd been to the Baltic coast once or twice, but then it was warm and people sunbathed on towels and children dug tunnels in the sand. I pulled down my hat over my ears and rubbed my hands together. The alcohol had dulled the edge of my fear and for a moment I even felt peaceful, glad to be alone. But then I heard a voice behind me.

"*Guten Abend*," the man said, as if we were two strangers who just happened to meet on the beach.

"*Guten Morgen*," I replied.

"Yes, I guess you're right—it's morning already. You're alone?"

"Yes."

He moved from my back to my side, and I noticed he was shorter than I was. He was wearing a bulky jacket with the hood pulled over his forehead. In the dim beam cast by my flashlight, I could just make out that he wore glasses and had a goatee. He told me to turn off the light.

"Thank you for coming," I said, my eyes trying to adjust to the darkness.

He laughed slightly. "Does one have a choice in these matters?" He didn't leave time for an answer. "So you're curious to learn more about Herr Gruhl?"

"Yes."

"He's not a nice man, you know. It's not safe for you to be here."

"Not safe for you either."

"No, but I'm used to it."

Are you? I wanted to ask, remembering how Johan had described him as paranoid. But maybe under the circumstances paranoia was a sensible adaptive response. "I want to learn more about his international dealings."

"I know, I know," he said. "Time to Act Press, his book *Sea Change.*"

"So he wrote that?"

"Oh, yes, he shipped that book from the warehouse all over the world, but mainly to your country, I confess. There appears to be a mutual interest. . . . "

"Unfortunately, yes."

"But that's nothing, you have to understand; the books and pamphlets are nothing. Just paper."

"What else is there?"

He was quiet for a few moments as if listening for any intrusive sounds, but the waves' breaking would have provided cover for anyone surveilling us. "I'm not sure," he continued, "but he's shipping illegal cargo. A month or so ago I was working the late-night shift when he came to the warehouse to speak with my supervisor. There was a South African man with him who had a heavy Afrikaner accent. An hour later a truck arrived with a container, and my supervisor went down to the docks.

"I don't know for certain, but I suspect the container was loaded onto a ship that night. Probably the night watchman and the custom agents were paid handsomely to turn their eyes away. Two weeks later my supervisor bought a new car, a Mercedes—that's impossible to do on his salary."

"What do you think was in the container?"

"I don't know. And I'm not sure which ship it was sent out on. But I know the date. November fifteenth. And the container had the name of a company I didn't recognize: Vetlans."

"Can you find out where it was sent?"

"I'm hoping you can."

"How?" I asked, rubbing my hands together again.

"I've made some arrangements, but it's up to you whether you want to pursue this."

"What kind of arrangements?"

"You've come at a good moment. Tomorrow night Rostock plays Dresden in an important football match. Everyone who works in the warehouse will be watching the match there on TV, and they'll be drunk, very drunk. Herr Gruhl is the team's main sponsor, so he'll be at the game. I'm going to give you the combination code to the side entrance of the warehouse. From there you go up the stairs to the office. The Turkish cleaner will leave the door open. He's a friend, a member of our group. You can go through the shipping bill files, but you must put everything back in place and lock the door after you."

"Will you be there?"

"I'll be drunk, just like the rest of them."

He gave me a map of the warehouse and explained the plan in more detail. "If you get caught, you don't know me, of course."

"Of course."

"I suggest you bring a pocketful of cash in case you need to bribe someone." He paused, and I wondered if he wanted a payment too, though Johan hadn't suggested that. I had nothing against paying people for information—in my kind of research, informants were taking a risk, after all.

"Shall I pay you something?" I asked finally.

"*Nein, nein,*" he rebuked me. "*Es geht nicht um Geld.*" This is not about money.

"What *is* it about?"

He paused again, pulling his collar more tightly around his neck and shifting his weight from one foot to the other. "There's a memorial on this island," he began, "close to the village of Timmendorf. Have you heard of it?" I shook my head. "Have you heard of the Neuengamme concentration camp near Hamburg?"

"I think so, but I don't know much about it."

"Well, near the end of the war the Nazis loaded ten thousand inmates from Neuengamme onto three ships sailing to the Bay of Lübeck. The inmates were to be murdered at sea. But before they could be executed, the British bombed the ships. Seven thousand people drowned. Many bodies washed ashore and were buried here. The memorial is named after one of the ships, *Cap Arcona.* My parents were interned at Neuengamme because they were Communists. They were on that ship."

"I see," I said, though maybe my words were lost in the wind. I tried to fix my eyes on the white lines of froth left by the waves. I tried to imagine the horror of the bodies washing up on the shore. Who found them first? Who dug the graves, the fishermen?

"So you see, I don't need to cast about for reasons. The others, they're always discussing things, reading books, playing with theories. Children's games. I only have one concern—that nothing like that ever happens again."

He thanked me before I could thank him, then shook my hand before he turned and disappeared into the woods.

The Reverend leads her into the back room. Al is behind them, probably training the rifle on her back, though she's too scared to turn around and see for sure. The Reverend tells her to sit down, so she does. Nelson's across from her. Avoiding his eye, she looks at the calendar above his head. It's from the Firestone dealer, and the December picture is a tire decorated like a wreath. Hank put the calendar up.

"Where's Hank?" she asks, before they have a chance to say anything. "I want to know where Hank is."

"He's in Chicago, like I told you, Lucy," the Reverend says.

"I don't believe it. He wouldn't miss Christmas."

"I ordered him to go there—for exorcism. The Devil got inside him."

"What do you mean the Devil got inside him?"

"He started to doubt, Lucy. He's gone down there to do some real hard praying, to find the way again." The Reverend pauses, and a look passes between the three men. "Don't you go astray now too. Don't let the Devil get inside. Hank's depending on you."

"What do you mean by that?"

"He means," Nelson says, his lips widening into something that is supposed to look like a smile, "he means that if you screw up we're going to blow his fucking brains out."

"I didn't say that, Nelson."

"No, but I am. If you walk out that door one more time without asking, Hank's going to die. Understand?"

She nods her head, looking at the Reverend and then at the calendar, counting the days left until the New Year: twenty-nine, thirty, thirty-one. Don is back on the thirty-first. She's waiting for the Reverend to say something, but he doesn't. "Is he right, Reverend?" she asks.

"I have faith in Hank, Lucy, and I have faith in you. All you need to do is stand behind that counter in the store and deal with customers. Do what you're told, and everything will be all right. Now take off your coat and make us some coffee."

Slowly, she gets up and walks over to the coffee machine, where she fetches the glass pot. She fills it at the sink and loads the filter with a packet of ground coffee. As she pours the water into the top, she feels the rifle barrel against her spine. "Al's just giving you a little back scratch," Nelson says. "Feels good, doesn't it?"

I had forgotten how much we depend on natural light to make us function. With the curtains drawn against the day, Michael and I felt more disoriented than we already were, stumbling around the cottage like drunks with bad hangovers, yet with senses keened to the slightest noise. Even birdsong was suspect.

We had made love in the early morning after my return from the beach, but it was too quick, too urgent, as if the goal were reaching the aftermath as fast as possible so we could lie in each other's arms and pretend we were safe. I didn't tell him about Sajit, it didn't matter then; all that mattered were the ghost ships, the bodies washed up on shore. I dreamed about them.

During that day, if you can call it a day, we sat in the kitchen

and studied the warehouse map the man had given me. "We don't
have to go through with this," I told Michael, so many times that
he finally ordered me to stop. We rehearsed various scenarios in
case we got caught, but none were very realistic. Our only real
defense was money. I hoped the man was right and the security
guard would take a bribe. Otherwise we would have a lot of
explaining to do, either in front of Karl Gruhl, who might not give
us the opportunity to explain, or the Rostock police. I preferred
the latter possibility.

Johan's friend came for us at seven. He told us Johan had been
followed all day, and this evening as a diversionary move, he was
going to pick up a couple who matched our description from a
local hotel and take his shadow on a tour of all the back streets of
Rostock. "How about yourself?" I asked him.

"They don't know me yet. Soon, maybe, after you leave, they'll
start looking more closely, but Herr Gruhl no longer has the secret
police at his disposal. That could change. He's planning to run for
mayor."

"Gruhl?"

"That's why he's given so much money to the football team—to
boost his popularity. He's president of the club now."

"Like Berlusconi in Italy."

"Yes, though fortunately Gruhl doesn't own any television net-
works. I don't know if he has national ambitions like Berlusconi.
For now he wants more local control, the opportunity to rearrange
certain public services—like the police."

"Can he win?"

He shrugged. "With unemployment the way it is, maybe. Many
of us will be cheering for Dresden tonight."

The boat ride was smoother this time. It was a still night with a smattering of stars in the uneven seams of cloud cover. I stayed on deck this time, glad for the fresh air after being inside the musty cottage all day. Michael stood next to Johan's friend, asking him nautical questions: simple male talk, which I found soothing, reminding me of my father and his fishing friends.

We docked at a different marina about a quarter-mile from the warehouse. We would walk from here and return to the boat when we were through. Then Johan's friend would take us to a town along the coast, where we would spend the night before going by train to Hamburg. "Most people are inside watching the match," he told us. "But if anyone's outside the warehouse, they'll wonder what you're doing. Pretend you're drunken lovers. Stagger if you have to."

Johan's friend was right—there was not a soul out as we walked to the warehouse. Guard dogs barked from behind chain-link fences, and here and there a TV set flashed in a window. Michael had his arm around me and we tried to play drunk, but we were too nervous, resuming a brisk pace between each inept attempt at a stagger. If someone was watching, they wouldn't be convinced.

My hand trembled as I punched in the code to the side door of the warehouse. We slipped into a dimly lit vestibule that smelled of cigarette smoke. I noticed a door to the main body of the building had been left slightly ajar. I didn't stop to look, but I could hear the voices of the sports announcers turned up high amid raucous cheering. I wondered about the man on the beach and whether I would recognize his voice.

We climbed the stairs to the office, where, as promised, the door was unlocked. A computer was on with a screensaver of tropical fish. A cyber water bubble rose to the surface and made a popping noise that startled me. Michael shined a flashlight along a bank of file cabinets across the back wall as I tried to decipher their labels. There appeared to be four deep drawers of shipping bills, but fortunately they were labeled and organized by date, so we went straight to the most recent one. It was locked, but Michael had brought tools and picked the lock easily.

I pulled out the November file and put it on the desk. The sound of cheering had ebbed downstairs, and I could hear people moving around, the sound of a toilet flushing—it was too early for the game to be over, but we hadn't reckoned on the half. I debated escaping down the stairs now with the file in hand, but I feared meeting someone at the bottom. "Stand by the door," I whispered to Michael. "Signal if anyone's coming."

I flipped through the file until I reached mid-November. Gruhl's warehouse had loaded freight on two ships on November 15. One was bound for Finland, the other to Canada, with the final destination Sault Sainte Marie, the locks at the meeting point of Lake Huron and Lake Superior, about two hundred miles from Houghton. I read down the list of freight, looking for the name Vetlans. It was at the bottom, in alphabetical order, and the freight was described as South African wine. It seemed an unlikely cargo for the Upper Peninsula, where most people drank cheap beer and rotgut whiskey.

After making a mental note of the ship's name, *Leuchtfeuer*— Beacon of Light—I closed the file. I was just about to put it back in the drawer when Michael warned me someone was coming upstairs. He grabbed a heavy vase from a shelf and stood by the side of the door, so if someone opened it he would be shielded from view. There was nowhere for me to hide, so I made a quick decision. I sat on the desk and unbuttoned the top of my blouse.

A key turned in the door. "Finally," I said in a slurred German as the door began to open. "I've been waiting up here for over an hour. Aren't I more important than the match? If I'm too late coming home, my husband will start to wonder, you know."

The security guard stood in the door frame and stared at me.

"Oh, it's not you." I laughed drunkenly. "Come in, come in. If he's not coming, maybe you will do. Let me see you better."

"Who are you?" the guard asked, as he stepped tentatively into the room. But before he had time to find out, Michael hit him over the head with the vase. He slumped to the ground and we ran out of the office and down the stairs.

Lucy can't sleep. She needs to know if Hank is dead or not. If he's dead, she can escape and nothing will happen to him because it's already happened and his body is lying somewhere, maybe buried already or dumped in the lake. But if he's alive, she has to go along for his sake. It would be easier if she still loved him; the choice wouldn't be a choice at all because she'd do anything to keep him alive, if he was alive. How can she know?

She summons the Voice, but it won't come to her. It's forcing her to choose, testing her, they're all testing her, like the special ed teachers who said she was slow but surprisingly fast with figures. Hard to diagnose, maybe nothing really wrong with her. She never told them it was seeing too much that slowed her down, not seeing too little. They wouldn't have understood.

At least her parents understood. They left her the cabin so there would be a place where it was OK to be slow, to watch the patterns on the water.

She'll never sleep again as long as Hank may or may not be dead, and Al stretches out on the couch in the living room, clutching his gun like a child would hug a stuffed animal. Her house isn't hers anymore. Nothing is hers except the breath that keeps going in and out of her body.

I wanted to believe everything would be all right. We reached the boat before the guard regained consciousness and sounded the alarm; we left the city before Dresden beat Rostock in overtime with a penalty kick scored by a black player. Soccer hooligans and neo-Nazis went on a rampage through the poorer sections of the city, smashing windows and beating people up.

I saw a report about it on television at the Hamburg airport. My plane was delayed because of fog in London, and Michael's had already left. As soon as he got back to Houghton, he was going to drive to Sault Sainte Marie to make inquiries about the ship.

There were no casualties, the TV reporter said, but two people had been seriously injured. One was a Serbian street cleaner—his wife cried into the camera before the focus shifted to his young daughter burying her face in her mother's skirt—the other was a middle-aged German man who was assaulted by a gang of thugs as he left his night job at a dockside warehouse owned by Karl Gruhl. Police suspected that the attack was motivated by anger at Gruhl for his team's defeat. A policeman had scared off the thugs just as they were about to push the man into the water. He had sustained a number of broken bones and internal bleeding and was still in a coma. They flashed a photograph of him. He wore glasses and had a goatee. I was almost certain he was the man I had met on the beach.

Sitting across from me, I noticed a young man in an expensive suede jacket studying my reaction. I caught his eye and he looked away, but in that split second of contact he had let me know I could be next.

CHAPTER 17

HITLER'S EXECUTIONER

I spent the flight from Hamburg to London weighing whether or not I should level with Sajit and make Marcy stay in Oxford. I was leaning toward the affirmative, but when I arrived, her bags were already packed and she wasn't speaking to her father. Without his permission, she had gone out and got her eyebrow pierced, and he viewed it as a serious personal affront. I was glad I hadn't told him about the pregnancy. Not that I was the child psychology expert, but I knew, or thought I knew, how to handle her better than he did.

On the way back to Houghton, Marcy and I were delayed in Detroit overnight because of heavy snow in the UP. We stayed in a funky airport hotel with no stars and no soap and no spare rolls of toilet paper. I wanted it to be a mother-daughter moment, to order up pizza and lie on the bed watching stupid movies, but neither of us was capable of that. I knew she wanted to ask me questions but was too scared of the answers.

Were her father and I going to get back together? She must have noticed the renewed intimacy between us, heard the bedroom door close in the middle of the night. I had made love with Sajit one more time. He knew I'd just been with Michael, and it gave his lovemaking a jealous edge—he was out to prove his manhood and win me back. But there was no *me* to win; my mind was too far away, focused on Rostock. I had e-mailed Johan from Oxford, and he confirmed that the man on the beach was the same one attacked by the gang. He was still in a coma.

In retrospect I realize I should have told Marcy about what happened in Rostock. It would have made all the difference. Instead, in the airport hotel I read a book while she watched TV, and in the morning we were more distant than ever as we ate the hotel breakfast of stale muffins and sour juice. It was January 2 already. The New Year had come and gone.

We arrived in Houghton in the early afternoon. It had snowed forty inches since our departure, and the snowbanks in the airport parking lot were beginning to look like tall retaining walls. The sky was gray, but a different gray from London, not as dark and more transparent, like a sheet of old tracing paper.

The house seemed smaller and flimsier than I remembered, the ceilings especially low. I turned up the heat and pressed the button on the answering machine. Seth had called three times for Marcy, and there were a number of hang-ups that were probably Evan. I checked my e-mail. Michael was back from Sault Sainte Marie and wanted to speak with me as soon as possible.

That evening I dropped Marcy off at the movies and then went to meet Michael in the bar of the old Grantwood Hotel, where two menacing gargoyles were perched above the front door. They stared far beyond me, snow between their teeth. The bar was a quiet place generally, but even quieter with the college students still away for the holidays. We sat at a table in the back, with a mock Tiffany lamp suspended between us and a Muzak polka playing over the sound system. The waitress looked to be in her seventies, and by the time the wine finally arrived it seemed to have aged too, bordering on vinegar.

Our hands touched briefly on the table, but I was too tired and tense to even contemplate sex. I found myself wishing he were just my student again, reporting the results of research on something boring and benign.

It was anything but that. His trip to Sault Sainte Marie had confirmed our suspicions. He tracked down a dockworker who had helped unload the *Leuchtfeuer*, and plied him with enough whiskey to loosen his tongue. The worker remembered the container of wine and said U.S. Customs hadn't checked it closely, only opening a case or two on the top; they assume goods coming from Germany have already been checked by agents in Canada. A man had arrived to pick up the freight and straightaway had it loaded onto another smaller boat. He remembered thinking that was strange. Usually, wine is transported by truck; there are two or three regular distributors.

"And then I asked him what this man looked like," Michael continued. "He told me he was tall and thin and had a long ponytail—that's what he remembered most, the ponytail. It sounds like the same guy I saw outside the church that night."

"Could be"—I nodded—"but we don't know for sure."

"I've been doing some research on the Web too. There's no wine distributor or freight forwarding company named Vetlans. The only Vetlans I could find was a South African medical supply company."

"Medical supply?"

"Based in Cape Town. I searched Lexis-Nexis and got an article on the South African Truth Commission. They questioned a Dr. van Houten about his role in the biological weapons program during apartheid. There wasn't enough evidence to convict him of any wrongdoing, but the article mentioned that he now owns a medical supply company named Vetlans. Here," he said, pulling a sheet of paper from his backpack. "Have a look."

While I was putting on my glasses, I noticed a man entering the bar. He looked familiar, and then I placed him as the man who had leered at Marcy in the sporting goods store. Michael had told me his name was Nelson. "Michael," I whispered, "don't look behind you, but we have a visitor."

"Who?"

"It's that guy Nelson, I think."

"I wondered if someone was following me. There was a car close behind me all the way from Calumet."

Nelson sat down at the bar without taking off his coat and ordered a drink. Michael slipped a ten-dollar bill under a coaster. "We'll just walk out now," he said, "straight past him into the lobby. Ready?"

I put my glasses back in my case and grabbed my coat from the back of the chair. There was no one else in the lobby except the receptionist, who was refilling a glass bowl with peppermints. "Better bundle up," she advised. "It's a cold night out there."

Lucy retreats to the bedroom even though it's only nine. Al's sitting in the living room watching TV, and she doesn't care to join him. In certain ways he scares her more than Nelson—he's too quiet. You know the words are rumbling around in his head, knocking against each other, getting angrier and angrier. Nelson's more out front, easier to read.

She gets in bed with her clothes on in case she has to run. Not that she'd make it—they'd shoot her before her hand even touched the window latch. Don's back from downstate now, but she can't call him, because they watch everything she does. Diane phoned yesterday and they had to let her speak to her sister, but she couldn't say much. She promised she'd visit soon. "Lucy, are you OK?" Diane asked. "Is Hank back yet?"

"He's still in Chicago," she replied. "I think he'll be back on Friday."

"Are you doing OK alone?"

"Just fine. You know I'm good at shoveling snow."

Shoveling snow is the only thing that brings her peace these days. It lets her forget what's going on and remember better things, like working alongside her father. When she was five, he bought her a little orange snow shovel, and she made a snow fort where she hid with Diane and spied on the neighborhood boys throwing snowballs at passing cars. Once David Hutterson threw one at the car of an off-duty policeman and got chased down the street, but he ran faster than the cop and hid in the snow fort along with Diane and her. He was always nice to her after that; in junior high he punched someone out for calling her stupid.

She closes her eyes, trying to remember more good things like that, because maybe there's no more time left and she might as well look back and not forward into the darkness. She just wishes the Voice would come to her again. Maybe it's waiting for her to go back so far there's no farther to go, and then it will show her the way, tell her the truth about Hank.

And so in her mind she shovels snow again, light powdery snow that doesn't stick to the shovel and makes a rainbow spray as it falls. She shovels until her mother calls from the doorway. "Lucy, come in," she says. "You've done enough for now."

Michael insisted on staying at the house to protect us. I told Marcy his furnace had broken and he needed a place to spend several nights. I could tell she didn't believe me; she believed we were lovers. That upset her enough that she didn't see the fear I wore like a long, heavy overcoat dragging behind me as I passed from room to room, locking windows and closing curtains.

It snowed so hard the next day they canceled school, and the three of us were stuck inside the house together. To avoid us, Marcy spent most of the time in her bedroom while Michael and I sat at my desk, searching the Internet for more clues to Vetlans.

For lunch I made a pot of lentil soup, which we ate together in the kitchen. Michael tried to make conversation with Marcy, but his questions inspired only one- or two-word answers. How was England? OK. Are you looking forward to going back to school? Not particularly. He gave up after a while, and I filled the vacuum by soliciting items for a grocery list.

In the afternoon, Michael and I came upon the Web page of an international physicians' group opposed to chemical and biological weapons. Its report on South Africa claimed that although the Mandela government had dismantled the weapons program there, former officials were selling old stocks and secrets underground. One had been caught making contact with Libyan agents. Among the bizarre weapons the program had produced were anthrax-tainted chocolates and cigarettes, cylinders filled with poison that could be inserted inside screwdrivers, and umbrellas with poison tips. There was evidence that several prominent antiapartheid activists had been poisoned through such means.

Another research priority had been to find a biological agent that would render only black women infertile. Project Pure, it was euphemistically called. All the information concerning Project Pure had been destroyed, but most experts believed it hadn't been successful since the concept itself was scientifically flawed. There is more genetic variation within races than among them, the report noted, and any agent that targeted black people would be likely to affect white people too.

The report also contained a Who's Who of the clandestine program. Van Houten's name was on the list.

When I read that, I turned to Michael and told him it was time for us to go to the FBI. "Not yet," he answered, his eyes still glued to the computer screen.

"Why not?"

"It's still speculation."

"You know that's not true. We have more than enough evidence now. They're following us. Let the FBI find out what they're hiding. Our responsibility ends here."

"They'll botch it up," he insisted. "Look how efficient they've been in finding Johnny's killers. This is a small place. Word will leak out and they'll get away before they're caught. We need to go back to the mine first—find out what they're hiding."

"I don't think so."

"You don't have to come."

"Michael, don't be crazy. They'll kill us this time." I looked at him then and saw what I'd been trying not to see—he *was* crazy; it took craziness to get this far, so close and so fascinated with evil. I had fallen in love with that craziness because he had crossed the line I'd never let myself cross, the line where I'd always turned back, turned another page, churned out another paper. And by making love with his craziness, I had helped it grow, watered and fertilized it, until his manhood was all bound up with it and me. I understood the fantasy of being Hitler's executioner, of doing on your own what it took whole armies to accomplish. For a moment I'd let myself be seduced by that fantasy too, but it was over now and I was older again, and I knew it was time to stop.

Time to stop him.

I made love with him late that night after Marcy went to bed. I was worried she would hear us but I had to; it was the only way left to reach him. This time I made love as an older woman, slowing him down, looking him in the eye, trying to make him follow me somewhere deeper than just pleasure, the place where souls meet and weave together like reeds in a basket. But he didn't want to be contained. His body was restless. He pulled out of me a few seconds after he came, rolled over on his back, and said nothing.

"Promise me you won't go to the mine tomorrow," I whispered.

"I won't go to the mine if you won't go to the FBI," he replied. Then he got up and returned to the living room, where he stayed up all night, his rifle pointed at the front door.

At ten-thirty in the morning a telephone truck pulls up to the store and the driver delivers an envelope for the Reverend. Lucy recognizes him from the church but doesn't know his name. He's around fifty and has a long, gaunt face on a pudgy body, as if someone put a Frankenstein head on a baby doll. He doesn't even say hello, just hands her the envelope and departs as fast as he can, leaving a trail of snow on the floor.

The Reverend and Nelson are in the back room, meeting with some men she's never seen before. They gave her strict instructions not to be disturbed, so she decides to wait. She feels the envelope—there's a cassette inside, probably another tape of Gillian and Marcy's phone calls. The Reverend doesn't trust her to do the listening anymore. She notices there's nothing written on the envelope, so she could open it, put the cassette back in a new one, and no one would be the wiser. Her Walkman is in her purse.

She goes into the bathroom and locks the door. Her hands are shaking as she opens the envelope and slips the cassette into the recorder. It's been so long since she's heard Marcy's voice. There it is. She's talking to her friend Seth.

"I hope I didn't wake you up," she says softly.

"What time is it?" he asks groggily.

"One o'clock. They're having sex right now, can you believe it? He is such a creep. And she keeps lying to me about it; she claims his furnace is broken. Yeah, right. She had sex with my father too. It's disgusting. And she's getting even more paranoid. I didn't call you today because she says I can't use the phone anymore—she told me to walk to the grocery store to use the pay phone. In the middle of a fucking blizzard."

"At least she doesn't look at you like you're some kind of pervert," Seth tells her. "At least she doesn't go off to her room and cry every ten minutes like my mother."

"Do you think she knows you're gay?"

"I didn't tell her anything, but she looks at me like she knows. And my father pretends nothing's wrong. It's weird, too fucking weird."

"Maybe you should just tell them. What are they going to do?"

"I want to see Gabe first. I need to talk with him about it."

"Then why don't you go see him?"

"I'm thinking about it, but I'm nervous. What if it's not the same? What if he has someone else already?"

"He hasn't said he does, has he?"

"No, he says he wants to see me."

"Then what's the problem?"

"I'm the problem. It was just so perfect this summer, and I keep thinking it will never be that perfect again."

"Maybe it won't, but it will be something else. It keeps changing with Evan, but that's just the way it is—sometimes it's good, sometimes it sucks, but we still love each other. You have to take the risk, Seth." She pauses and Lucy can hear her take a deep breath. "Do you want me to go with you? Wouldn't it be great to run away from all this crap for a few days? We could stay at Gabe's place and Evan could fly out to Green Bay. You said Gabe has a big place, right?"

"He inherited his grandparents' house."

"We'll skip school tomorrow and take the bus to Green Bay."

"What about our parents?"

"We'll send them a note from here before we go—let them know we'll be back in a couple of days."

"They'll be worried."

"Let them be worried. Maybe they'll treat us better after we get back."

"I'll call Gabe and see what he says."

"Get directions to his place too, so I can give them to Evan. I'll call you back in a little while. Don't call me. She'll freak out if she hears the phone."

When she calls Seth back, he tells her Gabe is excited about them coming. She calls Evan afterward, giving him the address: 145 Hawthorne Avenue in Green Bay.

Lucy switches off the tape. She can't stay in the bathroom too long; they might come looking for her, or a customer might show up. She flushes the toilet and slips the tape into another envelope. She wishes she didn't have to give it to the Reverend, but he's probably expecting it. She doesn't want him to know Marcy has run away. But maybe she hasn't—maybe she got cold feet. Lucy prays that she's not on the bus to Green Bay.

After Marcy went to school, I made Michael sit with me at the computer. I told him that whether or not we went to the FBI, we needed to assemble our evidence and write it up; there had to be documentation in case something happened to us. It was a grim task but one that I'm good at, and there was a certain relief in watching the sentences and paragraphs take shape on the screen. I also felt confident that by the end I would convince Michael that we needed help. He said very little to me that morning and kept a safe physical distance between us, measuring the space between my chair and his with a mental ruler. Finally, he retreated to the bedroom to get some sleep.

I didn't mind. I needed the space to think, not only about what I was writing but about Marcy. I hatched a plan to send her down to my mother's in Arizona, but I knew she wouldn't go unless I gave her a good reason why. I would have to tell her at least something about what Michael and I were doing.

When it was time for Marcy to come home in the afternoon, I stood by the window watching for the school bus, but it passed without stopping. She's probably at Seth's, I told myself, though she said she was coming home right after school. I waited fifteen minutes, then woke Michael up and told him I was driving down to the grocery store to use the pay phone. I called the Nicholsons, and Anne said Seth hadn't come home either. She wasn't concerned, figuring they had probably walked into town.

I wanted to believe her, but I couldn't allow myself the luxury. I put in some more coins and called the school. The secretary checked the attendance record: Marcy had been reported absent in homeroom. I asked about Seth. He had been reported absent too.

I called Anne back with the news. "They must be skipping school together," she said. "Seth complained a lot last night about going back. He's done this before—last semester there was an absence on his report card that he couldn't explain. We had a long talk about it, and Mark threatened to ground him if it ever happened again. But Mark's always saying things like that and never following through."

"Where do you think they are?"

"They're probably at a friend's house. I'll call around if you want."

"I'd appreciate that. I'll get in touch with you a little later. My phone's not working, so I'm calling from a pay phone."

After I hung up, I went back home and straight into Marcy's room. The top drawer of her dresser was open, and by instinct I went over to close it. She was like her father in that respect—they always left drawers open. She stored her epilepsy pills in that drawer. I looked for the bottle but couldn't find it.

It wasn't in any of the other drawers either. Where had she put it?

I looked everywhere, but it was gone. Some other things were missing too: the diary she kept in her bedside table and the little stuffed bear her girlfriend in Boston gave her as a going-away present. Probably, if I'd had the presence of mind to count them, a few pairs of socks and underwear.

My daughter has run away, an internal voice announced.

No, no, it can't be true, another responded. She still hasn't unpacked everything after her trip, or she's put them in different places. Keep looking, you'll see.

I searched and searched, but there was no sign of the pills or the bear or the diary.

Numbly, I drove to the pay phone again and called Anne about my suspicions. She told me to hold on while she checked Seth's room. She was crying when she came back. His toothbrush and razor were gone, as was the spare cash she kept in the checkbook. He hadn't been happy lately, she told me. He'd been having a hard time ever since she found that letter in his backpack. Mark had told me about the letter, hadn't he? But they hadn't talked about it with Seth. She should have encouraged him to speak to her, but she didn't know how. It was her fault, all of this was her fault—

I cut her off, I hope not rudely. I didn't want to hear her maternal guilt, I had more than enough of my own. I just wanted to know where they were. I forced us to become practical. I told her to call the school to see if any of his other friends were missing. I would call the bus station and get back to her.

The ticket salesman told me yes, that morning two young people had bought tickets for Green Bay. He remembered the girl because she looked foreign and had a pierced eyebrow. The boy was carrying a guitar case.

"Green Bay?" Anne sounded surprised when I called her. "Why would they go to Green Bay?" Then she paused. "One of his guitar instructors at Interlochen came from Green Bay. That's the only connection I can think of."

"Do you remember his name?"

"Gabe something. He called here once. I'll call the Interlochen office—I just hope it's still open."

"Have you told Mark?"

"He's coming home right now. Maybe he'll remember Gabe's last name; he has a better memory for names. Why don't you come over?"

"Thanks," I said. "I'll do that."

I hung up and looked outside, where the sunlight on the snow was so bright I was temporarily blinded. But when I stepped out and shaded my eyes, I noticed there was a blue pickup with Illinois plates in the lot.

CHAPTER 18

SNOW FORT

The Interlochen office was open, so Anne found the name and address of Seth's teacher—Gabe Latham, 145 Hawthorne Avenue, Green Bay, Wisconsin. They tried to phone him but no one answered, so we decided we would drive down. I went home first on the pretext that I wanted to pack a few things in case we stayed the night. I told Michael what was happening, and he agreed to stay at the house in case Marcy called. The Nicholsons picked me up at five.

It was one of the slowest drives of my life. Just over the Wisconsin line it began to sleet, forcing Mark to cut his speed in half. A car passed us, then spun out into the opposite lane, narrowly missing a collision with a truck. All three of us were so anxious we couldn't talk, and the classical radio station played what sounded like funeral dirges. It was after nine by the time we pulled up in front of Gabe's house. The lights were on and electric candles burned in the front windows. We could hear a live guitar duet as we made our way along the icy walk.

Mark rang the doorbell while Anne slipped her arm in mine.

The music stopped, and a few moments later a young man opened the door. He looked to be in his early twenties and was wearing a green cable-knit sweater, gray corduroy pants, and Danish clogs. He had short brown hair cut stylishly and an earring in one ear.

"Are you Gabe Latham?" Mark asked.

"Yes."

"Are Seth and Marcy here?"

"Seth is," Gabe replied, after a lengthy pause. "Marcy went out to dinner."

"I'm Seth's father."

"I see." He blushed slightly. "Please come in."

We stood awkwardly in the foyer while he insisted on taking our coats, pretending that there was nothing odd about our sudden appearance. Then he led us into the living room, where Seth was sitting on the couch, holding his guitar in front of him like a shield. I remember noticing that the room was impeccably clean and furnished with handsome antiques inherited from someone with old money and good taste. No one moved for a moment, and then Anne went over to the couch and bent down and put her arms around Seth.

"I'm sorry, Mom," he mumbled, "I'm really sorry."

"I didn't know they were running away," Gabe said to Mark, who stood rigidly by the piano like a novice at a recital. "They told me they were just coming to visit."

I couldn't tell if it was the truth or not, but it didn't matter. All I wanted was to see Marcy. "Where's Marcy?" I asked Gabe, puzzled that she'd gone out alone for dinner.

"She went out with her friend Evan to a Chinese restaurant."

"Evan's here?"

"He flew in from Boston. I loaned them my car. The restaurant's a couple of miles away."

"Take me there," I demanded, and then as an afterthought, "please."

Mark gave me his keys, but before we got into the car, Gabe offered to drive and I agreed. I stared silently out the window as his neighborhood of older homes gave way to a street of 1950s-style ranches, still twinkling with garish Christmas lights, and then to a strip of ugly franchises: Domino's, Burger King, and Big Boy, with the fat little mascot bulging out of his checkered overalls. Lights were on inside the restaurants, but their parking lots were deserted and we were the only car waiting at most of the red lights. Green Bay. Where was the green? Where was the bay? Memories of the hostile crowd at the abortion clinic came back to me and then the thought of Rollins's body lying listless on a motel bed. I hated this city.

We pulled into the lot of the Panda Gardens restaurant, which looked like a converted HoJo's with a pagoda-style roof on top. You could smell the kitchen from outside; the odor was neither sweet nor sour but acrid, probably from rancid oil. I walked faster than Gabe and pushed open the front door. Only a few tables were occupied, and I spied Evan at one. He had on the same vest he wore year in and year out, made of leather so soiled it looked like it had been cured in dirt.

Without a word I brushed by the hostess. Evan grimaced when he first saw me, then gave me his customary big, false stoned smile, which long ago I'd come to despise. "Where's Marcy?" I barked at him.

"In the bathroom."

I hurried through the restaurant into the back hall, where there was a phone, two restrooms, and a side exit door. "Marcy," I called, as I entered the ladies' room. The three stalls were empty and no one was standing at the sink. I recognized Marcy's lip balm on the counter and scooped it up, then rushed out into the hall and outside through the exit door. No one was there, although a car was pulling out at the far edge of the lot. I chased after it through puddles of slush, trying to read the license plate, but before I could it pulled onto the road and sped away.

She had to be inside. I went back in the restaurant, my shoes and pant legs soaked. Gabe was now sitting with Evan at the booth and I sat down too, pushing away a half-eaten plate of fried rice that must have been Marcy's dinner. "She's not there," I said.

"What?"

"I said she's not there. Where did she go, Evan? Did she run away when she saw me come in?"

He shook his head, dazed. "No, she just went to the bathroom, I swear. She'd been in there about ten minutes before you came. I was starting to get worried she was sick or something."

"Are there any stores around? Could she have gone out to buy something?"

"Everything's closed up by now," Gabe said, "and it's too far to walk."

"Then where the hell is she?" My voice rose high enough that the elderly couple at the nearest table turned their heads, but I didn't care. "Were you fighting, Evan?" He shook his head, but it wasn't convincing. "Tell me," I demanded. His eyes woke up then, or maybe it was just a momentary triumph of the uppers over the downers—his pockets were probably stuffed with a potpourri of drugs. Maybe he'd given Marcy something and she freaked out and was running through the slush or maybe, just maybe, she was making her way back to Gabe's house. "What happened, Evan?"

"We were just discussing things."

"What kind of things?" I kept my eyes fixed on him, though it was hard. He had been pretty to look at once—jet-black hair, pale skin, blue, blue Irish eyes—now he was junkie thin. All the boy had left his face, but no man had stepped forward to inhabit it.

"She wanted to call you, but I told her not to. She started to cry, and—"

"I'm going to call the house in case she's been in touch," Gabe said, pushing back his chair and standing up.

As he headed toward the phone, a waiter approached and inquired if I wanted to order anything. He was Chinese but second-generation with a flat Wisconsin accent. I said no and asked him if he'd seen Marcy leave the restaurant by the side door. He didn't think so, he told me, but he might not have noticed; he was irritated because two men had come in to order take-out but had left before it was ready. "Did you see them leave?" I asked.

"No," he answered. "They must have gone out the back."

The car speeding away. Was Marcy in it? Why hadn't I run faster and read the license plate? Panic twisted my stomach into a knot, and I felt faint from the pain. Just then Gabe returned to the table with the news that Marcy hadn't called, though Seth told him that Michael had just phoned for me and said it was urgent. "Maybe she's called home," I said, grabbing my purse. I ran to the phone and punched in my calling card number. It seemed an eternity for the call to go through. Finally, I heard Michael's voice on the end of the line. "Has Marcy called?" I blurted.

"Yes," he said.

"Thank God! Where is she?"

"They have her, Gillian. A man told me they took her from a restaurant in Green Bay. It sounded like he was speaking from a car. If we do anything, if we tell anyone about what we've found out, he said they're going to kill her. They let her talk to me for a few seconds. She said they're holding a gun to her head and we should just tell everyone she's on her way back to Houghton. She was calm at first—she even told me to tell you she had her pills—but then she started to cry and they hung up."

I didn't say anything for so long he thought we were disconnected. "Gillian, are you there?"

"Why did they take her, Michael?" I finally managed to say. "Why did they take her and not me?"

They're so busy now they forget to keep things from her. She knows that trucks are bound for Chicago with guns and explosives, that early tomorrow morning Al is going out to the mine to get something, that the Reverend is in charge. He's lost his sermonizing voice and sits at the desk in the back office giving orders, more like an army general than a minister. He treats her like a servant—*Get this, Lucy, get that*—but he doesn't touch her. Thank God for that.

She's cooking them a late dinner now at the house, some steaks Hank put in the freezer last time there was a sale at Food Fair. She defrosted them in the microwave, so they'll be tough, but she doesn't care. Now the baked potatoes are in there. She turns the microwave off and tests one with a fork. Still hard, so she punches the timer for five more minutes.

The phone rings and she answers, hoping it's her sister, but instead a man asks for the Reverend. "The phone's for you, Reverend," she calls into the living room. In the few seconds she waits for him to pick up the receiver, the Voice returns to her at last, instructing her not to hang up. She turns off the microwave and stills her breath, willing all the kitchen appliances to be silent.

"We're about an hour and a half outside Houghton," a man says. "Where do you want us to take the girl?"

"Nelson's cabin," the Reverend responds. "Remember where it is?"

"Where we had the meeting last month?"

"That's it. Bring her there."

As soon as he's off the phone, the Reverend shouts for her. "Is dinner ready yet, Lucy? Nelson and I have to leave in twenty minutes."

"Almost ready," she replies, turning on the microwave again. "Just a couple more minutes on the potatoes."

"Hurry it up, will you?"

She sets the table, folding the napkins, though she doesn't know why; they won't even notice. She puts out steak knives, a butter dish, salt and pepper. The table looks normal, as if a family might be eating there. As if nothing is wrong. As if they don't have Marcy.

Hank's dead now, the Voice tells her. You can't help Hank, but you *can* help Marcy.

Nelson's cabin, the Reverend told the man. But it's her cabin, not his.

She washes dishes while they eat, scrubbing the broiler pan

more than she needs to, removing every little drop of grease until the aluminum looks new except for the hairline scratches. On the windowsill above the sink there's a little spider plant Diane gave her. It just put out a new sprout that hangs off the side, connected to the mother plant by a thin runner. It would be so easy to break it off, so easy to break the girl. Nelson will break her if the other men haven't already. In her cabin, not his. Not in her cabin, *no*.

It seems so long until Nelson and the Reverend leave, though it's only ten or fifteen minutes. Al goes into the living room to watch TV. She turns on the dishwasher even though it's only half full and leaves the tap running. Her coat and boots are by the door, but they've taken away her car keys.

How long will it be until he notices she's gone? Where should she go?

She has to walk on the road because the snow is too deep on either side. There's a light on at the Sullivans' house, so she makes that her destination. She turns back to see if Al is following. Not yet. She rings the Sullivans' doorbell.

"Oh, hi, Lucy," Fran says, as she opens the door, holding a spatula in one hand. "What's up?"

"I wondered if I could use your phone. Something's wrong with mine."

"Sure, come on in. The phone's right there." She points to the hall table. "Just go ahead. I need to take some cookies out of the oven."

Lucy dials Don's number. "Please come get me," she says, before he barely has a chance to say hello. "I'll be waiting at the corner of Grove and Blackberry. There's a brown ranch there with a snow fort by the driveway. I'll be waiting in the fort."

"What's going on?"

"I'll explain later. Just come get me." She hangs up, then pokes her head into the kitchen. "Thanks, Fran."

"Want a cookie and a cup of coffee?"

"No thanks, gotta get back home."

Outside she turns in the direction of Blackberry Lane. It won't be long now until Al figures out she's escaped. She wishes she could run, but the road's too slippery; the snow is mixed with sleet. She reaches the corner when she hears the sound of a motor. The snow fort is so small she barely fits in. She hugs her knees to her chest and listens to the approaching vehicle. It's moving slowly and sounds like Al's pickup. She prays he won't notice the snow fort; he probably thinks she's stupid enough to keep walking on the road. She starts to shiver, a mixture of cold and fear. No matter, no one can see her, no one can hear her teeth chattering. What if Don doesn't come? What if he thinks she's crazy?

The sound of the pickup fades. She closes her eyes, thinking about Marcy now, how to free her. That's what the Voice wants her to do. The Voice tells her that Marcy's not a mud person, no one's a mud person. She knows that, she knew it before in her heart, where the Reverend never reached. She never really believed him. God made us all the same. Marcy's shivering too, but she's hiding inside herself. She doesn't have a fort like this one. God made us all the same.

By the time Don comes, Lucy's so stiff with cold he has to grab her hand and pull her out, then help her up into his truck. He puts a blanket over her legs and turns the heat up high. "Get out of here fast," she tells him.

"Your husband's after you?"

She shakes her head. "No, my husband's dead."

After the Nicholsons dropped me off at home, Michael tried to comfort me. He put his arms around me and drew me close, but I pulled away. I didn't want anyone to touch me. It was like the excruciating pain of childbirth when midwives and spouses try to hold your hand and guide your breath, but all you want is to be left alone. But no, that's not true, I didn't really want to be alone; I wanted Sajit. I wanted to fall down at his feet and beg his forgiveness.

But there was no time for that, no time for blame, though I suppose I blamed Michael too and that's another reason I couldn't bear to let him touch me. I had to decide what to do. No more thinking, just action, because they weren't waiting anymore. I took them at their word—that if I told anyone, they would kill Marcy. So I lied to the Nicholsons and said she'd called and was on the bus back to Houghton. Everything was fine. They were willing to believe me because they were so relieved to have Seth home. When they dropped me off at the house, Anne gave me a big hug. "We'll talk tomorrow," she said.

But what was tomorrow? The distinction between night and morning seemed artificial, and time was no longer time but a countdown until the moment they would decide it was no longer useful to keep Marcy alive. I sat down with Michael at the kitchen table, drinking a Coke to give me energy, but it was Marcy's soda and the sweet syrup tasted bitter in my mouth.

Michael was ready for battle, over-ready like a fresh recruit brought up on war movies, so full of energy he couldn't sit still and rattled his chair. He was convinced that we could stop whatever evil these men were planning to do, but I disagreed, declaring the first priority was to find Marcy. He said the two were the same thing, but I said no, they were different. He told me he was going out to the mine. I screamed at him that they would kill Marcy *and* him if he went out there. "Maybe they're keeping her there," he replied calmly, too calmly.

"And you'll save her?" I asked disbelievingly.

"Yes. Do you have a better plan?"

In truth I didn't, and I started to cry. He tried to comfort me again, putting his hand on top of mine, but it felt like paper covering rock in the old children's game. I pulled away once more and retreated to the bedroom, where I lay down and sobbed. He let me fall asleep, though I had asked him not to, and when the rapping on the window woke me at around four in the morning, he was already gone.

The rapping grew more insistent. Had they sent someone to shoot me? I wondered. But why would they bother to alert me? Had Marcy escaped? Who was it? What did they want? What did I have to lose?

Or did I even ask myself these questions? It's all a fog, at one with the dream I was or wasn't having. All I know is I pulled back the curtains to find a woman's face staring back at me. She gestured for me to open the window, and I pushed it up a few inches. "I know where your daughter is," she whispered. "Come with me; I'll take you there."

They can't drive to the cabin because Nelson will hear them, so the three of them walk along the road. Don dims the flashlight and they walk single file behind him, Lucy last. She has a rifle and so does Don, but Gillian doesn't know how to shoot and there's no time to teach her.

It must be almost six by now, but it's still pitch black. The snow has stopped and there's a fine mist, which catches in Lucy's throat. She muffles a cough. Soon they'll be within viewing distance of the cabin; soon Don should turn off the flashlight. She'll lead if he lets her. After night-hunting with her father, she's good at seeing in the dark. She's good at shooting too, killed a deer once, though at first Don didn't want to believe her. She had to beg him to give her his other rifle.

She can still remember the deer's face—how sadness mixed with pride when she saw the dark blood around the bullet hole. Right between the eyes she got him, so he died fast. Much better to kill than to wound, her father had told her.

A puff of wind blows a clump of snow from a nearby tree, and Don stops and points his rifle when he hears the thud. "It's only snow," she whispers, but he waits a few seconds before moving on. He wanted to go to the police, but she convinced him it was too risky; the girl would get caught in the cross fire.

The next time he stops, the sound is for real. A motor sputters, then starts up, and lights come toward them. They run into the woods, stumbling through the deep snow. A thorny branch catches Gillian's jacket, and Lucy has to free her. "Lie down," she orders, and Gillian burrows into the snow. Lucy dashes behind a bush, training her rifle on the road. She recognizes the Reverend's Cherokee as it passes. Nelson will be alone with Marcy now.

Close to the cabin they separate, Don going to the front, Lucy to the rear, and Gillian keeping watch by the road in case the Reverend returns. Only Nelson's truck is in the driveway. A rhododendron grows by the back window, covering the glass, so the shade is usually left up. Lucy squeezes between the bush and the window and stands on her tiptoes. The shade is pulled about two-thirds down, but through the gap she can see into the living room.

Marcy is lying on the couch, her arms and feet bound. Nelson is standing over her, holding a gun in one hand while he unzips his fly with the other. He reaches down and unzips hers, then pulls down her jeans and underwear. He unties the rope around her legs. As he kneels over her, she starts to jerk uncontrollably, her head rolling from side to side. Nelson grabs her by the shoulder and shakes her, but her body just goes limp.

Don bursts through the front door, aiming the rifle at Nelson's back. But Nelson's quick; he spins around, shoots, and Don falls. Like the deer. Don falls.

The Voice comes fast, like a flash of light, like the smashing of glass as her rifle butt knocks through the window. Nelson grabs Marcy and holds her in front of him, the gun at her head. "I'll shoot her!" he yells, but he doesn't see Lucy, just the broken window, because she's not there anymore. She's running to the side window. She breaks it too and he shoots at it, but she's gone already, to the back again.

"Marcy!" Gillian is screaming from outside the cabin. "Marcy, I'm here!"

For just a second Nelson is distracted by Gillian's cry and turns his head away from Marcy's, but a second is enough. The Voice directs the rifle between his eyes. The Voice tells Lucy she won't miss. She won't hit the girl. She will shoot Nelson dead.

Marcy had Nelson's blood on her when I grabbed her, but I didn't notice it until later when I took off my stained jacket in the police station. I was prepared to lay her down and treat her seizure, but she was fully conscious. She had been faking it, she told me. She was shaking but I was too, and we held on to each other for a long time, not even thinking about the other body on the floor.

Lucy was with him, and when I finally was able to turn in that direction, I realized Don was still alive. The bullet had hit above his heart and he was unconscious but still breathing. Somehow Lucy had had the presence of mind to call 911, and then she kneeled down by his body and prayed.

I don't remember getting into the police car, but I remember lying back, resting my head on the back of the seat, feeling my adrenaline giving out and the warmth of Marcy's body next to mine, wanting sleep as I had never wanted it before. But it was too soon for that. I would have to summon the energy to explain everything to the police and send them out to the mine to find Michael. I didn't think then to thank Lucy. That would come later.

What would come first was a crackling voice on the police radio announcing a series of six bomb explosions in Chicago. One was at the offices of a prominent financial investment firm, Cohen, Liebermann & Kahn. The other five were at busy commuter rail stations in black neighborhoods on the South Side. The preliminary estimate of casualties was over one thousand.

THE RING OF TRUTH

It took me a long time before I could mourn the death of Michael, before I could give flesh to the bare, bleak words I read in the police report.

They found him outside the mine, a few yards away from Al, who was already dead when the police arrived. Michael stayed alive just long enough to tell them what had happened. After he left my house, he had skied in to the mine and surprised Al, who was loading canisters onto the back of a snowmobile. Michael shot first, but Al caught him in the groin before falling. Michael dragged himself over to the snowmobile, but couldn't lift himself up and lay in the snow semiconscious and bleeding. He might have survived if he'd still been able to lift his gun and shoot before the Reverend shot him. There wasn't even a battle. The Reverend put three bullets into his chest before escaping with the canisters.

I wondered if Michael asked about Marcy or me before he died, but the police said no, he died telling them about the Reverend. So I have to make up that part. I have to pretend he died knowing we were safe. I make up other endings too. I hold his hand, I stop his bleeding, I save him. I make love to him in my dreams.

In the investigation that followed his death, I told the police and FBI everything we knew and everything we surmised. They arrested two men in Chicago, who later testified that the bombs were a decoy to divert the police from the Reverend's plan to release a biological agent on the South Side that would kill tens of thousands of black people. But there was never any real proof of biological weapons, and they couldn't pin anything on Karl Gruhl either. After his soccer team won the National Cup he was elected mayor of Rostock.

Mark Nicholson suggested I take a leave from the department until the investigation was completed, but I knew he wanted me to leave for good. I had violated just about every rule of academic ethics, and a student was dead because of it. He didn't want to have to fire me, so I resigned and retreated to Oxford.

It was there that I began to perform my penance. Sajit and Marcy wouldn't forgive me, not for what I'd done but for my failure to tell them about it, to warn them, to seek their advice. I watched them grow closer as I shut myself in the study and stared out the window at the canal and the sedentary house-boats, wishing for more movement on the water besides inter-mittent drops of rain. Sajit arranged for Marcy to be tutored at home, and it seemed to suit her. Occasionally, she even deigned to tell me about a book she read. In early June I returned to Houghton to pack up our remaining things and sell the house. That was the superficial reason anyway. The truth was, I had to go back.

It was high spring in the Upper Peninsula, and the land was a green I hadn't experienced before, dark and deep as if the soil had bled into the roots of even the thinnest grasses. As I crossed over from Hancock to Houghton, the drawbridge rose for a commercial boat and I had a few minutes to take in the view. It was a clear day and the water was blue, the buildings along the bank distinct; I could easily make out the patterns of their bricks and shingles. The clarity was overwhelming. I longed for snow to blur my vision and cover my tracks.

The FOR SALE sign in front of the house was almost obscured by weeds, but it didn't matter; I had accepted a bid two weeks ago. The realtor had hired a cleaner for the inside, so when I opened the door, disinfectant mixed with the smell of moldy carpet. I opened all the windows before bringing in my bag. For over an hour I pretended I was strong enough to make it through—all I had to do was sort through our things and call a shipper to box them up—a matter of a day or two at most.

There was still tea in the cupboard, so I put on a pot of water. When I sat down to drink it, I saw Michael at the table, his hand reaching for a cup that wasn't there. I remembered the ring that had once been on his finger, the ring he'd buried for Johnny. In the end, avenging Johnny's death had been more important to him than anything else, more important than me or Marcy or even his own life. That's why he went out to the mine alone.

Somehow I made it to the store that afternoon to buy some provisions and then went through my bedroom closet, sorting through the clothes I hadn't taken with me. I saw them like costumes I'd worn on a movie set, and the scenes revolved around Michael: the tunic that had attracted his eye at the Nicholsons' party, the ski jacket I wore during our lessons, a wool blazer I had on during the train trip from Hamburg to Rostock. It felt adolescent, this association of clothes with love, Barbie doll–style wardrobe romance. But my infatuation with him had been adolescent, that was the point, even if our mission had been deadly serious. I owed him more.

I was so jet-lagged I fell asleep early that night. I don't know what I dreamed, but when I woke up the next morning, I knew I had to retrieve the ring. After breakfast I picked up a map at the Forest Service office in Houghton and bought a spade and tape measure at the hardware store.

I retraced the route Michael and I had taken through the Porcupine Mountains, passing the picnic ground where we stopped for lunch. It was midweek and no one was there except for a park vehicle collecting trash. The forest was thicker than in the fall. Even the evergreens sprouted new growth, filling the spaces where light had once filtered through.

When I turned off the highway, I worried that the rental car wouldn't make it over the muddy back roads, but it hadn't rained for the past few weeks and the ruts were almost dry. I kept stopping to look at the map, hoping I would remember where Michael had turned off Forest Road Number 17 to the logging road with the pull-over. Was it a left or right? I had to roll up the windows against the mosquitoes and blackflies swarming outside.

Maybe Michael guided me, I don't know. Maybe I was just crazy enough to be lucky for once, because I made the right turn and stopped where I was supposed to stop. Where Johnny had stopped. Where Nelson and Al had shot him.

Of course I didn't know for sure they were the culprits, but I was certain enough. There had to be some rough justice in Michael's sacrifice.

I covered myself with insect spray before I left the car, but even so the mosquitoes buzzed around me. I didn't want to swat them, I wanted the moment to be purer than that, just me and the silent woods. Now I realized that silence only comes with snow, and even then the noise is still there, trapped between ice crystals, waiting for the sun to free it. If I wanted silence, I would have to look deeper within myself.

In the clearing I found the two pine trees, and in the same way as Michael I used the tape measure to determine the point equidistant between them. The ground was hard and rocky and it took me awhile to unearth the ring. The leather pouch had started to deteriorate, but inside, the silver ring was surprisingly untarnished, the turquoise as blue as the day Michael buried it. I put it on my finger even though I knew it didn't belong there. I needed to feel him again, if only for a moment, because I needed his forgiveness too.

Or was this search for forgiveness a shield against the love I couldn't or wouldn't allow any of them to give me, not Michael or Sajit or Marcy? How much more could I really blame myself for what had happened? I hadn't set it in motion, I hadn't stood here with a gun and shot Johnny, I hadn't made Michael's choices for him. I entered the play after it started and had to invent my lines. And so I faltered and made mistakes because I didn't have a script; no one did; no one was the hero of the last act, because there wasn't one; no curtain fell to a standing ovation. If there was any hero or heroine at all, it was Lucy, because she had saved my daughter's life.

A voice came from deep inside me. Instead of guilt, I should feel gratitude. Marcy was still alive.

Lucy sits on the cabin porch, waiting for Gillian. It's screened in now—she used some of the money from selling the store to fix up the cabin and make it her place again. The FBI warned her that she shouldn't live out here alone; they even offered to move her somewhere and give her a new identity, but she's tired of living with fear. She knows she's safe. The Voice told her the Reverend won't come back. He's somewhere else now, somewhere far away. Other people need to worry about him, not her.

She's made a fresh pot of coffee for Gillian, but she's out of milk; she hopes Gillian drinks it black. She was too tired this morning to drive back to Houghton to the grocery. Don's convenience store is closed now because he's moved back downstate. It took him getting shot for his ex-wife to appreciate him, and they're living together again now. Lucy misses him, but it's OK, he had to go back to his kids. And he gave her what she wanted.

It's his baby, she knows it. Not Hank's or the Reverend's. The baby that came to her that day when she gave the ghost baby back to Marcy.

A fish jumps on the lake and she watches the circles on the water swell, then fade. One day when she was little she counted how many fish jumped in an hour. You can spend a lot of time watching water. That's what she did when her father took her fishing. Diane didn't like to go because she hated to put worms on the hook.

Diane says she'll help take care of the baby when Lucy needs to go back to work. She can probably live a year on the store money,

maybe longer if she's careful. Hank gave all their savings to the
Reverend and never told her, but she can't be angry with him now.
He's dead, and besides, he didn't know what he was doing. In the
spring they found his body under a thin layer of ice in the swamp
near the mine.

She hears the car coming and stands up, slightly dizzy—she
should probably have something to eat. She's never been so
hungry in her life. What will she say to Gillian? What if she takes
milk in her coffee?

She walks down the steps to meet her. Gillian gets out of the car
with a bouquet of flowers in her arms—roses, it looks like, mixed
with white carnations. She hands them to Lucy and then embraces
her, taking care not to crush the flowers. "Thank you," Lucy says.

"No, I wanted to thank you," Gillian begins, but before she can
say anything more, Lucy interrupts.

"I'm going to have a baby," she says.

"That's wonderful!" Gillian smiles and gives her another
embrace, closer this time, close enough to feel the baby in her
stomach. Lucy looks over her shoulder and spots another fish
jumping on the water. The ring it makes is so big it seems to
spread all the way onto the land, enclosing them, if only for a
moment.

In my absence Sajit and Marcy forgave me, though I no longer
needed forgiveness. I needed us to be a family, whatever it took,
my sacrifice or his or no one's at all, just accepting the spaces
between us and forgetting them when we came close, touched,
slept together in the same bed.

We are doing all right now, not great but all right. I have a job in the Bodleian library as an archivist of early-nineteenth-century German manuscripts. It's boring, but it fills the time. Maybe I'll apply for a teaching job when I have more energy.

Sajit made me promise that my days as a political researcher are over. I don't tell him about the e-mails I still receive from my colleagues in Rostock who are keeping a close watch on Karl Gruhl. Or that every time I read about the threat of biological terrorism, I wonder where the Reverend is and what is contained in those canisters.

I don't know how long I can keep living in this safety zone, I hope long enough to see Marcy safely out of adolescence. Something keeps pushing me out—too much knowledge, I guess—or maybe it's the same need that propelled Michael into my office that first morning: the need to avenge a death. I buried his ring in a forest near here, equidistant between two pine trees. Maybe one day I will find the Reverend and earn the right to wear it again.

ABOUT THE AUTHOR

Elizabeth Hartmann is the Director of the Population and Development Program at Hampshire College in Amherst, Massachusetts. She speaks widely on development issues, reproductive rights, women's issues, and human rights. She has written for *Ms.*, *The Progressive*, *The Nation*, and many scholarly journals. She is the co-author (with James K. Boyce) of *A Quiet Violence: View from a Bangladesh Village*, which was written after she lived in Bangladesh and India for several years. In 1987, she published *Reproductive Rights and Wrongs: The Global Politics of Population Control*, which was issued in a revised edition in 1995.